BERSERKERS

Unliving . . . self-replicating . . . the ultimate enemy of everything that lived . . . and they raged across the Galaxy.

Before Harivarman could speak or move, the connecting door burst fully open. That intrusion was accompanied in vacuum-silence by the destruction of the adjacent wall, as a large object that was too wide for the doorway came through it anyway on six long mechanical legs, stone bursting and erupting around it. The berserker's half-gutted belly still hung open, a cable or two trailing from the site of Harivarman's surgery. The legs were all unfolded now and at least four of them working, performing at least well enough to propel the huge berserker at the speed of a walking man.

Their purpose was the elimination of all life and unimpeded they would succeed.

Look for all these Tor books by Fred Saberhagen

BERSERKER BASE (with Poul Anderson, Edward Bryant, Stephen R. Donaldson, Larry Nivens, Connie Willis, and Roger Zelazny) Trade
BERSERKER: BLUE DEATH (Trade)
THE BERSERKER THRONE
THE BERSERKER WARS
A CENTURY OF PROGRESS
COILS (with Roger Zelazny)
THE EARTH DESCENDED
THE FIRST BOOK OF SWORDS
THE SECOND BOOK OF SWORDS
THE THIRD BOOK OF SWORDS
THE FIRST BOOK OF LOST SWORDS: WOUNDHEALER'S STORY (Hardcover)

FRED SABERHAGEN

THE BERSERKER THRONE

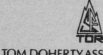

A TOM DOHERTY ASSOCIATES BOOK

THE BERSERKER THRONE

Copyright © 1985 by Fred Saberhagen

First Tor printing: December 1986

A TOR Book

Published by Tom Doherty Associates, Inc.
49 West 24 Street
New York, N.Y. 10010

Cover art by Vincent DiFate

ISBN: 0-812-55318-7
CAN. ED.: 0-812-55319-5

Library of Congress Catalog Card Number: 85-2021

Printed in the United States of America

0 9 8 7 6 5 4 3 2 1

Chapter 1

Around the green and lovely world called Salutai, the sky was clear of terror, as it had been now for many years. Today the planet's dayside sky was almost clear of clouds as well, and at midday the face of the land beneath it blazed with the thousand colors of midsummer flowers.

It was the Holiday of Life today on Salutai, the planet's greatest yearly festival, and at the meridian of noon the central procession of the festival was passing through small town streets strewn with fresh-cut blooms.

Through this particular small town ran many canals. They were clean, open waterways, and almost as numerous as the streets. And today in the canals as in the streets of Salutai the masses of summer blooms were prodigally distributed, those on the water floating and drifting in the controlled current. The streets and canal banks and buildings of the town under the noonday sun echoed with celebration, with ten kinds of music all being played and sung at the same time. The buildings, streets, canals, as well as the people in them and on them and the living plants that made archways above, were all mad with decorations.

At the center of the slow-moving ceremonial procession crept the broad, low, bubble-domed groundcar in which the Empress of the Eight Worlds was riding. The parade extending ahead of her car and behind it was not really very long, but it took its time, so that everyone in the town who wanted to see the procession and the Empress at close range had a good chance to do so. And there were many, in this town and across the planet, who did want to see. The crowds, here on Salutai composed exclusively of Earth-descended humans, cried the name of their Empress in several languages, and some of the people in the crowd waved petitions and raised banners and placards, promoting one cause or another, as her clear-topped groundcar crept past.

Though the procession was not moving with much speed, neither was the town large. The sun of Salutai was still very nearly directly overhead when the central groundcar and its escort of marchers and other vehicles emerged from the confinement of the old town's narrow streets, and entered abruptly into a countryside that was approximately half in well-managed cultivation, half still in what looked like virgin wilderness.

As the short parade left the last of the hard-paved streets behind, the crowds surrounding it grew no less, but rather greater. Here, amid a vast, parklike expanse that provided more room in which to assemble, a larger throng was waiting. This crowd was made up partly of government workers and dependents drafted into action and tubed out from the nearby capital city; still, most of the people had come here freely, to cheer a monarch popular enough to draw spontaneous affection from many of her people.

Here a substantial minority of the crowd had in mind other things besides the offer of uncritical affection. Live news coverage of the procession was notably absent, but still there were occasional protests. Whenever these protestors and placard-bearers grew too numerous or noisy, security people in uniform and out appeared in sudden concentration, moving to break up the gatherings as gently and as quietly as possible. There were no injuries. The people of Salutai knew a long tradition of courtesy, and they were almost universally unused to the organization of violence, at least against their fellow humans and fellow citizens.

Now, still surrounded by flowers, and by a slow wave of noise that was still predominantly happy, the procession paused on the bank of a broad, open canal. Amid a suddenly increased presence of uniformed security forces, the Empress, still tall and regal despite her advanced age, stood up out of her low car, and amid much ceremonious escort walked down a few steps to a dock. There she stepped aboard a heavily decorated pleasure-barge that waited to receive her, rising and falling gently amid the floating drifts of flowers.

She had to delay briefly then, looking back toward shore, to give her attention to a delegation of schoolchildren who were about to present her with a special bouquet.

To a young man who was watching from the top of a small hill a hundred meters distant, amid the scalloped outer fringes of the crowd, the whole scene, of applauding throngs, welcoming children, and the endless visual bombardment of blossoms, made a very pretty picture indeed.

The young man's name was Chen Shizuoka, and with his curly dark hair surrounding an almost angelic face he looked very earnest and nervous at the moment, more so than those around him. He said to his companion: "Listen to them. They still love her."

The two of them, Chen and the young woman who was standing with him, had been waiting for several hours on the hilltop, along with a handful of other people who had with foresight chosen this place for the clear view that it was certain to provide of the Empress and the parade. For the last few minutes Chen and his companion, whose name was Hana Calderon, had been watching intently the stately and joyful approach of the procession. Chen loved the Empress, as did so many of her people, and he would have liked to be able to get closer to her now, near enough to cry out some heartfelt personal greeting, and perhaps even to meet her eyes. But today he had a duty that precluded the gratification of any such personal wish.

Hana Calderon was not really so young as Chen; at the moment she looked quieter, less nervous, and somehow more effective. She raised a hand and brushed back straight black hair from dark oriental eyes, narrowed now in calculation.

"I think," she said, her tone suggesting that she was mildly chiding the young man but being careful how she went about it, "that what most of them are really cheering is the Holiday of Life."

As if by reflex Chen glanced up at the clear terrorless sky, from which it was always possible—and this year perhaps more probable than last—that terror might come again.

"I suppose," he said to his companion, avoiding argument as usual, "that feelings are strong again this year. With the news."

Hana Calderon nodded, moving her chiseled classical profile up and down without turning the gaze of her dark eyes away from the Empress's barge. The presentation of the special bouquet had just been completed, and the vessel was now almost ready to carry the Empress out on the next, waterborne leg of her progress.

The young woman said in an abstracted voice: "I suppose they are." Then, still not looking away from the barge, she reached out a hand to touch Chen. In a suddenly crisp tone, she added: "Are you ready?"

Chen Shizuoka's right hand had been for a long time ready in his inner pocket, gripping a small plastic object. It seemed to him that his fingers had been clutching that object for an eternity. "Ready."

"Then let it go. Now!" The words were an order, given sharply and decisively, though Hana's voice was too low for anyone else standing nearby to hear her through the noise of the surrounding crowd.

A hundred meters downhill from where they stood, the barge was just getting into motion. Chen Shizuoka withdrew the tiny device he had been gripping, and with a different pressure of his fingers activated it. A signal even subtler than most electronic emanations was sent forth.

From among the tight-packed crowd below, there rose up sudden screams.

Don't be afraid! Chen wanted to reassure them. He knew how harmless the large inflatable devices were that now came popping up out of the canal, in front of and around the barge that bore the Empress. The great rough shapes, surfacing like huge gray hippopotami of old Earth, were blocking the decorated barge completely. The devices, inflating themselves at Chen's signal, were all moored to the bottom of the canal so as not to be easily pushed out of the way. As large as hippos, they were of various shapes, all intended to represent particular models of berserkers, but in no more than a clumsy cartoon fashion. Chen himself had insisted on that point, so that not even a single startled child in the crowd should be able to mistake them for the terrible reality. What the planners of the demonstration hoped to create in their audience was thought, not terror.

A considerable amount of work had gone into fabricating the inflatable devices, and the effort and strain of planting them secretly in the canal had been, Chen thought when he looked back on it, more than he ever wanted to go through again. Not that he would have refused to do it all again, and more, if he thought that doing so would get the Prince recalled to power, and some of those who currently served the Empress in high places exiled in his stead.

Up out of the water the odd shapes came, shiny-wet and dark and in the cartoon crudity of their forms unmistakable as to what they were supposed to represent. One after another in rapid succession broke the surface, the swift bobbing lunges of their rising pushing aside the drowning masses of flowers.

The crowds near the canal were in great turmoil.

"It's working," Chen crooned softly, happily to the young woman at his side, not turning his head to look at her. "It's going to do the job."

Suddenly there were sharp thrumming sounds from below, and more yells, and an even greater turmoil among the crowd, the start of real panic. Some of the more trigger-happy security people had pulled out handguns and were actually opening fire, with devastating effect upon harmless inflated plastic. Chen, with sudden helpless concern, as if he had seen a distant child toying with a dangerous weapon, recalled how there had been hurt feelings among the populace, injured protests at the mere announcement that this time when the Empress traveled among her people she was going to be accompanied by a strong security contingent.

And the many citizens who had protested the security arrangements had been right, Chen thought, there were the supposed protectors now, blasting away with guns and endangering lives. It was not as if they could really believe that they were confronted with a plot to *hurt* the Empress. No one was going to do that; not to the Empress; certainly not here on her home world of Salutai.

The brief outburst of gunfire ceased, evidently on some order, as abruptly as it had started. But the uproar and panic in the surrounding crowd continued at an alarming pitch. Looking downhill, Chen observed that some of the clumsy-looking waterborne devices had been destroyed. But enough of them remained in place to at least impede the forward movement of the barge. A dozen in all of the inflatable things had been put into position—Chen could still remember the feel of the bottom mud, the taste it gave the water when it was stirred up, the thrill of terror recurring each time there was some alarm and he and the others thought that they had been discovered at their task.

Some of the placards borne by the ugly gray shapes had not yet been blasted into illegibility. One of them read: THE ENEMY IS NOT DESTROYED. And another: RECALL PRINCE HARIVARMAN.

"Let's get going," said Hana Calderon suddenly, speaking quietly into Chen's ear. He nodded once, and with that they separated, with nothing more in the way of farewell than one last glance of triumph exchanged. Except for the unexpected outbreak of gunfire, and the resulting panic—maybe someone really *had* been hurt; Chen certainly hoped not—everything was going smoothly, according to the carefully rehearsed plan. No one in that crowd below would be able to ignore their message. Everyone would carry it home and talk about it. Approvingly or disapprovingly, they would be forced to think about it. And eventually, inevitably, it would be accepted. Because it was the truth.

Chen turned away from Hana and from the scene

below. Without either delay or haste he started walking
his own planned path down the side of the hill away
from the canal and the confusion around the barge. He
didn't look for Hana, but he knew she would be making
a similar withdrawal, moving on a diverging course. He
would meet her later, in the city. No one appeared to
take any particular notice of him as he retreated. He
dropped his plastic control device into a trash disposal in
passing. He felt certain already that their getaway was
going to be as successful as all the other previously
successful steps in the elaborate plan.

Even now, out of direct sight of the demonstration
that his hands had triggered, Chen could hear in the
crowd's roar behind him the kind of impact their show
had achieved. At least as great as anything he had dared
to hope for. Now from the same direction sounded sharp
reports, what must be the sound of more inflated dum-
mies being shot to fragments. And the roar of the crowd
went up again.

His imitation berserkers would shortly be destroyed,
but no one of the thousands who had been here today
would be able to ignore or forget the messages that they
had carried.

Chen listened carefully as he retreated, savoring the
crowd noise behind him. It was fading gradually as he
moved away, and now for some reason it held more
anger and fear than he had imagined there would be—
because of the actions of the security people, he supposed,
and who could blame the crowd for that?

Some fifty meters down the hill, moving amid a
slowly growing crowd of other people who had pru-

dently or timidly decided to be somewhere else, Chen came to an inconspicuously parked groundcycle. When he straddled the machine it started quietly, and within moments it was bearing him at a greatly increased speed away from the tumult and the crowds.

He had less than a kilometer to travel on the cycle, traversing a network of smooth pathways that laced the lovely countryside, before he reached a subway station whose entrance was almost hidden, set into the side of a flowered embankment. He abandoned the cycle outside the station, confident that a confederate would take it away later so it would not be traced to him. Once underground, Chen was able almost at once to board a swift tubetrain that brought him in a few minutes underneath the capital city.

Disembarking from the train, riding a stair to ground level, into the usual swarm of people at one of the central metropolitan stations, Chen felt a wave of bleak reaction as he melded himself into the population of the streets. It was almost a sense of disappointment at the ease of his and his friends' success. It seemed in a way unfair, as if the security people had never had a chance of stopping the demonstration, or of catching up with him or Hana afterward; now all was, would be, anticlimax.

Of course, most of the other members of Chen's protest group had kept telling him all along that the demonstration would be a great success. Hana had certainly been confident, and he himself had really expected nothing less than success. . . .

The plan now called for him to go home, that is to

return to the student's room where he lived alone, and there await developments. But there was no particular hurry about his getting to his room. Chen delayed, watching a public newscast that was evidently running somewhat behind events, for it showed nothing about a demonstration interrupting the progress of the Empress. He moved on to a favorite bookstore, dallied there a little longer, then walked on unhurriedly. If he ever should be questioned, for any reason, about his where-abouts today, he'd have an answer: Why yes, he had been out there, watching the parade. When things started to get noisy and rowdy, and he heard actual shots, he had simply decided that it was time to leave.

Chen passed another public newscast, and dawdled before the elevated holostage long enough to be sure that the news still contained no mention of the demon-stration; by now, he felt sure, that omission must be deliberate. On Salutai such blatantly direct government control was unheard of, even in these times; the situa-tion made him uneasy.

When Chen reached the street where he lodged, and approached the block on which his room was located, his uneasiness led him to look about him with unwonted caution. He saw with a sinking sensation, but somehow no real surprise, that there were security people here, cruising in their cars, two or three cars of them at least, observing. He had learned to recognize the type of unmarked groundcar that they favored. They appeared to be trying to make themselves inconspicuous, but there they were.

Something had gone wrong after all. He could not

help believing that they were here waiting for him to
show up. The sinking feeling was becoming a steady
sickness in his gut.

Chen stepped around a corner into a cross street. He
paused in the doorway of an apartment building, and
stood pondering what to do next.

He leaned out of the doorway to look back along the
way that he had come, and the sound numbed him for
an instant with its sudden shock, a frightening impact
against the wall immediately beside his head, as if an
invisible rock from some invisible catapult had struck
there. There was another component to the sound too, a
sharp thrum, a louder echo of the police weapons at the
demonstration, much louder and closer than he had
heard them from the hill. This came from a rooftop or
an upper window across the street. Someone over there
was shooting at him, shooting to kill.

In sudden cold terror Chen dodged out of the doorway,
heading down the street in a fast zigzag walk, the
movement blending him at once into the flow of other
hurrying pedestrians. Still his whole back felt tensed and
swollen, one enormous muscle tightening uselessly against
the killing blow that was to come any second. The sky
that had been free of terror an hour ago had turned now
to blue ice closing him in.

Now he thought that one of the unmarked cars of the
security people was keeping pace with him along the
street. He dodged quickly into a smaller side passage for
pedestrians, leaving the vehicle behind.

He fled through the complex and crowded heart of the
city, heading instinctively for areas where the conges-

tion would be greater. Once, then twice, he dared to hope that he had shaken his pursuers off. But each time, even before hope could really establish itself, he saw that such was not the case. They had perhaps lost sight of him for the moment, but he knew they must be everywhere, in vehicles and afoot, in uniform and in civilian clothes. Anyone who glanced at him might be Security . . . and Chen had to assume that they were all after him.

Organize a simple demonstration, just a demonstration, and they hunted you like this. Tried to kill you on sight, out of hand . . . it was a bad dream, and he was caught up in it, and there was no use hoping to be saved by any rules of sanity and logic.

What did they want to *kill* him for, what had he done that even they should think was terrible to that degree? If a free citizen could no longer even protest openly without being hunted like a dangerous animal, then things on the world of Salutai were already even worse than he and his friends had been telling one another. Far worse.

Exhaustion overtook Chen quickly. It was as if he had been running steadily for hours, enduring steady fear and tension more tiring than mere physical exertion. In one of the tougher neighborhoods of the city, a couple of kilometers now from his own apartment, Chen entered a crowded square of shops and other buildings, some of them little more than hovels. A few derelicts were camped, amid litter, on the grassy plaza at the center.

Chen had taken his last turning seeking a complication

of pathways, but realized as soon as he had entered the square that the move might well have been a blunder. There were only three or four ways out of it again. Should he turn back right away . . . ?

It was already too late for that. One of the slow-cruising groundcars had just stopped, a little way behind him. They must be losing him and picking him up again, trying to close in. Quickly he slid around a knot of people, getting them between him and the car, and moved on with them. If the crowds of pedestrians ever thinned out, he was lost. He was better dressed than most of the people in this neighborhood, on the verge at least of being conspicuous because of that.

Walking, waiting in exhaustion for a blasting death, he scanned the storefronts rapidly for a place to hide. If his pursuers were willing to shoot him dead, they were certainly not going to be put off by the necessity of searching for him inside a store, or anywhere else that he could think of. Nothing that he could do to throw them off was going to give them too much trouble.

Except, perhaps . . .

On one of the storefronts ahead there loomed a large sign, of a type familiar all across the Earth-colonized portion of the Galaxy. It was seen on most worlds, as here, more often in the poorer neighborhoods than in the well-to-do:

THE FIGHT FOR LIFE HAS NOT BEEN WON.
THE TEMPLARS NEED YOU.

Just beneath the sign, a poster with its lifelike picture

animated by electronics showed an appealing child in the act of cringing away from a grasping metal menace. The berserker android on the poster was a far more barbed and angled and poisonous-looking portrayal of the ancient enemy than any of Chen's balloons had been.

And as if this poster were indeed another menace from which he needed desperately to be saved, Chen stopped in his tracks, recoiled slightly, and glanced hastily, hopelessly, around the square.

His situation here looked indeed hopeless. Already he thought that he could see a checkpoint being established, or one already functioning unobtrusively, at each possible exit.

And suppose he did manage, somehow, to find another way out of the square. The search for him, a manhunt of this intensity, was obviously not going to be broken off simply because he managed to dodge it one more time. The hunt was going to go on. And he could think of no place in this city, on this planet, where it could not reach him; no place to hide. Chen certainly had no intention of leading these murderous monsters to any of his friends.

This kind of a hunt, Chen saw, could end only when they had caught him. And he had seen and felt evidence that being caught would not simply be a matter of being arrested—matters had gone beyond that already. Incomprehensibly, the security people had shot at him. He kept coming back to that fact, being brought up short by it, stumbling over it. But there was no way around the fact. For some reason that could make sense only to their mad arrogance, they were really trying to kill him.

He was walking forward again, moving in a daze, a condition which on these poor streets made him less rather than more conspicuous. The door to the Templars' recruiting office was again immediately in front of him. To Chen that open doorway had a look of unreality, but now everything about him did; everything except the fact that someone was now trying to accomplish his death. That had a reality of a transcendent kind.

"What can we do for you, sir?" A bland-looking sergeant behind a counter, no different in appearance or manner except for the uniform than any other salesman in any other shop, raised his head and spoke as Chen entered. A couple of other young men, with some kind of fancy paper readouts in their hands, were just turning away from the counter, about to leave the office.

Chen moved up close to the waist-high surface of the counter, and rested his hands upon it. There came and went in his mind a last fleeting thought that perhaps it would be enough for him to spend a little time in this office, off the street; perhaps if he did that the killers out there would get tired of looking for him and go away . . .

. . . that hope was not worth even a fleeting thought. He had to get on with what he perceived as his only remaining choice.

Chen cleared his throat. "I—if I were to enlist right now, how soon could I get off planet?"

"Soon as you want." Experienced eyes sized Chen up with calculation. The sergeant was carefully unsurprised.

Chen pressed him: "Today, maybe?"

The sergeant checked the timepiece on the wall. Now he looked more than ever to Chen like a salesman, one accustomed to not show surprise at a customer's strange request. Certainly it seemed that the question was not entirely new to him.

"Why not today?" The sergeant's voice was matter-of-fact, perhaps carefully so. "If you're in something of a hurry to get elsewhere, that's all right with us. Soon as you sign the enlistment form, and take the oath, then you're officially a Templar. We'd drive you to the spaceport enclave today anyway. That's Templar diplomatic territory. If, maybe, just for an example, there were angry relatives looking for you here, or maybe creditors, they wouldn't have a chance. We've even had people come in who were in trouble with the law, with the cops hardly a jump behind them. The cops have no chance either, not of arresting someone who's officially a Templar. Not for something the man did before he enlisted." The recruiter looked at Chen steadily; it sounded like a speech that had been well thought out, one that had been given before.

Chen cleared his throat again. "That's about what I thought; I . . ."

Something in Chen, ever since he was a child, was always stirred by stories of adventure, had always looked forward in daydreams to this moment: to becoming a Templar, entering a world of physical adventure, risking all in a most worthy cause. In real life, other considerations had always until now prevailed: a distaste for what he foresaw the military life would be like; a wish to be a student; a strong desire to be free to act in Eight Worlds politics.

And in the daydreams, Chen had never thought that it would be the desperate need for escape that would drive him to this step, as it had driven so many characters in adventure stories. But there was no arguing with reality, which evidently after all had no prejudice against trite melodrama. Those guns in the hands of the men outside were real.

Chen signed the document placed before him by the recruiter, not bothering to read it, either before or after. "Now what? Can I wait here?"

The sergeant, still as calm as before, came around from behind his official barricade. "Yeah. But first, to make it official, you take the oath. I need another live witness for that." He went into the back room and came back with a young woman, who wore on the shoulder of her Templar uniform an insignia that Chen thought meant she was a clerk.

The oath, like the paper he had just signed, went by him without its words really registering in his consciousness; he could only hope that it would serve as a magic curtain, an incantation, to render him invisible to scanning gunsights.

Now he was led into the back room and told to wait. It might have been the back room of any office, holding information transmission and storage equipment, with miscellaneous bins and closets. There were also a few chairs and two desks, at one of which the young clerk went back to her paperwork.

A couple of hours passed—for Chen, as in some

endless dream—as he sat numbly watching the clerk go about her duties. Her work was largely electronic, and did not appear to be all that arduous. Once or twice he tried to make conversation, and got in return short answers, and looks that had in them the faintly amused tolerance of the veteran.

Before the first hour of Chen's wait was over, there came from the front office a sound of new voices, too low to be fully distinguishable, as if several men had entered at once and were in conference with the sergeant. The voices might have represented no more than some group of friends coming in together on a routine recruiting inquiry, but Chen thought that they meant something else. He waited fatalistically, but nothing happened, except that the voices ceased presently and the men went out again. And shortly after that unusual conversation in the front, the sergeant came briefly into the back again, for no other reason than to give Chen a long and unreadable look.

After the second hour of Chen's wait, two young men, not the same two who had been in the office when Chen entered, arrived and were ushered into the back to join him in his waiting. These two, he thought, were certainly real recruits. They exchanged nods with Chen, and had no more success than he had had in making nervous banter with the clerk.

Shortly after their arrival, ground transportation arrived to take all three recruits to the Templar facility at the spaceport. They were led by the sergeant out a back door of the office into an alley, and at once urged into the vehicle, a high-built van.

The windows of the groundvan were set for high one-way opacity; it would be very hard for anyone outside to look in. During the drive to the spaceport Chen observed a security car or two, or what he thought were such; it was hard to tell if their occupants might be taking any particular interest in the Templar vehicle.

Inside the van, the ride to the spaceport was mostly silent; it was beginning to sink in on the other recruits, perhaps, what sort of a major change in lifestyle they had embarked upon.

Listening to the few words that his two companions exchanged between them, Chen gathered that basic training for all Templar recruits from the Eight Worlds now took place on the planet Niteroi, only about two days' travel from Salutai at c-plus speeds. Chen hadn't bothered to ask where he was going, having, as the sergeant evidently realized, quite enough in the way of other matters to engage his thoughts.

Now in the back of Chen's mind the faint hope—he wasn't sure it really amounted to a hope—had arisen that he might, now that he was officially a Templar, get a chance someday to see the Templar Radiant, and perhaps even the opportunity to meet or at least set eyes on the man who was the chief object of all his political action, the exiled Prince Harivarman. The Prince had been held at the Radiant in Templar custody for the past four standard years. Well, maybe some day that chance would come. Right now Chen was willing to settle for exile himself, or imprisonment or just about any terms on which he would be allowed to live.

The recruiting sergeant, who had come along in the

van to deliver his shipment, eyed Chen closely again when they were getting out of the vehicle at the spaceport, already behind the closed gates and gray walls of the small Templar enclave there.

"I hear you were out there demonstrating for the Prince." The sergeant's face was still unreadable. His voice no longer sounded exactly polite—Chen was no longer a civilian who had just walked into his office as a prospect—but the tone did not seem to express disapproval either.

"That's right," Chen said proudly.

The sergeant did not respond in any way that Chen could see, but turned away and went on about his business.

Other recruits, gathered from elsewhere on the planet, were waiting within the walls of the spaceport Templar enclave, already being kept separate from civilians. More than a dozen freshly enlisted young men and women were aboard the shuttle when it finally rose from Salutai.

Chapter 2

For hundreds of years Earth-descended humanity had observed and tried to explain the class of astrophysical objects called gravitational radiants, but still no wholly satisfactory scientific theory existed to account for them. Only nine of the objects, including the Templar Radiant, were known to exist in the entire Galaxy. Each of the nine was a fiery paradox: a mild source of comparatively harmless radiation, and, what made them unique, each a center and source of inverse gravity. Centuries ago human effort had rendered the Templar Radiant unique even in its class by enclosing it completely within a vast spherical fortress of stone and metal and fabricated forms of matter.

Commander Anne Blenheim was enjoying what was almost her first look around the vast interior of the ancient Templar Fortress that enclosed the Radiant itself, and of which she had very recently assumed command. Looking up, she saw the Radiant as a sunlike object, not much bigger than a point in its apparent size, though only about four kilometers directly above her head. The reversed gravitational influence of the Radiant naturally prevailed here, and the sunlike point would be in the same directly overhead position for anyone standing anywhere on the inner surface of the Fortress, whose basic shape was that of an enormous hollow sphere.

The reasons why that form of construction had been used—or indeed the reasons for the Fortress having been built at all—were lost, along with much else in the early history of its creators, the Dardanians. They had disappeared from Galactic society centuries ago, and to historians of the present day they formed one of the most enigmatic branches of Earth-descended humanity.

Still, the thought behind one aspect of the construction was obvious; the inner surface of the Fortress had been fixed at a distance of approximately four kilometers from the Radiant itself, because at that distance the reverse gravity of the Radiant, pushing the inhabitants of the Fortress against the faintly concave surface, was equal to Earth-standard normal.

Commander Blenheim stood, neatly uniformed, just outside the main gate of the Templar base; around her the little, self-contained world rose up in all directions. One square kilometer after another mapped itself out conveniently for inspection on the interior of the surrounding and supporting globe of rock and metal. The inner surface was lined with streets, dotted with houses, with buildings of all sorts except that none were very tall. The commander knew that many of the buildings, possibly even a majority of them, were now unused.

There were also great blank spaces on the map, kilometers of raw rock that might once have been occupied, but had been scraped clean of surface detail in some remodeling project of centuries ago, and were now abandoned. Now again remodeling activity was in progress, especially in and around the Templar base itself. There was a lot of greenery in sight too, plants from Earth and other worlds genetically redesigned to thrive in this mild steady light. This massive effort at planting was a development that Anne Blenheim understood was fairly new, and of which she heartily approved both esthetically and as an affirmation of life. Orchards and single trees and even miniature forests were visible everywhere across the inner sphere that made itself a sky.

Close by the small parklike space where the commander was now standing, the main gate of the Templar compound was busy with pedestrian and vehicular traffic, either military people or those on business with the military. A great many of the people passing through glanced at Commander Blenheim as they went by; she had been on board the Fortress for only one standard day, and her arrival as the new commanding officer was, she was sure, the biggest topic of conversation among the few thousand people who made up the whole civilian and military population here.

Because she was now standing just outside the gate and not inside it, salutes from the passing military were not forthcoming, and the commander was spared the distraction of having to return them. But the quick glances at her continued. Military and civilian passersby alike were all doubtless wondering just why the new base commander might be standing here in apparent idleness—taking a traffic count, perhaps? Waiting for someone?—but in the twenty-four hours she had been on the Radiant, no one had become a close enough acquaintance to pause and try to find out.

In her imagination she framed an answer anyway: "Waiting to make a diplomatic contact of sorts. With a certain—gentleman." Then she smiled at the strange gaze that answer evoked from her imaginary questioner. A diplomatic contact, here? The Templars were of course as active in that field as anyone else, if not more so— they had to be, with no home land or planet of their own. But the place for diplomacy would seem to be out in the mainstream of human civilization, out where the other power brokers moved.

Or perhaps her hypothetical questioner would understand at once. After all, the Prince had been here on the Fortress for four standard years.

If instead of talking about diplomatic contacts she were to say that she was waiting for her prisoner to show up—well, that would have been at least as accurate, but the reaction perhaps less fun to watch.

And this, she decided, must be the eminent gentleman himself approaching now. The groundcar easing its way toward Commander Blenheim through moderate traffic was of a type unremarkable on the streets of the Fortress, though it would have been conspicuous almost anywhere else. It was a special model that could maneuver as a slow and very short-range spacecraft as well as an atmospheric flyer. Two such vehicles had been assigned for the Prince's use, and both of them had been modified to radiate certain identifying signals continuously, tracer transmissions that allowed Templar spy devices to follow their movements. But the cars—or flyers—bore no special markings visible to the casual eye.

Commander Blenheim had met the exiled Prince Harivarman for the first time yesterday, but only in a brief formal introduction on the day of her arrival. She had promptly accepted the Prince's offer to give her a tour today of Georgicus Sabel's old workroom; she had chosen to wait for him outside the gate, arriving a little early so she could keep an eye on the progress of some of the remodeling work nearby while she was waiting.

The Prince—no, she reminded herself, she must now cease to call him the Prince, even in her own thoughts, even if everyone on the Eight Worlds still called him that; the regulations that were part of the Compact of Exile said that he was now to be addressed as General Harivarman—the general, then, the exile, had been a quasi-prisoner here in the Fortress for the past four years. The commander's intelligence reports informed her that he was becoming something of an enthusiast about the local history. Well, for such a small place, there was certainly plenty of history available here; more than some whole planets had to boast about, Commander Blenheim had often thought while doing her homework on it as part of her preparation for her new job. And from her new point of view as the general's chief jailer it was of course much better for him to be absorbed in history than taking too strong an interest in current events.

Everyone in the Eight Worlds knew the Prince's story. And a good many had heard it beyond the Eight, out on those hundreds of worlds composing what its members considered to be the human mainstream of Galactic civilization. Since the news had spread of her assignment as commander here, it had sometimes seemed to Anne Blenheim that everyone in the inhabited Galaxy had an opinion on the Prince—the general—and each was ready to give her their version of good advice on how to deal with the great man who was now in her charge. Some said quietly that, though of course it was not in her power to do so, he really should be released. Some said he should be executed, that the Council of the Eight Thrones would never be safe until he was dead. And there were plenty of intermediate opinions. The Council should restore him to power as Prime Minister under the Empress. Or they should send him as ambassador plenipotentiary to Earth. Or confine him in a solitary cell for life.

As she kept telling other people firmly, her new job really gave her nothing to say, even in an advisory capacity, as to which of those courses should be adopted. The Compact of Exile, a complicated agreement by which the Templars had accepted responsibility for Harivarman's confinement and welfare, left her as base commander little room for altering the terms of the general's existence. And *jailer* was not really the right word, not the correct job description for the relationship of the base commander on the Fortress with the eminent expatriate.

Of course, what exactly the right word was for that aspect of her job was something she had not yet worked out to her own satisfaction. The Compact of Exile, like many another important document, had been deliberately left somewhat vague. And Colonel Phocion, her predecessor here, had evidently taken too different an approach than hers for his ideas to be very helpful.

The approaching groundcar was rolling to a stop within a few meters of where Anne Blenheim was standing, just at the entrance to the small park. She could see now that there were two men in it. In front, a driver—more a ceremonial position than anything else, for naturally the car really drove itself—and a passenger in back. Commander Blenheim, who had naturally done some homework on the history and present condition of the exile, was sure that the human driver could be no one but a man named Lescar, who was the Prince's—there she went again—who was *the general's* faithful servant and longtime companion.

Four years ago, at the beginning of his exile, General Harivarman had arrived at the Templar Radiant with an attractive wife and an extensive staff of aides and servants, more than twenty people in all. The wife had made brave, self-effacing statements about loyalty. Now he was down to one devoted companion, the remainder— wife included—having for one reason or another opted to depart.

The man who now stood up out of the car, to greet the commander somehow less impressively than she had expected, was informally dressed, dark, angular, and muscular of build. His face, not particularly handsome, was of course immediately recognizable. It was somehow surprising that, except for his hands and perhaps his feet, he was not really physically large. General Harivarman was obviously past his first immaturity of youth, and it was equally obvious that he was not yet greatly burdened with years; it would have been difficult for any casual observer to pin his age down much more closely than that. But Commander Blenheim knew that he was notably young for one of his achievements, in fact just thirty-seven standard years, only slightly older than herself. Lucky the leader, she thought, who had that kind of ageless look; her own appearance, peach-complected and a little plump, made people sometimes assume her to be even younger than she was—especially before they got to know her.

In a moment, routine and rather formal greetings having been exchanged between commander and exile, she and the man she kept reminding herself to call the general were settled in the back of the car and under way, the back of the driver's graying head fixed in place before them.

Ever since yesterday's brief introduction, she had been wondering what this second and more leisurely encounter with the general would produce, in terms of mutual understanding. Well, the first moments of it were already something of a disappointment, though Commander Blenheim was not sure why.

As the car began to move the man beside her had been gazing off into the distance. Now he turned his head and was looking at her closely, in an almost proprietary way. No way to win points with her, but then he probably didn't care.

He said now in his deep voice: "No doubt you've done your homework, Commander, about Georgicus Sabel? I don't want to inflict a tiresome rehashing of a history that you already know."

"I've had to do a fair amount of homework recently on other topics. I know what everyone knows, of course, about Sabel . . . but go ahead, you tell me."

Her seat companion looked thoughtful. He seemed to be taking the assignment seriously. "Well. Two hundred and five years ago, right here—that is, right in the workshop that we're going to visit, and right under the noses of the Guardians—Georgicus Sabel encountered a functioning berserker, a remnant of their attacking force of several hundred years before *that*. He tried to bargain with it. He proposed giving it something it wanted, for something, scientific information, that he thought he could get from it in return. . . .

"To deal with a berserker, to play the role of goodlife, wasn't what he had started out to do, of course. He began by seeking Truth, you see. That's Truth with a great big scientific capital T."

"But since he dealt with a berserker, he *was* goodlife. Wasn't he?" Commander Blenheim knew the story very well, from the relatively inaccessible official Templar records as well as from the public histories. She knew what Sabel had been. He had been goodlife without a doubt. Guilty of that which in the Templar universe of thought was still the one great and unforgivable sin, the act that negated any possible good intentions—the provision of service and aid to a berserker, one of those murderous robots that went about its age-old programmed task of eliminating from the universe the blight of life. To Templars—to any human being except the perverted goodlife, but to Templars in particular—berserkers were malignance personified in metal.

So much Anne Blenheim knew, beyond a doubt, about Sabel. But she wanted to learn at first hand what the Prin—what the general thought on such a topic; and she also wanted to know how the general talked, to watch him and listen to him, to get a taste of his famous persuasive magnetism.

The man riding beside her remained thoughtful. "Technically, yes, Sabel was goodlife. Legally, yes. He would have been convicted, there's no doubt, if he had been brought to a Templar trial."

"Or to a trial in any other impartial human court."

"I suppose. Under the existing law. But if you mean did he really want to see berserkers wipe the universe clean of life, or did he want them to kill even a single human being, or did he in any sense worship the death machines—as real goodlife always do, in some sense— then the answer must be no."

It was a heavy answer to a heavy question. Sabel had been dead and gone for centuries, and Commander Blenheim had no wish to get into a heavy argument about him.

She and her companion rode on in silence for a while, through clean, almost unpopulated streets, past experimental buildings and plantings, past refurbished houses and new-grown groves. In Sabel's day, she remembered from her reading, the interior cavity of the Fortress had been allowed to remain in vacuum, people living and building their houses all around the interior surface with their breathing air held tightly under clear bubbles; only in the last few decades had the necessary engineering been completed to maintain a film of atmosphere over the whole interior surface.

She asked: "And how did you happen to become an expert on the history of the Sabel case, General? I gather that you really are."

"Oh." There was a faint tone of disappointment, as if she might have chosen to raise a more interesting point of the many available. "In the beginning, you see, when I first took up residence here, the subject of Sabel didn't interest me particularly." The general spread large, capable hands in an engaging gesture. "But gradually, over those first months . . . well, if one wishes to remain intellectually active here on the Fortress, what can one study? The choices are somewhat limited. There's physics, of course, like old Sabel himself, trying to wrest some new truth from nature. But if real physicists have been staring at the Radiant for centuries and haven't got very far with it—well, there's not much hope for an amateur."

He said it with such conscientious diffidence that the commander felt compelled to comment. "I wasn't warned that you'd be modest."

The general grinned, showing the first flash of something extraordinary that she had seen in him. "Modest, perhaps. Self-effacing, never." Then, looking out of the car, he pointed ahead. And, of course, up at an angle.

Only half a kilometer ahead of them now was an angled shape that had to be Sabel's laboratory, or the roof of it anyway. The commander had noticed that most of the buildings here in this now airy but still virtually weatherless space, even the most recently constructed ones, still had roofs, many of them sloped and angled as if to shed nonexistent rain or snow. The conspicuous roof ahead of them was a series of angled and curved surfaces, studded with the small protrusions of old-looking instruments, and marked with holes where other instruments had evidently been taken out long ago.

Of course the laboratory, like everything else on the concave dwelling surface, had been basically within view of the groundcar's occupants all along. Now the building vanished briefly as they drew near, disappearing behind one of the many newly planted lines of tall trees, and then remaining out of sight behind a high stone wall that looked like some of the original Dardanian construction. Of course the whole vast inner curve of the Fortress was no more than one face of the ancient Dardanians' enigmatic and grandiose creation. The supporting shell outside and around the face was approximately two kilometers thick, much of it hollowed by a vast honeycomb of rooms and passages of unknown purpose. The whole Fortress had an overall outside diameter of approximately twelve kilometers. Even without counting the single vast interior space where burned the Radiant itself, some six hundred cubic kilometers of stone and steel and smaller spaces were enclosed inside the shell.

The car had come to a stop now in a deserted-looking public street, at a point very near their apparent goal. The two people who had ridden in the rear seat now got out on their respective sides. All around them was a pervasive quiet, strikingly noticeable after the hum and murmur of activity around the base. Anne Blenheim had been told that sound sometimes carried or was muffled strangely in the artificially created and maintained atmosphere pressed by inverse gravity against the inside of a round shell. The whole central space inside the enormous Fortress was of course not filled with air; most of it was vacuum. The repulsive force of the Radiant increased exponentially with nearness to it. Not that the relation could be mathematically expressed in any formula as neat as variance with the square of the distance, in a simple reversal of the way that normal gravity behaved; no, here things were more complex as well as backwards. Not even the most powerful interstellar drive—the experiment had been tried—could force a ship within half a kilometer of that mysterious and fiery central point. And one result of the inversion was that the infused breathable air was effectively held as a film only a score of meters thick around the inner surface of the Fortress, where it was prevented by forcefield gates from escaping into the labyrinth of uninhabited outer chambers, and thence to space.

All in all, thought Commander Blenheim, as she had thought several times an hour since her arrival yesterday, all in all a most fascinating place.

As if he were able to sense the present train of her thoughts, the exile asked: "Do you expect you'll like it, then? Your tour of duty here, I mean?"

She granted him a faint smile. "I expect that I just might."

"Good. Oh, by the way, I haven't gone through the usual formalities of asking you about your trip."

"The journey was quite pleasantly uneventful, thank you. Routine, until we were in our close approach here. Even from outside, the Fortress is—impressive."

"I'd rather see it from outside." His voice was flat, and he was watching her steadily.

If the general was testing whether he could unsettle her by referring so baldly to his quasi-prisoner status, she trusted that her response was disappointing. "I've seen other exiles in much worse confinement. Not to mention other people who are under no legal sanctions at all."

"Political, surely." Then when she looked at him he amplified: "The sanctions, I mean. In my case. You said 'legal.' "

"I have a habit of saying what I mean, General Harivarman. Shall we go in now and take a look at this famous laboratory?"

"Of course. Follow me." The tone was briefly one that a Prince—or a general—might use, giving orders to a mere commander.

As the two of them walked away, the driver remained sitting wordlessly in the car. An old-style servant, what little she had heard about Lescar suggested; part of the machinery.

Commander Blenheim followed her guide into a nearby building through an unlocked door, thence into a passage that promptly led them down one level below the street. The lighting panels in the ceiling were all working, and the air was circulating freshly. The interiors here, like the streets outside, were clean and ordinary-looking. Still, thought the commander, everything here had an aura of being little used.

Harivarman, leading the way, stopped presently at another unmarked door, this one also of commonplace appearance—but at a second look, not quite.

The general was pointing to certain traces at eye level on the wall beside the door. He told her: "The Guardians' seal was placed here, when Sabel's contact with the berserker was discovered. It wasn't removed until about twenty years ago, according to the best information I can discover."

"The Guardians," Anne Blenheim reminded him, "were disbanded well before that." They had been a fanatical sub-order of the quasi-religious Templars—more religious then than now—a segment devoted mainly to anti-goodlife activity. Almost everyone now agreed that they had overshot the mark in their devotion to that excellent cause, employing methods that more than once degenerated into witch hunting, and sometimes even proved counterproductive, arousing interest in, and even enthusiasm for, the cause they so fanatically opposed.

She added: "Nor am I a 'closet' Guardian, in case you have been wondering where on the spectrum my own political and ethical sympathies lie. Though I suspect I am somewhat more conservative than my predecessor here; I hear that you and Colonel Phocion were on the verge of being—what's the old term?—'drinking buddies.' Nor do I, or anyone else as far as I know, suspect you of secret goodlife sympathies.''

That last was worth a shared smile; Harivarman's record as a fighter against berserkers was as well known as were his later political difficulties with the human leaders of Salutai and other worlds. Commander Blenheim had even read one unconfirmed report that in a hero-worshipping way speculated that the Prince (*general!*) might be a descendant of the berserkers' human arch-enemy, the legendary Johann Karlsen.

"I am glad to hear it," Karlsen's descendant—if it were really so—noted solemnly. And lightly bowed her forward. "Shall we go in?"

There were several rooms inside the laboratory, all of them spacious, well-lit, free of trash and essentially empty. There was, in a practical, scientific sense, hardly anything left of the place to see. It was just about as the commander's reading had led her to expect. Centuries ago the Guardian witch hunters had gutted this labora-tory down to the bare walls, and in some rooms deeper than that. But the very thoroughness of the process of search-and-destroy remained as evidence, first-hand testimony, about the Guardians if not about Sabel himself.

There was little here to comment on, beyond that fact. Their stay in the place was not very long.

Presently she and the general were back in the rear seat of the car, and the car was under way again, returning her to the Templar base. She had been half-expecting an invitation to visit the general in his quarters, but it was not forthcoming. The human driver had still not spoken a word in the commander's presence. Somehow she doubted that she was missing much in the way of brilliant conversation.

"I see you are manning the old defenses again," the Prince commented, after a few hundred meters of the return journey had rolled by in smooth silence. For a long time the Fortress had been more of a museum and a relic than anything else; real fighting, real danger, had been elsewhere. But that was now changing again, or at least starting to change. Anne Blenheim's appointment as base commander here was not the subtle insult to an ambitious officer that it might have been a few decades ago. Far from it. Her superiors expected her to accomplish a great deal.

Following her companion's gaze, Commander Blenheim could observe activity that she had ordered yesterday, one of the old defense control centers being given preliminary tests by a staff of technicians, many of whom had arrived on the same ship with her.

She said: "Yes; the war is far from over."

Harivarman, sitting beside her, sighed. There could hardly be any doubt in his mind which war it was that she or any Templar ever meant. That war which all humanity—except of course for the few evil-worshipping goodlife—had to be always and everywhere ready to fight, for survival against berserkers. He said: "If only I could be sure that the Council felt that way."

The two of them, Anne Blenheim realized, were certainly in agreement on the need for humanity to unite and press on with the berserker-war to victory; she had known that all along. But she was not going to discuss politics with her prisoner, and that first halfway political statement that she could not disagree with would certainly lead them into talk of real politics if she agreed.

Rather than do that she changed the subject. "There's a lot of empty space here, isn't there? I mean a really enormous amount. Oh, I suppose I knew before I arrived that it would be so. But it never really struck me until now, getting my first good look at it from the inside."

The general looked around and up, past the fiery point where the Radiant burned in vacuum, its inverse force pressing the atmosphere, their bodies, everything else, away from it. He said: "Oh, yes. Literally millions of chambers and passages back inside the shell. Room enough, of course, to run away and hide if I were so inclined. Hundreds of cubic kilometers of room. But ultimately, of course, nowhere to go."

Again a sudden complaint about his status as a prisoner. Well, what more natural? It was just that somehow Commander Anne had expected more stoicism from this man, because of what she had heard about him; but she supposed she would complain too, in his place. But she was not going to commiserate with the general on his problems. Instead she gave her own viewpoint. "A lot of volume to try to defend, with the number of people and the material I'm being given to work with. Not, I suppose, that defense is actually going to become a practical question within the next year or two."

"Let's hope not." In the past year or so increasing

berserker activity in the region of the Eight Worlds had made the possibility loom larger.

He didn't elaborate on his answer. The whole Fortress was obviously still much more a museum than the real Fortress it once had been, that real fortress neither of them had ever seen.

The smooth progress of their car now drew them in sight of a group of tourists, people from various planets taking a more formal tour of the Fortress in a larger, open-sided vehicle. Commander Blenheim wondered if they would stop at Sabel's old laboratory too. Tourism was no longer as much of a business here as it had been in Sabel's time; nor was the City's population nearly as large.

Making conversation, Anne Blenheim mentioned this to the general.

He agreed. "The population in Sabel's time was over a hundred thousand, did you know that? I don't have any current official figures, but I can use my eyes. The total is obviously now down to something much less than that. A great many of the civilians are tourist-facility operators, or civilian base employees. There's a crew at the scientific station. And your Templars, of course, who make up a large part of the total."

"There'll be more people here soon. Military and civilian both."

"Oh?"

"We're relocating the Templar Academy here. The first class of approximately a hundred cadets is due to start arriving in less than a standard month."

"That's news." The general seemed strongly interested.

She supposed that any change, especially one that promised more people at the Radiant, must be interesting to him. He asked her: "Where are you going to put them all? Lots of room, as you say, but not that much of it under atmosphere and in good repair."

"We're looking for sections, preferably buildings near the base, that will be easy to repair and refurbish. And perhaps areas for training, out on the outer surface of the shell. I may request that you give me another tour some day—I gather you have been emulating Doctor Sabel, in your enthusiasm for exploration, at least."

"I'm at your service when you want to go." He shook his head. "It really is exploration. Reconstruction would be difficult out there. Out in the desert places—no demons to report as yet." He looked at her as if he wasn't sure she would get the allusion; well, she really hadn't, but at least she realized that it was one. *Demons.* She would look up the word.

She said: "With the influx of cadets we may be in crowded quarters for a while, but it shouldn't be that hard to expand. As soon as the first group of trainees learn some basic elements of space survival, we'll make it part of the next phase of their training to refurbish some of the old facilities. Where did the good Doctor Sabel find his berserker, by the way?"

"He came upon it in one of the remoter corridors. A long way even from the areas where I usually poke around. A long, long way, even then, from the inhabited portions of the Fortress."

After the Sabel debacle, she knew, the more remote corridors had been rather thoroughly searched for any more machines that might become active. Of course the damned machines could be good at concealment, at playing dead, as they were good at many other things; and to this day it was not completely certain that all the active units had been found. There might even, possibly, be more of them out there somewhere, frozen into the slag of ancient battle as the object of Sabel's efforts was supposed to have been when he discovered it.

Then the commander wondered suddenly if that might be what the general was really after in his exploration—one more metallic dragon-monster. Not, of course, that Harivarman would be one to play the perverted games of goodlife. But, to find a foe still dangerous, to re-enact the combat glories of the days not long ago when Prince Harivarman had been a hero to everyone on the Eight Worlds—and incidentally to show up the Templars, for having been in control of this place so long and still having left one of the enemy functional and deadly dangerous—yes, she could see how that might be attractive to him.

At her request the general let her out of his car just at the main gate of the base, very near the spot where he had picked her up. She saw to it that their goodbyes were brief, because she had a lot of work to do. A pity. She would have liked to talk to him longer.

She would probably, she thought, soon take him up on his offer of another tour now that they had begun, as she felt, to understand each other.

As she walked through the gate and into the base, briskly returning the guards' salutes, she was wondering what his wife, or former wife, might be like.

Chapter 3

Like most citizens of most worlds with Earth-descended populations, Chen Shizuoka had never traveled outside the atmosphere of the planet on which he had been born. In human society there were a few jobs that required space travel; otherwise it was for the most part an activity of the wealthy or powerful. Chen, a poor student from a poor family, was and had always been a long way from either of those categories.

Of course he had—again like most people—read descriptions and experienced re-creations of the generally mild sensations of space flight. So nothing about the early stages of his first journey away from Salutai really surprised him. From the spaceport a shuttle lifted him and its gathered handful of other recruits up to an interstellar transport craft that was awaiting them in orbit. Except for its Templar markings, the transport was an

51

almost featureless sphere, impressive in its size to those aboard the shuttle as they drew near. Some of Chen's fellow recruits, gathered at a viewport, talked knowledgeably about the type and designation of the ship they were about to board. Chen knew almost nothing of such technical matters, and was not greatly interested in them. He supposed that now some such interest might begin to be required of him, depending on what kind of an assignment he drew after his basic training. He wondered, too, where he would serve. The Templar organization, many centuries old, and independent of any planetary government or league of planets, existed in almost every part of the Galaxy to which Earth-descended humanity had spread.

But Chen's thoughts, instead of being focused on the new life that he was entering, remained primarily with his friends back on the world he had just left, and at which he now took a lingering last look as he was about to leave the shuttle for the transport. He had been for most of his life a shy youth, not one to make friends very easily. And they were really his best friends, those people who had gone out of their way to welcome him into the political protest group. They had helped him find a direction for his life, had shared their dreams with him, along with the work and risk of organizing the demonstration. The inflatable berserkers had been his idea, though, and he was proud of it.

Chen's chief concern at the moment was whether any of his friends were also being shot at. He fretted and wondered how soon he might be able to communicate with them again. He would send mail, when he had the chance. He would of course have to try to write between the lines about his real concerns, assuming that what he wrote would be read and censored somewhere along the way. That wasn't commonly done, or at least he hadn't thought it was, but if they were ready to shoot people down . . .

Who would he write to? Hana? They weren't what you would call lovers; thank all the powers that he hadn't made any permanent connections along that line.

Whose mail was least likely to be intercepted, among the people he would trust to see that his messages got passed along? There was Vaurabourg, and Janis; but they were in it about as deep as he. There was old Segovia, who Chen thought was probably Hana's real lover if she really had one. Chen had only seen him with her once or twice, in the university library, and thought the older man probably had some post on the faculty. But Segovia had never shown up at the meetings of the protest group. And what if he considered Chen a rival?

Now Chen thought miserably that he wasn't at all good at this intrigue business, though only hours ago succeeding at it had seemed childishly easy. But then he supposed that almost no one on Salutai was very good at it. Their demonstration in front of the Empress's boat had been effective only because the authorities were at least equally inept at playing their part of the game.

Chen kept coming back to it in silent marveling: The security people back there in the city had actually *shot* at him, had really tried to kill him. Who would have believed it? He couldn't get over it at all.

It just demonstrated that things were worse even than

the most radical of his friends had tried to tell him; therefore it was even more vital than any of them had realized that the Prince be recalled to power. Prince Harivarman ought to be raised to greater power than before; he was needed to serve as the strong right hand of the Empress herself, sweeping aside the other advisers who had led the government so badly astray. Yes, that was obvious. The situation cried out for action to make that happen.

Not that he, Chen, was going to be able to take any further part in politics for some time. The Templars, welcome almost everywhere, had a reputation for being politically neutral. Fighting berserkers was their business.

So, no more politics for the time being. Unless, of course—just suppose—he should somehow be assigned to the base at the Templar Radiant itself, and there be able to meet the exiled Prince in person, and . . . but no. Chen was reasonably sure that Templar basic training was not conducted at their old Radiant Fortress which, as he understood matters, now was little more than a shrine or museum. A few words caught from his shipmates' conversation informed him that basic training for recruits from the Eight Worlds would be conducted at Niteroi, a lightweight world in the same stellar neighborhood, that shared its sun with a swarm of nearby small planets and satellites. An ideal planetary system, Chen supposed, for teaching people how to handle themselves in a variety of physical environments. Realistically, it would be a long time before he saw the Templar Radiant, if he ever did; and he could hope that the

Prince would be recalled from exile well before that happened.

Shortly after boarding the interstellar transport the recruits were assembled in the ship's passenger lounge. Chen heard official confirmation that they were bound for Niteroi, and that the voyage would occupy something like eight days, four times longer than the usual direct time. The reason was that there would be stopovers at two more worlds to pick up recruits.

The days of the voyage began to pass, Chen remaining too much occupied with his own worries to take much interest in the experience. The recruits' territory aboard ship, already somewhat restricted, began to seem crowded when more came on at the first stop. Still, the addition this time was predominantly female, and social life aboard took on a decidedly different tone. There were fascinating language and social differences to be explored. There was plenty of time for socializing; the Templar crew of the ship was making no attempt to begin training the recruits or even to enforce discipline beyond mere safety rules. All that could wait for the attention of those who did it properly, the permanent party instructors at the basic training barracks on Niteroi.

The great majority of the other recruits began to enjoy the voyage energetically at about this point. Chen would have done the same had the conditions of his enlistment been different, but as things stood enjoyment was out of the question for him. He kept trying to reassure himself that the Templars' behavior toward him so far proved that the traditional law still held—enlistment in their order gave immunity to prosecution under any planetary code. If his information was accurate—it had been acquired in large part from adventure stories, a fact which tended to worry him—the only exceptions to the rule of immunity should be a few capital crimes, matters like high treason. And no mere demonstration, he assured himself, no matter how noisy, effective, and offensive to the political establishment, could possibly be forced into that category. So he saw no reason why the traditional legal immunity should not apply to him; yet he would feel much easier when he was absolutely sure.

A few more days of interstellar travel passed, comfortable and dull. With the transport's viewports closed in flightspace, and the artificial gravity functioning smoothly, Chen might almost have been confined in a few rooms of his home city, among a gang of half-congenial young strangers.

Then the transport entered another solar system, materialized out of the realm of flightspace mathematics into the shared conventional spacetime which humanity tended to think of as normality. The ship settled comfortably into planetary orbit, and received still more recruits from yet another shuttle.

Shortly after this second brief stop, with the transport in deep mathematical flight again, the stars once more invisible outside the hull, two of the career Templars who made up the ship's crew came into the recruits' lounge. And there amid a group of his shipmates they confronted Chen.

Both Templars were older men, strong and capable-looking veterans. "Recruit Shizuoka," said one.

Chen looked up, startled, from the game upon which

he had been trying to concentrate. "Yes. Yes sir, I mean."

"On your feet. Come this way." It was by no means a request.

One of their hands on each of his arms, they escorted him out of the lounge, away from his wondering fellow recruits, and out of familiar territory into a portion of the ship Chen had not been allowed to see before. There, behind closed doors in a small private cabin, to his surprise and sudden outrage, he was ordered to strip and then thoroughly searched. His clothes were efficiently searched too, scanned with electronic devices before they were handed back to him.

Chen's questions and protests, first fearful and tentative, then injured and angry, were ignored. He would have been more loudly angry, he would have resisted violently, if he had dared. A single look at the men who were searching him assured him that such resistance would not be wise.

Dressed again, he found himself being conducted to another, even smaller room.

He was given no explanation at all, no words of any kind beyond monosyllabic orders. The door of the tiny cabin closed behind him, shutting him in alone; it was a very strange small room indeed, very sparsely and peculiarly furnished.

Still, it took Chen a moment more to understand that he was now locked up in the ship's brig.

"Recruit Shizuoka."

Chen looked around him wildly for a moment; the voice was issuing from an invisible speaker or speakers, concealed somewhere in a bulkhead, or amid the spartan furnishings.

"W-what?" he stammered.

"You will be confined until we dock at the Radiant." It was a male voice, sounding almost bored. "Pending further investigation there."

"Until we . . . we dock at the *what?*"

There was no answer.

Dock at the Radiant. That was what the voice had said.

Chen stood with his mouth open, on the verge of shouting back more questions at the wall; but there could really be no doubt of what the investigation would be about. Interrupting a procession with a protest appeared to have become something on the order of a capital crime. And he had no doubt that the voice had said that the ship was going to the Radiant. Not to the Niteroi system, where the recruits aboard had been repeatedly told that they were bound.

But why?

There was a viewscreen in the brig, taking up a large portion of one bulkhead. But there was no way Chen could discover to turn it on. Evidently if they wanted to show him something they could. Otherwise . . .

There was a clock too, built into another bulkhead panel, and it was running; Chen supposed that they could turn that off as well when they chose. But the clock continued to keep time. If Chen had known how far away the Templar Radiant was, knowing the time might have been some help.

His meals arrived punctually, trays automatically delivered in a bin above the waste-disposal slot, trays hold-ing acceptable food, no better and no worse than what he had been getting as one more anonymous recruit. The spartan plumbing worked. For entertainment the cell was furnished with a couple of old books and a reader, and as the next days passed Chen came to know the old books well. He tried to amuse himself by imagining discipline problems arising among the nineteen innocent recruits still presumably partying it up out there; would he get company if so? Somehow he doubted that he would.

He wondered what the other recruits had been told about his arrest and confinement.

Up until that last planetary stop the attitude of the Templar crew toward Chen Shizuoka had been all mild indifference, as it was toward everybody else. But imme-diately after that stop he had to go into the brig, and certainly not for anything he had done aboard ship. Therefore some word about him, some story about what he had done or was accused of doing, had already reached that planet from Salutai, and had come up with the latest batch of recruits on the shuttle, and been passed on to the officers of the Templar transport.

Whatever the Templar crew had heard about Chen Shizuoka at that point, they had had no time to commu-nicate with their superiors elsewhere. They had been forced to make a decision on the spot, and on their own initiative, and they had decided not to take him to Niteroi as scheduled; instead they were taking it upon themselves to divert the whole shipment of recruits off to the Radiant Fortress.

What could they possibly have been told?

The brig's lone inhabitant received no warning at all that an end was imminent to the last leg of his first space flight, any more than he had been warned of his incarceration. Not until the journey's last few minutes, when there came a subtle twisting of the artificial gravity, and then a slight jar felt through the deck like that of a boat grating on a sandy bottom. That, Chen knew—the adventure stories again—was the interstellar drive cutting out, and the forces employed to move the ship in normal spacetime taking over.

A few more minutes passed in isolation. Then suddenly the door to the brig was sliding open. A Templar voice said: "Come along. We're getting you off first."

And at last, being escorted watchfully along a hull passage, Chen passed an unshielded viewport again and had a good chance to see where he was going. They were still in space, and he discovered that the Fortress of the Templar Radiant, seen from outside and at close range, had a certain resemblance to the descriptions that he had heard and read of the larger spacegoing berserkers; it was an enormous, rough-skinned sphere, replete with cracks and wounds from ancient battles, and still formidable-looking with what Chen supposed were varieties of offensive and defensive armament. Heavy shadows occluded much of the sphere's rugged surface, because here a lot of the background space was dark nebula instead of stars. The Eight Worlds and their spatial environs, of which this was an extended part, were somewhat isolated from the rest of the Galaxy by enormous Galactic clouds of dark dust and gas, and were accessible only by circuitous passages from the hundreds of other human-occupied planets whose people tended to think of themselves as making up the mainstream of Galactic civilization.

The vast sphere ahead of the transport grew quickly larger, until to Chen's inexperienced eye it had assumed what looked like planetary dimensions. Then the interstellar ship that he was riding, that had looked so large to Chen when he approached it aboard a shuttle, went plunging into a mere pore of the onrushing planet's surface. This comparatively narrow passage, Chen soon observed, did not lead straight in to the dock facilities, which he assumed were near the center of the enormous Fortress, or at least somewhere on its inner surface, but made many turns. And presently he realized that this zig-zagging of the passage must have a defensive purpose too.

There had evidently been some preliminary radio communication between transport and Fortress concerning him because, immediately after the transport docked, Chen was hustled offship ahead of anyone else. Surrounded by his silent Templar escort, he was made to walk in what felt like normal gravity along a narrow paved way that appeared to be some kind of a city alley, though it was much cleaner than most of the alleys he had seen.

Resting in another dock nearby was a tourists' ship, a huge but perversely normal object. What looked like almost normal sunlight was filtering down through nearby branches, vine and tree, their small leaves quaking in a breeze that after Chen's days aboard ship certainly suggested the openness of a planet's surface. That wind had to be, he realized, somehow artificially induced and managed.

Before Chen thought to look up at the famous bright enigma that here served as a sun, he had been hustled underneath a roof and into shadow.

Now he was ordered to sit on a stone bench and wait, a sturdy and uncommunicative Templar on each side of him. But he had hardly sat down before they were dragging him to his feet again.

"The base commander wants to talk to you," warned an approaching officer. "Watch your manners."

And here she came, at a brisk walk, with escort. The base commander surprised Chen somewhat by being a young woman—well, not really that young, he supposed. He supposed also that he ought to salute, or something, as some of the people around him were doing. But as yet no one had officially taught him how.

He tried to read hope into the lady's blue-eyed stare as she came to a sharp halt before him, confronting him at close range. But what he saw there looked more like menace.

Words issued crisply from her soft mouth. "I am Commander Blenheim. I understand that you have enlisted in the Templars in order to avoid legal prosecution on Salutai."

"Uh . . . yessir . . . ma'am . . . uh."

Half a dozen other officers, including the captain of the transport ship, were standing by now, all faintly grim, almost expressionless. But they were all deferring to Commander Blenheim, and though they were looking at Chen as if he were endlessly fascinating, they showed no intention of asking him any questions themselves. This was going to be their boss's show.

The commander asked Chen, quite reasonably: "Are you guilty of this crime that you're accused of?"

"Ma'am . . . maybe I need legal advice."

She continued to be reasonable. She even, to Chen's surprise, sounded a little like his counselor at the university. "Yes, quite likely you do. Or will eventually. You see, if there are to be any proceedings against you, in a matter like this, they won't take place here. When the time comes, I'm sure you'll be provided counsel. Look here, young man, what I'm hoping for is some statement, some evidence, something from you that will demonstrate that this is all some dreadful error. That there's no need to start that ball rolling, to hold you for extradition for high treason and for murder. Maybe that's too much to hope—"

"*Murder?*" That word didn't, at first, make any sense to Chen. It was gibberish, nonsense. It came almost as a relief. It proved there was a mistake, that she had to be talking about someone else.

And then the whole thing began at last, insidiously, to make a dreadful kind of sense. Murder. And high treason, too. And being shot at . . .

The commander was studying him carefully. He looked back at her, holding his breath. But now, somehow, he knew the awful truth before she spoke.

Her gaze continued to hold him steadily, while her crisp voice said: "Her Supreme Majesty the Empress was assassinated, in the midst of a holiday procession on the planet Salutai, no more than a few hours before you enlisted in the Templars, in the capital city of that world . . .''

The base commander had not yet finished speaking. In fact she had hardly started; but Chen for the moment could hear nothing more.

Chapter 4

Lescar was in the dock area of the City, a district in which he was usually to be found shortly after the arrival at the Fortress of any kind of interstellar ship. Today, as usual on these occasions, he had occupied himself in moving from one place of business or amusement to another, quietly doing his best to gather as soon as possible any news of other worlds that might have been brought to the Radiant by the visiting crew or passengers.

In the course of today's effort along those lines the graying little man was talking to one of his regularly cultivated contacts, a minor functionary at the port facility, when word reached them of the arrival of a second ship, this one quite unexpected. The word was that a Templar transport had just been contacted on radio and would be docking at the Radiant soon.

Moving quickly, Lescar got himself to one of his favorite vantage points for observation, a public balcony near the interior docks. He was barely in time to observe the arrival of the interstellar transport ship. The great spherical shape came nudging its way up out of one of the hundred-meter-wide mouths of the vast ship channel that tunneled in through the kilometers of the Fortress's rocky shell to form the terminal of the docks. The blunt round shape of the transport came easing up into atmosphere through a forcefield skin that stretched and thinned itself before the ship. The forcefields parted slowly and gently to grant the vessel passage, while retaining in the interior of the Fortress the atmospheric pressure that they were designed to hold. For an aperture of the required size, the forcefield system worked better than a mechanical airlock.

Lescar stared at the new arrival. Yes, it was certainly a Templar transport, and it had certainly not been on today's shipping schedule. Something at least mildly unusual must be going on.

It wasn't possible for Lescar to observe directly who might be getting off the transport, or who was getting ready to board it, or what cargo was going to be loaded or unloaded. The shape of the huge docks, and the height of the walls that partially encircled them, pretty well prevented that. He could see little more than the uninformative curved top of the great ship's hull as it rested in the dock, graying and glistening as it grew a thin film of ice from atmospheric moisture.

Lescar did not stand and watch the ice develop. Instead he resumed his round of visits to certain nearby places where he had found that news from the docks was most likely to make its first unofficial appearance.

Within an hour, before even the arrival of the transport had been officially announced, he had the shocking news. It was, in a way, too startling not to be believed. And moments after Lescar had heard the words repeated, confirming them as well as he could without undue delay, he was hurrying away on foot. Keeping his sharp-featured face as expressionless as usual, he was carrying a message of world-shaking import to the Prince. What effect the Empress's assassination might have on their exile was beyond Lescar's powers to calculate, and he did not try. But he never doubted that the Prince would instantly grasp all of the implications.

Prince Harivarman, his servant knew, was at the moment about as many kilometers away from the City and the docks as it was possible for him to get, spending the day in the archaeohistorical research that had gradually come to occupy him more and more. It took Lescar only a few minutes on foot to reach the exiles' large house on the City's fringe. On arrival there, he went at once to the garage where they kept their two permitted vehicles, and got behind the controls of the one flyer that now remained in its parking space.

After making sure he had a spacesuit aboard, Lescar turned on power and eased the vehicle free of the surface. In the flyer, no point anywhere within the Fortress was more than a few minutes distant. Once out of the garage, still under manual control, he turned in the direction of the nearest forcefield gate allowing vehicular access to the airless outer regions of the Fortress.

Lescar thought he knew approximately where the Prince was working today. Still, the problem of finding another small flyer somewhere in the vast maze of the Fortress's outer chambers and corridors could have been well-nigh hopeless, except for their vehicles' locator devices, transmitting constantly. Of course the real purpose of the locators was to make it easier for the Templars to keep track of the two exiles at all times. But a fortuitous side effect was that they could always find each other with a minimum of difficulty. Their jailers had no fear that the exiles might be tempted to try to use the spaceworthy vehicles to escape; the flyers' comparatively simple spacedrives would be quite useless for such a purpose. Without a vehicle equipped with a true interstellar drive, the tricky spacebending technology that made it possible to travel effectively faster than light, there was nowhere for an escapee from the Radiant Fortress to go. Nowhere, at least, that could be reached in a mere human lifetime, of a few centuries at the longest.

On the panel in front of Lescar a glowing plan showed the main outer corridors of the Fortress, and a colored dot near one main line the location of the Prince's flyer. Tapping in a simple order, Lescar directed his own craft to proceed to the same place.

Already he had reached the portal in the floor of the inhabited surface, a miniature version of a shipping dock, that would pass his vehicle out of atmosphere. The gray veils of the forcefield gate beneath him began to work, imitating in reverse the cycle by which the larger gate beside the docks had admitted the interstellar transport. The field stretched in a gray pattern over the bubble of Lescar's cabin, then opened for the flyer, and then fell behind it, receding ever more swiftly as the vehicle accelerated.

Now around Lescar's small ship there extended great darkness, relieved only by the flyer's own lights. Those lights showed Lescar the rough stone walls of a little-used small-ship channel. The walls of the endless tube of stone went rushing by in vacuum-silence, faster and faster still.

With his autopilot now switched on, Lescar was able to spend the brief journey getting himself into a light spacesuit; the Prince would probably not be in his own flyer, but he would be somewhere near it.

The Prince was busily at work in a remote outer branch-corridor of the Fortress, where he had set up his own small battery of artificial lights, as well as a temporary shelter useful in certain of his experiments. In the brightness that his lights afforded he was looking at pictures partly incised and partly painted on the walls of ancient stone. He found the Dardanian artwork or decoration endlessly fascinating. There were frequently patterns in it, esthetic connections between one painting and another, but they never seemed to repeat themselves exactly. And, even after all his study, the pictures were still more than half incomprehensible, like art or artifacts from the old prespace age on Earth. Harivarman was of course not the first to undertake a study of the Dardanian artistic record here on the Fortress, but he thought that he was surprisingly close to being the first in modern times to approach such a study systematically.

There was much more here to investigate than the Dardanian inscriptions and pictures on the walls, though there were easily enough of those to keep a researcher occupied for several lifetimes. The sheer volume of the Fortress and its contents had prevented any thorough or comprehensive investigation. Digging into chambers sealed centuries ago by accident or design, opening closets and mysterious containers long forgotten, Harivarman had found artifacts of many kinds, some utterly mystifying. He had recently discovered some recordings of Dardanian music, and now, even as he worked, he was listening to the sounds of unidentifiable instruments, untraceable melodies.

The voices, he sometimes thought fancifully, of Dardanian ghosts . . .

At the moment he worked drifting almost weightlessly in his spacesuit, surrounded by riches of old inscriptions, kilometers of ancient stonework, and mazes of rooms, some of them containing chests made of metal and of unknown materials, still-sealed relics of Dardanian days.

When the Prince had first become interested in this exploration he had been continually amazed that there was no army of investigators here digging away already, no horde of busy archaeologists and historians from a hundred worlds competing with him. That he should have all this to himself still seemed odd. But the Templars since acquiring the Fortress centuries ago had always been cool at best to exploration by visitors, and had themselves worked at the task only desultorily. Not that they had ever raised an objection to Harivarman's efforts. He realized that they probably thought it kept him out of trouble, distracting him from dangerous political schemes.

Against one lightly curving wall of a broad corridor, a wall bearing a set of inscriptions that he had at first thought would be of special interest, the Prince had set up his temporary shelter, essentially an air-filled bubble of clear tough plastic equipped with an airlock. Drifting and thinking inside this bubble, finding these particular wall carvings less interesting the more he looked at them, Harivarman suddenly became aware of movement, shifting shadows, the dim advent of far-reflected lights. They signaled what had to be the approach of a flyer, coming down one of the main corridors nearby. It would be Lescar, he supposed. The Templars patrolled these outer portions of the Fortress only infrequently, and hardly anyone else ever bothered to come out here.

From certain familiar subtleties in the pattern of the onrushing, quickly brightening lights he was sure that it was Lescar's flyer. The Prince, turning off his Dardanian music, listening now for some communication, wondered a little that Lescar was preserving radio silence as he drew near. That in turn probably meant that the little man was bringing what he considered important news, and wished to minimize the chance that enemies were listening when he conveyed his excitement to his master.

If there were really any reason for secrecy, to have conveyed the news, or even the fact of news, by radio, even in code, would have been chancy. Once, long ago, some kind of Dardanian communication system must have linked all these puzzling shafts and chambers. Or, perhaps not . . . there might have been some ritual, ceremonial, or artistic purpose in the lack. And no real evidence of any such system now remained. The Dardanians, Earth-descended like most of the rest of the known Galaxy's intelligent inhabitants, had long since disappeared, and no one understood them any longer—if anyone ever had. Under present conditions, for various technical reasons, radio communications within the Fortress tended to be erratic, occasionally unreliable. But the exiles had for four years operated on the assumption that the Templars could eavesdrop on any conversation in or near the flyers they had so considerately placed at the disposal of those who were their unwilling guests.

Lescar's vehicle came drifting to a halt immediately outside Harivarman's temporary shelter, and by its autopilot stabilized itself in position there. The gray little man, emerging suited from the flyer's hatch, at once signaled to Harivarman in their private code of gestures that he wanted an immediate conference under conditions of radio silence. Harivarman beckoned him into the inflated shelter, which he considered as likely as any place to be secure against eavesdropping. And there he immediately heard his servant's news.

When Harivarman learned of the Empress's death, he drifted in silence for a few moments, now and then touching the wall with boot or glove, just as in gravity of normal strength he might have paced the floor. This far from the Radiant a drifting body took a long time to fall.

Looking at the inscribed wall that only minutes ago he had found so fascinating, he could see it now as nothing but an enormous and solemn toy. Worse, a means of self-hypnosis. Such was the impact, he thought, when the real world, the world of politics and power, intruded bluntly.

Briefly, memories of the Empress came and went in the Prince's thoughts. Not a blood relative of his at all, but still she had been to him at some times, and in some good sense, like a mother . . . and, later on, something of an enemy. It was she who had sent him here. Regret now at her death was mingled with overtones of vengeful triumph.

All of this emotional reaction was quite natural, Harivarman supposed, but it was quite profitless as well. Almost immediately the Prince's mind moved on. The point he had to consider at once was the effect of her assassination upon the political situation, the balance of power, particularly in the ruling Council of the Eight Worlds. When next those eight powerful representatives gathered on their ceremonial thrones, the choice of who should now occupy the great throne in the center—the choice of the next Empress, or Emperor—would be up to them.

Lescar was also drifting inside the shelter, waiting with a kind of impassive eagerness for his master's words of wisdom. Turning back to him, the Prince asked: "Did you get a look at this young man who is supposed to have done it? But no, I don't suppose you had a chance to see him."

"No, no chance of that, sir. A university student, the story is, a native Salutain, who after he'd killed the Empress joined the Templars to escape pursuit."

"Ah, yes. I see. But why should the Templars bring

him here, knowing extradition must be enforceable in such a case? More importantly, is there any reason why they should want to help such a man at all?''

''I don't suppose, sir, that they really would.''

''Then it's interesting that he should be brought here, don't you think?''

''Sir? There was something else—though no special importance was placed on it by the people I heard it from.''

''Well, what?''

''That just before the assassination—it took place in the Holiday of Life parade—there were political demonstrations. One demonstration in particular, in favor of your recall. This young Chen was apparently one of the chief organizers of that.''

Harivarman fell silent again. He drifted in thought. He could perceive several vague outlines in the situation, all of them ugly. ''And then right after that he killed the Empress? Or at least they think he did. Ah. That's all I need.''

The Prince paused. Then he continued: ''Then it looks like I'm going to be accused of conspiring to kill her. At the least it's very likely. Matters have been so arranged. So, if I'm going to do anything to protect myself, I have to see him, this supposed assassin . . . I wonder. Perhaps they brought him here to the Radiant, just to arrange a confrontation with me?''

Lescar shook his head. It was his belief, frequently stated in the past, that his master sometimes tried to think too many moves ahead. ''My thought, Your Honor, is that they brought him here simply because they had already recruited him before they found out what he'd done, or was accused of doing. Then they were in something of a panic. You know the Templars can't just hand over one of their own to any planetary authorities on demand. Not even if it's only a new recruit. They don't do that; any Templar officer who did so would be . . ."

"Yes. You're right."

Lescar's face twitched; for him, that was something of an emotional demonstration. "But they didn't know what else to do with him, and so they brought him here. This rock is the Templar headquarters, all the home territory the Templars really have, and they must feel more secure here than at the training grounds at Niteroi."

The Prince was musing aloud. "You may be right. You probably are. They could have taken him directly to their Superior General for a decision, but he's said to be almost constantly on the move around the Galaxy, and they probably didn't know where to reach him . . . you know, there's no authority presently on this rock who can decide Templar policy on matters of such importance. Our creamy-cheeked new base commander? No. No one—unless someone else came in on the same ship?—no word of that, hey? Then they'll have to wait for word from no one less than the Superior General. And he'll quite possibly want to come here and talk to the accused man before he decides the question. There'll be demands for extradition certainly . . ."

Lescar appeared to consider the idea of extradition very thoughtfully before he agreed that it was likely.

There was no one else around to fill the role of political counselor for the Prince, and so Lescar had assumed the job, and he gave it his best, just as he did the jobs of valet and cook. "Yes—naturally I suppose that's what they'll do. And you say you'll have to see this Chen too, Your Honor—is that wise?"

"How would my refusal to see him help? And yes, if I am to judge him, to try to determine the truth about his killing the Empress, I must see him—does he deny that he's guilty, by the way?"

"I have no idea, sir."

"Hm. Whoever this Chen really is, whatever his story or the truth of it, I expect our gracious hosts will sooner or later want to arrange for him to meet me. So they can observe our interactions, and then try to judge my part . . . thank you, Lescar, for bringing me this news so promptly. It's going to mean a change of some kind for us, certainly. And soon."

Lescar as usual accepted his master's thanks with a faint look of embarrassment. "Are you coming back to the City at once, Your Honor?"

"No." Harivarman brought his gentle drifting to a halt by taking a firm grip on a projecting bas-relief. "There's no rush about my appearing on the scene. Or not that much of one, at least. You go on back. I want to be alone, and think a little." He glanced at his inscriptions again. "And possibly decide what I'm going to do out here. If I'm going to be able to go on now with any of this work at all."

"Yes sir. I'll see what else I can find out."

"Do that, certainly. And if the Templars tell you they

are in a tremendous hurry to talk to me, tell them they can find me here without any trouble.''

Within a minute Lescar and his flyer were gone again. Harivarman was once more alone with the Dardanian presence; but those gentle ghosts had faded suddenly, making even fanciful communication with them much more difficult.

Looking out through the clear plastic of his shelter, the Prince watched the last fantastic reflections of the lights of Lescar's vehicle die away. Now only his own lights held the great darkness back.

The Empress dead. Certain implications, for the most part grim, were immediately obvious. His serious enemies, Roquelaure and the others, would now have a freer hand in trying to get rid of him permanently. What was not so plain to the Prince was the best way for him to try to deal with his enemies now, or at least avoid their wrath. Indeed, that became less plain the more he thought about it. He could wish now that he had heeded Lescar's frequent pleas during the first two years of exile that they try to arrange an escape. They could by now have had an emergency plan in place.

Slowly, the Prince resumed the bodily motions of the investigating archaeologist. He told himself that it might be easier to think while engaged in a physical routine of measurement, note-taking, photography . . . but a few minutes of going through the motions convinced him that it was not going to work. He could no longer believe that his energy should now be going into this research. And the job deserved to be done right; he was never again going to be able to work on this job properly.

At least he was not going to be able to go on with it properly today. And suddenly it had become difficult to predict anything about tomorrow.

Moving with practiced skill, the Prince quickly closed himself securely into his own spacesuit. Then he deflated the shelter, took it down and stowed it away in his flyer. That craft waited nearby, just out of his way, anchored by its autopilot in a passage that was no more than barely big enough to accommodate the vehicle's modest diameter. Sabel, the old records indicated, had used a similar machine, custom-narrowed for these confining corridors.

Though his lonely work had suddenly become unsatisfying, the Prince realized that there were things about it he was genuinely going to miss when it had to end. Even if the end should come in a triumphant recall to power. That, too, was now suddenly a possibility, he supposed, though not a likely one.

He would miss this work, and at the present moment he didn't even know whether he was going to be able to come back to it tomorrow.

Harivarman had already packed much of his equipment back into the flyer, when a nagging sense of untidy incompletion grew great enough to be uncomfortable. This particular short section of corridor held a pair of doors that he had been looking forward to opening. According to his experience of exploration in this area, doors placed like these should have behind them a couple of rooms, or perhaps one large room. Whatever was behind them had not yet been investigated. Those doors, he thought, were likely to open into one or two of the rare chambers that had never been entered since the Dardanians' time.

There was no need for the Prince to unpack the shelter once more, or to get much in the way of equipment out of the flyer again. One quick glance inside the room, or rooms, would be enough for now. If what he saw inside appeared sufficiently intriguing, he would have something to look forward to when—if—he got back here.

Extracting what he considered to be an appropriate tool from his packed kit, Harivarman launched himself in vanishingly small gravity and drifted in a long, free, practiced dive that brought him in a gently curving path almost exactly in front of the door he wanted. That door was of molded metal fancifully decorated. He could see nothing on it that looked like a lock. But he had tried this door gently before, on his first look around at this end of the corridor, and he was certain that it was blocked or stuck somehow. Probably, he thought, it had just become sealed with the metal-binding grip of centuries.

His tool, a combination vibrator and power hammer, soon took care of that impediment. Now the door could be slid back.

The room exposed was, naturally, completely dark inside. Harivarman shone his helmet light around, through emptiness. It was, for this part of the Fortress, a surprisingly large, deep chamber. There was another door that must connect with the as-yet unopened room adjoining. Once there had undoubtedly been functional artificial gravity. . . .

Then for some seconds Prince Harivarman did not breathe. He had thought at first that the large room was empty. But it was not. Against the rear wall, looking somehow crouched and defensive and small amid the room's emptiness, as if some enemy might have cornered it there, was a machine. The metal of it looked like armor, gleaming dully in his light. It was not really small at all, but almost as large as his flyer though of a different shape.

In this undisturbed place the minimal gravity had had time, plenty of time, to press the machine firmly though very lightly on the floor, so that now it was as motionless as the rock slabs of the walls. And the machine was no longer functional; Prince Harivarman in the first second of looking at it felt very sure of that. He would doubtless be dead already if it were.

Not an android. On second look, it did not really approach his flyer in size, but it was considerably bigger than a man, and shaped more like an insect, or a vehicle. Nor did it represent any of their most common types of comparatively simple combat units. No, this was something larger and more complex. The shape of the outer surface—perhaps it should be called a hull—suggested spaceflight capability; and there, near the bottom of the thing, within the pale of the six great folded and motionless spider-legs, was a bulge that resembled a corresponding curve on the lifeboat of an interstellar liner. That form surely indicated the presence of some kind of miniature interstellar drive.

Details were still doubtful, but one fact was certain.

There was no doubt in Prince Harivarman's mind that he had found a relict berserker, and one whose existence was undreamt of by the Templars or any other human being.

Chapter 5

By the time Chen had recovered from his faint, the base commander had departed. A different set of uniformed Templars now had Chen in charge, and they were half leading, half carrying him along a passage.

As soon as Chen had his wits about him again, he started protesting loudly.

"Look, it's crazy to think that I would have killed the Empress! Why would I have done that? I wanted to persuade her to recall the Prince! I didn't even know she'd been killed until I got here."

No one argued with him, on that point or any other. No one agreed with him about anything either. Rather it was as if they just weren't listening. All they wanted to do right now was put him away safely. They turned aside presently into a small room, where they deposited him on a plain couch.

He lay there, under the watchful eyes of his silent captors, until a couple of additional people arrived. These turned out to be a medical team, and they rushed Chen through an examination. This checkup took no more than five minutes, and evidently it revealed no conditions that required special handling, for presently its subject was on his way again, still under heavy escort and being treated no more or less gently than before. Chen was more than half expecting to be thrown directly into some kind of military prison—did Templars still call their lockup the "stockade," as they did in the adventure stories? But the room he was actually locked into was more comfortable-looking than he had expected, and it did not appear to be within any kind of prison complex. Instead, the surroundings suggested the corridor of some comfortable hotel.

Now one of the junior officers who had been hovering about took the time to explain to Chen that until further notice he was going to be confined to quarters.

"Does that mean I'm under arrest?"

"Confined to quarters."

"I know, but does that mean—?"

It was a noncom who answered Chen this time; the officers, including the one who had spoken, had all disappeared even as Chen was trying to question them. A sergeant said, "You haven't been formally charged with anything. The ship's crew who brought you in can't charge you, because all they know is hearsay, what they heard about you after they left Salutai."

"But when will I get out?" He called that question hopelessly after the sergeant's departing back.

"I don't know." By now almost everyone was gone; the only one left to answer Chen was a young uniformed woman standing in his room's doorway, evidently his sole remaining guard. The tone of her reply was doubtful, as if she were ready to admit her lack of experience in things like this, or perhaps a lack of experience of things in general. She was rather small, with a proud figure, and evidently an ancestry of dark races. Her nametag proclaimed her Cadet Olga Khazar.

The attitude of Cadet Olga Khazar, poised as she was in the doorway, strongly suggested that she was about to go out and close the door behind her.

Chen sat up straight in the chair where he had been deposited. He asked, as if the answer were not already obvious: "And now you're going to lock me in?" And at the same time he thought it strange that they had left one low-ranking guard here, and the door not yet even locked.

She replied almost timidly: "Yeah, that's orders. You're not going to kill yourself, are you? We'll have to watch you every moment if you're suicidal."

"Kill myself!" Then Chen was speechless for a moment, unable to imagine any words powerful enough to comment suitably on that idea. "If I'd wanted to die, believe me, I wouldn't have had to come all this distance to arrange it."

Now Chen could see a shifting of shadows just outside his door, and hear that a small gliding vehicle of some kind was rolling to a stop just behind Cadet Khazar, who evidently had not been left as much alone on the job as had first appeared. The cadet turned round to look at the arrival, and a moment later Chen saw her stand at attention and salute.

A moment after that, Commander Blenheim stuck her blond head into Chen's room. He got up from his chair and tried to stand at attention. She asked him: "Feeling better?"

"Yes ma'am, thank you. Look, Commander, I didn't kill anyone—least of all the Empress. What makes anyone think I did?"

The officer shook her head with what might have been sympathy, moderated with a large mixture of wariness. "Recruit, I really can't tell at this distance what you did or did not do on Salutai. All I know for sure is that the authorities there appear to want to question you about the crime. Someone on Salutai evidently thinks you did it. So you are confined to quarters until we can find out more. You have not been formally charged with anything as yet."

Chen murmured: "Or someone there wants everyone else to think that the authorities want me."

"That I suppose is a possibility." The commander nodded thoughtfully. "Who would want that?"

"I don't know, ma'am. I don't know who or why." But then in what felt like a flash of insight he perceived the shadow of an answer, or thought he did. "It's about the Prince, isn't it? Some of his enemies, I guess, will stop at nothing."

If the commander had any opinions on the Prince, or on political matters, she was keeping them to herself. Poker-faced, she eyed Chen silently, as if hoping he would say more.

Chen didn't know if what little he had said so far had helped his cause or damaged it.

He looked around the little room. Encouraged by something in the way she looked at him, he asked: "Ma'am, please, don't I get out of here for anything?"

"We'll have to arrange some kind of exercise period, since you may be in here for many days . . . and there are certain safety procedures in which training is mandatory for all Templar people on the Radiant. We'll have to arrange for you to have that as well. Otherwise, sorry, I think not. For now."

There was a robotic-sounding radio voice outside the room. It sounded as if it might be coming from the commander's vehicle, out of Chen's range of vision, and she turned away, Cadet Khazar throwing another salute unnoticed after her.

A moment later Chen could hear the older woman's voice asking: "Another ship?" Then there was some kind of radio reply, too low for him to make out. A moment after that, his room's door shut and closed him in. He got a final look, almost of sympathy, from Cadet Khazar before he heard the less subtle finality of the lock.

Chapter 6

Before he climbed back into his flyer to return to the City, Prince Harivarman unpacked some of the exploration gear that he had loaded aboard the craft only minutes ago, and stowed it away in one of the empty rooms nearby. The chamber he chose for this purpose was one of the innocent rooms off the same corridor as the room in which he had just made his great discovery.

The Prince created this cache of tools and emergency equipment with no fully reasoned plan in mind, only a half-formed idea that once he returned to the City he might find himself in need of a good reason or excuse for coming back out here, and retrieval of the cached equipment would provide one. Exactly why he thought he might soon have to begin accounting for his movements he could not have said. And of course he could demonstrate to any observer of his return trip that he was coming back *here*, to this innocent room, not *that* one down the corridor . . . it was, he thought, like a positional move in chess, made out of an educated instinct, though no immediate tactical advantage could be discerned.

The job of creating his innocent cache was quickly done. Then, with his mind in a bleak turmoil, Prince Harivarman went to look once more into the room where he had discovered *it*.

There against the far wall the berserker crouched. Or at least the long, bent insect-legs of metal made it look like it was crouching. It had not moved—no, of course it had not moved. The uppermost bulge atop the metal shape, what would have been the thing's head if it had had a head, was tilted a little sideways, and from the center of this head the roundness of a lens faced Harivarman. It was as if the berserker were regarding its visitor quizzically.

Harivarman looked a moment longer, then closed the door on it again. Quickly returning to his flyer, he boarded it and immediately headed back toward the City.

He was an imaginative man, at least at certain moments, and he thought he could feel the stare of that dead lens even now, boring into his back.

He drove the flyer slowly, cruising under manual control, as if he were observing the walls of these passages closely on the way, reading more inscriptions and locating artifact-sites. But in fact the Prince's thoughts, for the second time in an hour, had been jolted into an entirely new frame of reference.

Without consciously planning it, he had started his

trip back to the City along a different route than usual. He was heading not for the house where he and Lescar lived, but directly toward the Templar base, where he was going to report his discovery immediately.

It was an automatic reaction. Reporting a berserker machine of any kind was not only a requirement under any human law; it was, one knew without having to think about it, the only thing a decent citizen of the Galaxy could ever do—like reporting an unexploded bomb if one should ever happen to come upon one somewhere.

Still, he was proceeding slowly. Something told him that he had to think.

From what the Prince had seen of this particular berserker unit in his two hasty glimpses of it, it did not appear to have been badly smashed up in the old fighting. Doubtless it had come to the Radiant as part of an assault wave in the last berserker attack here hundreds of years ago. It must have been damaged in the fighting then, for it was certainly inert. Quite possibly at least a part of its brain had been destroyed. But equally obvious was the fact that much of the unit was still intact. Harivarman, calling up its remembered (never to be forgotten!) image, decided now that it must be some type of small but advanced lander, probably capable of functioning as a small independent starship, designed as part of a team to make a sneak attack on the Fortress. . . .

Harivarman suddenly slowed his flyer. He turned out of the small ship channel he had been following, and down a branching passage. He had come too close to the City too quickly; he needed more time to think before he got there.

His thoughts were now focused on the shape of the berserker's lower hull. Looking at that shape in his mind's eye, he was increasingly sure that it must possess an interstellar drive. In such a comparatively small package the drive would have to be an elementary affair, not much different from that of a lifeboat carried on a large human vessel.

Small or not, for all Prince Harivarman knew, the berserker's interstellar drive might still be functional—*and, if so, it might offer a means of escape.*

With some finite amount of effort—impossible to say just yet how much work might be required—he and Lescar might be able to gain possession of a vehicle that could, in a pinch, get them away from the Fortress. If not all the way to a friendly planet, then at least to some shipping lane where they could broadcast a distress signal upon re-entering normal space, and have a good chance of being picked up by a friendly ship.

At best, such an escape would be neither safe nor easy. It would be very dangerous. Just to begin with, there was the astrogation system, or rather the probable lack of one, to be considered.

And at worst such an escape plan would turn out to be suicidal madness. And preparation for it would mean a lot of work, an intense effort. And to have even a minimal chance of success, Harivarman would have to involve Lescar in the project. And now there might no longer be enough time.

Now, if the Empress was truly dead, Prime Minister Roquelaure, or one of the Prince's other enemies, would soon be sending killers after him. The more Harivarman thought about it the more certain he was of that. His would-be executioners might appear in uniform or out, they might be armed with warrants or only weapons, but they were almost certainly already on their way. He doubted that he had very many days left.

If there was a plan now that offered him any chance at all of getting away from the Radiant, he could hardly afford to be particular about its details and risks.

It had been the Empress who sent him into exile, but it had been no part of her plan to have Prince Harivarman die. He still thought that, had she lived, there was an excellent chance that sooner or later she would have called him back. Harivarman's mere existence served as a check and balance to other factions in the great game that the Empress knew how to play so well, the perpetual contest of intrigue and politics. But there were other powerful players in the game, most notably the prime minister, whose goals and ambitions were immoderate. If certain of those players came into power now, or even, as they were sure to do, became more willing to use the power they already had, then Harivarman in exile, isolated, would be virtually helpless against them. He still represented a potentially great danger to them, as long as he remained alive.

With the news of the Empress's death, the Prince for the first time since his arrival at the Fortress had known an urgent craving for escape. He had at first suppressed the feeling subconsciously, he supposed, because there seemed no possibility of acting on it. But now, suddenly . . . there might be.

There just might.

The flyer cruised slowly on toward the City, with the lone man aboard it lost in thought.

Before he decided on anything so drastic as using the berserker hardware in an escape, he would have to gather all the news he could about the reported assassination of the Empress. He would have to make absolutely sure, to begin with, that it had really happened, that the story was more than some madly tangled rumor. The commander would know the truth of that, if anyone on the Radiant did. Or she might at least have more evidence to judge it by. Perhaps she would be willing to share her knowledge with Harivarman openly.

He also had to try to obtain the most recent information possible on the general political and military situation in the Eight Worlds, and on what the Templars were thinking now. In particular he must learn how likely Commander Blenheim would be to turn her eminent prisoner over to his enemies if they came now to the Fortress to present her with what they said were valid extradition documents. He suspected she would have a hard time refusing them.

Depending on how long it took to locate the Superior General and apprise him of the situation, it might be weeks or even months before any decision made by that official could be expected to arrive at the Radiant by courier . . . or the SG, Commander in Chief of all Templars, might want to come here in person before deciding. He might even want to convene a synod or consistory of senior Templar officers. That was a rare event, and Harivarman could not recall offhand its proper title.

Deep in thought, the Prince moved his fingers lightly on the flyer's controls, altering his first choice of destination with as little consciousness of deliberate planning as he had experienced in making it. Avoiding the Templar base by a wide margin, he instead entered the City from his usual direction. Once surrounded by the usual City traffic, he shifted his vehicle into its groundcar mode, and proceeded straight to his garage.

Lescar's vehicle was in ahead of him, already occupying its customary spot. From the garage the Prince walked directly into his connecting private quarters, consisting of about eight rooms. The apartment was not particularly luxurious, but he had never cared much for luxury, and had been satisfied that the place was large enough for some elaborate entertaining. As things had turned out, he had very seldom had any occasion for that.

Harivarman was half expecting to find a message waiting for him, telling him in more or less diplomatic terms to contact Commander Blenheim promptly. She might of course have reached him by radio at any time while he was in his flyer, and bluntly directed him to report to her immediately, thus demonstrating the firmness of her control. He wasn't quite sure yet whether she was the type who had to demonstrate authority, but he could hope not; at least they had got through their first couple of meetings without much of that.

But no message of any kind was waiting for him, on either screen or holostage. Evidently, and this did not surprise Harivarman either, the commander was simply not in that much of a hurry to question him or join him in speculation about the assassination. Doubtless she

preferred to consult first with her advisers on her own
staff, and certainly she would send a robotic message
courier—or even a manned ship carrying some trusted
lieutenant—off to the Superior General, at emergency
priority, asking for instructions. Again Harivarman wondered if she even knew where the Superior General was;
the current holder of the office had a reputation for
keeping on the move.

Lescar was nowhere to be seen when the Prince walked
through their apartments. But the servant returned almost at once, as if some special sense had alerted him
to the Prince's arrival. Lescar's expression as he approached the house on foot showed that he must be
bringing with him, as the Prince had hoped, at least a
few more crumbs of news.

Not that Lescar entered their house babbling his news
freely.

Their dwelling was of course well provided with subtle,
hidden listening devices, carefully installed and moni-
tored by their jailers. Or at least both men had always
operated on the assumption that such was the case, even
though they had never found one of the gadgets. There
were moments when Harivarman seriously doubted that
the Templars, not known in these modern times for their
skill at intrigue, had even bothered to spy on him. But
the Templars would be listening now if they ever listened;
and now, for once, there was information to be exchanged that demanded privacy.

The Prince intercepted his hurrying servant at the
door. "Come for a walk with me, Lescar. I feel restless."

Outside, Harivarman turned not into the convenient

nearby park, site of most of his casual walks, but to a common City street nearby. It was a street on which people were generally scarce, winding as it did through a neighborhood only sparsely inhabited.

When the two men had achieved such a degree of security as seemed possible, the Prince told Lescar in a quick casual voice something about his find. He spoke only of a possibly intact interstellar drive unit suddenly discovered and available. He did not even hint at the unit's berserker provenance.

The graying man took the news calmly, as he took or tried to take everything that happened. His expression showed that he understood and accepted Harivarman's plan at once, without requiring details. He knew as well as his master did that there were certain commerce lanes in deep space, regions in which astrogation and drive conditions tended to be advantageous, that were favored by the vessels of regular interstellar trade. In one of those lanes, any kind of improvised lifeboat's signal would give a small craft at least a worthwhile chance of being picked up.

"We'll get right to work, then, Your Honor. Dardanian, is it, this unit?"

"I suppose it must be." The Prince considered that he had always been an accomplished liar. The secret, he had always thought, lay in believing what you said yourself, at the moment that you said it; it was the required answer, therefore the right one, and therefore it was true. He certainly wasn't going to have to convince Lescar; from the start of their exile he had always been in favor of working out some scheme of escape. Other

possibilities had existed from the start: There were ships'
crews constantly coming and going and there was the
steady tourist traffic, all this human interchange afford-
ing a means by which confidential messages and perhaps even small amounts of material could be passed—
they were going to have no time for that sort of thing
now, of course. And there were friends of the Prince in
high places on certain worlds, friends who could be
counted on for help, once some contact with them was
established. There were even one or two worlds out of
the Eight on which the Prince, once he reached them,
might hope for protection and even honor.

Always before when the possibility of escape had
been discussed between them—usually at Lescar's
insistence—Harivarman had weighed the chances and
decided to wait, hoping for an official recall instead.
This time the situation was different.

Lescar walked in silence for a little while, obviously
thinking things over. But still he asked no questions. He
had grasped the technical point at once: one of their two
special flyers could provide the tight hull and minimal
life support needed for an emergency spacecraft. And
Lescar would have grasped as well that at best there
would be a lot of work to do . . . and that at best the
risks would not be small.

Their path looped around through other City streets.
Lescar still had his own latest news to communicate, and
now began to speak in a low voice. His news concerned
the most recent arrival at the docks, the day's second
unexpected ship. In the exiles' experience, two such
landings in one day formed an unprecedented event.

The second ship, too, had come from Salutai. Other than that Lescar had been able to find out little about it, though one rumor-monger had said it was a private yacht. There was certainly some effort by the Templars to maintain secrecy about it. Lescar wanted to go back to the dock area soon and try to learn more. But he had thought that the mere fact of this second ship should be reported to his master first.

The Prince whispered: "If they've come here to arrest me already . . . well, then they've come. Too late to do anything about it now."

As they approached their dwelling again, Harivarman felt an almost irresistible urge to run to the garage, jump back into his flyer and return to the place of his discovery, there to throw himself immediately into the work of trying to salvage the needed drive. But to go back to the outer regions now, at this hour, would have been a drastic departure from his daily routine, something he was reluctant to do on the day of the great and terrible news. And one day's work on the drive would in itself be meaningless.

This time a message was awaiting him when he returned to his house. At first sight of the indicator, Harivarman braced himself internally for disaster. But it was not Commander Blenheim's face or voice that greeted him when he called up the recording. The face was that of a younger woman, of fragile loveliness, her familiar voice asking the Prince to call her as soon as possible.

His hand moved over the communications panel. Soon the recording was replaced by a live image of the same lovely face, framed in a cloud of red hair that seemed to drift immune to gravity, though its owner dwelt here on the inner Fortress surface only a few kilometers away. Even in exile, could a young Prince and a great man (so Harivarman sometimes asked himself in interior mockery) ever have a consort who was not breathtakingly beautiful?

"Harry, have you heard the news?" She seemed to be trying to suppress elation, and he wondered why.

"About the Empress? I've heard it, Gabrielle."

"Can I see you? Tonight?" She was eager.

"Of course. Where? Your place?"

"Take me out somewhere, Harry, won't you? I feel like going out."

Why did she ask that now, of all times? But he agreed, thinking that he had never taken Gabrielle out very much in the past. She hadn't seemed to mind. There weren't that many places to go anyway, in the tiny City. Why was she eager now? Was she already subverted or tricked, setting him up for an assassin team? He was capable of pondering such a question about her coldly. But it was too soon for such treachery; it couldn't have been arranged just yet, he reassured himself. In a few days, possibly.

Coming out of the shower, getting ready to go out, he looked at himself in his true-image, corner-reflector mirror, trying to assess the image objectively. He thought it more than likely that he was going to add Anne Blenheim to his list.

Chapter 7

After he had showered and changed, Harivarman went to meet Gabrielle in the City. Their rendezvous tonight was on one of the least quiet of those generally quiet streets, at a place that they had visited in the past—where in the small City had they not visited, in the two years of their relationship?—a place of entertainment, still called the *Contrat Rouge*, as it had been in Sabel's day.

Tonight, looking with changed perspective at that establishment's street sign, a sign that he must have passed at least a hundred times during the past four years, Harivarman found himself really wondering for the first time what old Sabel had experienced, dealing with a hidden berserker.

Not, of course, that his situation and Sabel's were really all that much alike.

In Sabel's time this area of the City had been, as it was now, a glassed-in mall. It had been then, as it still was, the chief district for entertainment and amusement. The decor must have been changed innumerable times during the intervening centuries, and parts of the architecture had been altered too—Harivarman had seen old holographs and models—but the overall look, like the nature of the business, was pretty much the same.

The exterior of the *Contrat Rouge* was not impressive, being mainly the same mottled brown and gray stone walls that you saw on half the buildings of the City. Neither did there appear at first glance to be anything special about the interior, thinly populated this early in the evening. The place gained a distinction of a kind when you sat in one of the booths and began to play with the optical controls that altered the appearance of everything seen through the booth's walls, which were transparent or translucent in varying degrees depending on where the controls were set. And that was only the simplest of the visual effects that could be achieved.

Harivarman found Gabrielle waiting for him. She was fine-tuning the booth's optics absently, so that the images of other patrons and of the human staff came altered through the walls of the plastic enclosure. The computer system managing the optics identified human images and clothed or re-clothed them to order. Gabrielle, in a modern green dress as fragile-looking as a spiderweb, currently had everyone who passed the booth dressed in some kind of fancy historical costumes, from a time and place that Harivarman was unable to identify.

What surprised the Prince was that Gabrielle was not alone. Sitting with her was a vastly older but still marginally attractive woman, dressed in somewhat outdated elegance. Brown ringlets hung past the older woman's hollow cheeks and arresting eyes.

Gabrielle jumped up happily when she saw Harivarman appear in the opening of the plastic wall that made the single doorway of the booth. "Harry, guess who I've found for you at last!"

For the moment, his mind filled with other matters, the Prince had not the slightest idea what this girl was talking about. "Found for me?" he asked. And then it came to him who the other woman must be, just as Gabrielle pronounced her name.

"Greta Thamar, Harry." The young woman's tone almost reproached him for having forgotten. Even after two years, Gabrielle was still faintly awed to find herself the intimate companion of a real Prince.

Now Harivarman could remember. When he had first heard that Greta Thamar, Sabel's old companion, was still alive, he had in Gabrielle's presence expressed a wish that he might meet her sometime. At that point he hadn't known that Greta Thamar might still be on the Fortress, or might return to it. And Harivarman, in the press of other recent events, had temporarily forgotten his wish to meet her.

Now he bowed lightly, extending a hand in perfect correctness. "Prince Harivarman," he introduced himself.

The woman made only a token gesture toward rising. She was not in the least impressed, evidently, and she took her time about replying. The Prince recalled that she had once in her youth undergone memory extraction at the hands of the Guardians—it was all part of the well-known saga of the treacherous Sabel—and he supposed that some permanent mental damage might well have resulted. At last she reached across the table to take his hand, and gave him a close look and a knowing nod. It was as if she believed they shared a secret.

"The management here has hired Greta again," put in Gabrielle, filling an almost awkward little silence. "It's new management now, of course. I mean—"

"They think I can bring in some tourists." The old woman's voice was surprisingly deep. Now that Harivarman had the chance to study her, her face and figure looked much younger than her actual age of centuries. It was, he thought, as if entering into legend might have helped somehow to preserve her.

Harivarman looked up involuntarily to see the metal plaque that he knew was high on the wall near the front entrance of the *Contrat Rouge*, visible above surrounding booths. The fancy optics Gabrielle had evoked in their booth's walls did nothing to change those letters on the metal.

In the year 23 of the 456th century of the Dardanian calendar
Greta Thamar, lover and victim of Georgicus Sabel, danced here

"She's actually been living here in the City all this time, Harry. Or for most of it." Gabrielle sounded tremendously proud of her find.

"Fascinating," said Harivarman. He realized that his voice sounded a touch too dry. Well, Thamar's story was really a fascinating one, he supposed. Or it would be, for a man who had the time to think about it.

The figure of an ethereally lovely human waitress approaching the booth in historical costume turned into the prosaic inhuman shape of a robotic waiter as soon as it reached the opening through the walls. The three of them ordered drinks and food, the Prince putting them on his bill; fortunately the terms of exile had not condemned him to poverty.

Gabrielle, the Prince decided, seemed unreasonably cheerful about everything. And in good appetite, ordering a substantial dinner. Maybe she was putting on an effort to cheer him up.

Harivarman, mostly out of a habit of wanting to make polite conversation, said to Greta Thamar: "I wish, then, that I might have met you sooner."

"I haven't been socializing much for a long time. But I'm going to be out now. I might even dance again." Traces of some handicap or oddity, perhaps the old woman's long-ago ME, were more in evidence, the Prince thought, the more she spoke.

"That's good," he commented. "That is, it'll be good if you really want to dance again."

"I used to live for dancing."

"I look forward to seeing a performance."

Gabrielle beamed at him for being nice to the old lady. And Greta physically did look as if she still might be able to dance, though Harivarman supposed it wouldn't

be the kind of dancing that customers ordinarily came to
a place like this to see.

Suddenly Gabrielle asked him: "Where are you going,
Prince?"

"I—" He hadn't made any move suggesting that he
was going to leave the booth, at least none that he was
aware of. "Nowhere at the moment." Suddenly understanding came. She meant that he would soon be leaving
the Fortress, under some terms that would bear discussion in public, and that he was going to have a choice as
to where he went.

He realized that Gabrielle didn't understand the situation at all. Perhaps she thought, no, she must think, that
the Empress's death meant he would be recalled to some
form of power. No wonder she had been so eager to
meet him here tonight.

Music came wafting into the booth from somewhere,
and faint laughter from the next booth. He sat there
looking closely at Gabrielle, who gazed back at him
from within her cloud of red hair, still appearing
unreasonably pleased. Gods of all space, but she was
beautiful.

Greta Thamar asked him, unexpectedly: "What do
you do, Prince? Where do you spend your time?"

"I'm an exile here, you see. Not a tourist."

"I know that." Her tone said he was a fool to think
he had to explain that to her; it was a rather sharp tone
for even a celebrity to use to a Prince. Age in some
ways had more privileges than mere rank. Greta Thamar
repeated: "But what do you *do?*"

"I spend a fair amount of time doing historical, archaeological research. Mostly out in the outer corridors."

The woman fell silent, nodding slightly, gazing into space, as if that answer had struck her as something that had to be considered seriously.

Gabrielle had been playing with the optics again, and the Prince did not recognize Colonel Phocion among the giant apes now moving in the aisles past the booth, until the man with drink in hand stopped in the open entrance.

The colonel, flushed and tending toward chubbiness, raised his glass in a light salute to Harivarman. "Cheers, Harry." He had been much less free with that informal name when he was still officially the Prince's jailer. "How are you and the Iron Lady getting on? I hear you took her sightseeing the other day." Phocion accompanied the statement with a wink. He was graying, getting along in years and in fact nearly ready for retirement, though still nowhere near as aged as Greta Thamar.

"There was nothing very exciting about our outing, I'm afraid," said Harivarman.

"What you always say in the early stages, old boy, as I recall. Well, if true, too bad. Maybe I'll call on the lady m'self. No reason why you should have all the crop attending you." And Phocion made a bow, his version of gallantry, to the two ladies.

"Have a drink with us?" Gabrielle inviting him confirmed that she was really happy about something. "You won't be on the Fortress that much longer, I suppose," she commented.

"Nor perhaps . . ." Phocion gave the Prince a look with a mixture of sharp things in it, and drowned the rest of what he had been going to say in his glass. He was waiting to get a ship that would take him away, either to an early retirement that Harivarman knew he did not want, or some uncongenial assignment that would amount to a demotion. The SG had evidently not been pleased with Colonel Phocion's performance of late.

"Nor am I going to be here much longer," said the Prince as cheerfully as he could. "And there's not much perhaps about it. You're right." He raised his own glass, returning the salute, and drank.

The colonel looked at the ladies, apparently assessing them in his quietly arrogant way; he'd already met Gabrielle, naturally, and now he looked at Greta Thamar as if he knew her too. But he still spoke only to the Prince. Now he would do his best to be bracing. "I suppose there's an excellent chance that you'll be recalled now."

"To power? Hardly." Harivarman spread his big hands. "Arrested is infinitely more likely."

Phocion's return look said that he had realized that all along, but had wanted to hold out hope.

There was a faint sound from Gabrielle across the table. The Prince looked at her, and saw incipient shock. He'd been right; it appeared that until this moment she really hadn't understood. Maybe he should have tried to break it gently.

Then she rallied suddenly. "Harry, for a moment I thought that you were serious."

Around them the interior of the *Contrat Rouge* was slowly filling up. The passage of falsified figures, costumed, bestial, or mechanical, past the booth was becoming almost a steady parade. Now a little knot of tourists passed, their appearance altered again in mid-transit by some perhaps automatic readjustment of the optics. Then some military people going by the other way created a brief distraction.

One of the tourists could be heard stage-whispering to another on the subject of how one should address a real Prince.

Phocion saluted Harry sadly and moved on, from all indications going in pursuit of one of the tourist women.

Gabrielle glanced at the woman beside her, who appeared to be far off somewhere in her own thoughts. Then she leaned across the table. "Harry, what did you mean, really? *Arrested?*"

Harivarman reached absently to give the set of optic controls on his side of the booth a random shuffling. Now the people passing were suddenly all nude, and certainly the booth made handsomer nudists of them than nature. The optics computers were biased toward subtle flattery in one mode, in another toward total exaggeration, enough for comedy. That mode did not come into play so often.

The Prince said gently to Gabrielle: "I meant arrested. I take it you've heard about the Empress?"

"Of course. But I don't see what that has to do with—you."

"Being arrested these days is nothing," said Greta Thamar suddenly, and Harivarman looked at her; she was looking past him. "Not like it was in the old days," she said, and suddenly peered at him closely.

"What do you really do, out there in the outer corridors? That's where Georgicus Sabel met the berserker."

Harivarman could feel his nerves draw taut. He told her: "I stockpile heavy weapons, oxygen, food supplies. So that when my friends land in a rescue expedition I'll be ready. I rather wish that they'd hurry up."

Greta was gazing past him. "I'm going to dance," she said.

He was about to say goodbye, and wish her luck on the resumption of her career, when he realized that Greta was not getting up, that her gaze was directed at the large holostage in the center of the room. The optics in the booth walls had been trained to let the holostage images come through unaltered.

And now, on the holostage, Greta Thamar's two-hundred-year-old image began to dance. It was an old holographic recording of a performance done live, perhaps on the very same stage, and here sat the woman herself, watching it with them.

She spoke, in a hushed voice, as if the recorded performance deserved reverence. Harivarman could not hear very clearly, but she was trying to tell them something about Sabel, and Harivarman could feel his scalp creep.

The image on the stage was that of a girl of eighteen, twenty at the most.

The first segment of the dance ended. Greta Thamar sitting in the booth appeared to come to herself, to realize that she had been rambling somewhat.

"The memory extraction still gets me sometimes. The Guardians could still use that then. Being arrested now is nothing." And now, moving somewhat stiffly, the old woman slid out of the booth and departed.

Harivarman grinned wryly, or tried to grin, at Gabrielle's worried face.

"Harry, tell me once and for all, what the Empress's assassination is going to mean."

"To me, a lot of trouble. Serious trouble. To you . . . well, I suppose that depends."

"On what?"

"On how closely you associate with me. No, it's too late to worry about that. On what my enemies think about you. On what mood they're in when they get here. On . . ."

Gabrielle was becoming intensely frightened, looking this way and that, as if those who bore his death warrant with them were here already. "Harry, if they do come after you . . ."

"Oh, they're coming. Naturally you want to know if they'll be interested in you as well. Quite natural." He felt less hurt by her attitude suddenly, and more sorry for her. "I wouldn't think so, Gabby, though of course I don't know for sure. But you're not political, everyone knows that. I shouldn't worry too much if I were you."

But it was hard to reassure Gabrielle. "I'm going, Harry."

"You haven't had your dessert." But then he relented. "Then leave. I'll stay. But I don't think it's going to matter, at this point, if you leave or not. Everyone knows that you and I have been—"

She was gone. He spun the optics control, watching her vary with the optics as she hurried away. The last spin dealt her nudity, in this case not doing justice to the original.

But now for some reason she was hurrying back . . . no, the optics had confused him, this wasn't Gabrielle at all.

Harivarman's heart gave a surprising leap.

He looked up, at close range, to see his wife standing beside the table at which he now sat alone.

Beatrix, darker, compact, in every way less spectacular than Gabrielle, said: "I waited till your girlfriend left."

"Thank you." He heard his own voice, sounding almost meek. "Will you sit down?"

She sat, pushing used dishes indifferently from in front of her. "Not the most enthusiastic welcome I have ever experienced." Beatrix was of course in her own way, in her own style, a lady of great beauty, fit consort for a Prince. As Princess she had lived here on the Radiant with Harivarman long enough to know his habits here and his haunts, and she had known where to find him this evening. She was, like him, an old experienced berserker-fighter, though few would have guessed the fact from looking at her demure loveliness now.

He said: "You were on the second ship, then, from Salutai. The one that just came in a few hours ago."

"I was. It's a private yacht. I'm not supposed to say who it belongs to, though that strikes me as silly. Anyone who really wanted to find out could. Suffice it to say that you still have friends, and not all of them are broke. Or afraid to admit they know you."

He put out a hand, to take hers on the table. "Thank you."

"Oh, don't mention it. Things were dull."

"That won't last long, I suspect." He studied her. "I suppose it's unnecessary to ask whether you know what you've got yourself into, by returning now."

"I've never divorced you, you know. Not formally. So I figure that I'm into it already."

"I guess you're right," Harivarman said after a while, and held on to his wife's hand.

Chapter 8

Next morning Harivarman awoke abruptly, with a
sense of inward shock, as if from some dream already
faded beyond recall. Yet he had the feeling that what
had roused him from sleep was a clear call from the real
world.

He awoke alone. He had insisted on Bea not moving
back into his house. He owed her that much at least, he
thought.

Fully awake, he lay for a few moments listening. The
house was quiet and untenanted around him, Lescar
nowhere in evidence. On rising, the Prince at once
checked the communication stage and screen for incoming messages, but there were none. Evidently Commander Blenheim was still in no particular hurry to
communicate with him.

Lescar, as usual an early riser, was already up and

gone. The little man, who liked to avoid electronic messages whenever possible, had left a handwritten note indicating that he was off to seek further information from some of his sources near the docks.

And no message from Beatrix. Well, Harivarman had told her to keep her distance.

The Prince, moving unhurriedly, hiding his impatience from whatever spy devices might actually be functioning within his dwelling, prepared as if for another day of nothing more important than pursuing his hobby of archaeology. When he had breakfasted and dressed, moving methodically, still restraining his impatience, he boarded his flyer in a leisurely manner and headed out alone.

In a few minutes the Prince had left behind him the Fortress's thin inner layer of atmosphere and civilization. Now he began to watch, as carefully as he could, around him and on his instruments, for any sign that he was being followed or spied on. Still he saw nothing to indicate that the Templars were keeping him under observation. Maybe, he thought, the flyers had no spy devices hidden in them after all.

By the time Harivarman had reached his destination, the remote corridor of yesterday's labor and discovery, he had got himself into his spacesuit. He parked his flyer almost exactly where he had left it on the previous day, not many meters from the chamber containing his great find. Now abandoning his pose of patience, he approached the berserker's room, drew a deep breath, and opened the door again.

His suit light showed him everything in and about the

chamber exactly as he remembered it from yesterday. The machine was inert, waiting for him in the position it must have been holding for the past two hundred years. Now the Prince could recall vaguely that the berserker had figured somehow in his dreams last night. He remembered again the inward shock, the sudden waking.

This time Harivarman approached the immobile death machine more closely, though still with slow ingrained caution. Now he could see the damage that must have knocked it out. Along one of the machine's flanks, on the side that had been hidden from him earlier, there ran a scar that could only have been inflicted by some powerful weapon. Maculations of molten metal, long ago hardened into slag, rimmed a head-sized hole that stabbed deep into the berserker's body. Small wonder that it was inert.

Straightening from his first inspection of the machine's wound, Harivarman dared to give the tilted headpiece a solid rap with the tool he had in hand. A film of dust, that must have been electrostatically acquired over lifetimes, jumped up to drift in vacuum. Certainly the thing was currently incapable of attacking anyone. There might of course be some last booby-trap built into it somewhere, but that risk the Prince had already decided he must accept.

Then on with the job.

Within a few minutes the Prince was well on the way to setting up his temporary workshop. He already had some lights in place around the dead machine, and had brought in some more tools from the flyer, and had about made up his mind on the best way to begin. It would probably be best first to disconnect the drive unit somehow from the larger portion of the berserker's body, and then move either the drive or the rest of the berserker away into another chamber. If he did that, then the origin of the device he was working on might not be so glaringly obvious. And then, when he brought Lescar out to help him, he might possibly be able to convince Lescar that the hardware they were trying to use was really Dardanian. Lescar's loyalty to his Prince was unshakable, Harivarman had no doubt at all of that; but the Prince also understood that the graying man lived with a monumental fear and loathing of berserkers.

Once he had the necessary minimum of tools and equipment in place, the Prince got to work. It was easy enough to decide to separate the drive unit from the rest. But there was of course the berserker's combat armor to be dealt with. And even here in near-weightlessness the inertia of some of the massive parts was going to make them hard to handle. Of course Harivarman had in the flyer a power-lifter that he could use.

Fortunately, these days even amateur archaeologists were often equipped with high technology. The Prince had an elaborate toolkit already assembled in his flyer. Enough equipment, perhaps, to enable him to get by, at least through the early stages of the job. If he needed more equipment, he could probably invent some convincing story that would let him obtain it.

It was time, he thought, that was going to be his real problem. It seemed certain that he was not going to be allowed the days he needed.

Several hours after his arrival at the site, the Prince

had his bubble-workshop inflated. Not in the chamber where he had found the berserker, but in the one adjoining, which fortunately for his plan was connected to the berserker's room by a closable door. Inside his large plastic bubble there hung, almost drifting in the weak gravity, the interstellar drive. Still in its inner casing, it was a massive pod two or three times greater in volume than a man's body, and considerably heavier. Harivarman had tied it to supports in three dimensions to keep it more or less positioned where he wanted it.

Another hour passed. Now that portion of the berserker's control system that seemed to directly concern the drive had been extracted and was already in the process of being spread out for dissection, like some rare and complex biological specimen, on a series of folding boards. The Prince was probing into the control system's electronic nerves with a series of tools, several of which were connected to his flyer's onboard computer. He had had to move the flyer a little closer to the site, wanting to run cables to the computer and not use a wireless link whose signals might conceivably be intercepted.

The Prince's first objective in this examination was to see whether the circuits commanding the interstellar drive unit remained functional at all. The preliminary indications were positive. He had studied berserkers intensely in the past, the better to fight them, and he now had a fair idea of what he was looking for.

And presently he raised his head, sighing. Yes, he could assume now that these control circuits were functional. But how he was going to get them to function under his control was something else again.

Harivarman pushed on with his examination. More time passed, unnoticed by the man who had grown totally absorbed in what he was doing.

But less and less was he thinking of his plan for escape. Eventually an hour had gone by in which the thought of arranging a means of escape from the Fortress had not entered the Prince's mind at all.

He was, instead, making a discovery. The revelation was proceeding only in small steps, but they were steps whose sum was truly breathtaking.

Almost from the start it had been apparent that some very peculiar control information seemed to have been left in the memory banks connected to the interstellar drive of this particular berserker. And Harivarman very soon got the impression, from a certain lack of organization in the way the data was stored, that it might have been left where it was inadvertently. It was chiefly the nature of that information that concerned him now.

Near the beginning of the fourth hour of his investigation, the Prince really paused for the first time. He had to pause. And he had to put down for a while the electronic probe, because his hand was cramped and shaking from gripping it so hard in his excitement. Closing his helmet, resealing the spacesuit that he had been wearing half open inside the shelter, he went out through the shelter's airlock and out of the antique room, its walls almost the same color as those of the *Contrat Rouge*. In the airless, almost lightless corridor outside the room he paused, clinging to the rough stone wall. In one direction the corridor ran straight for a few hundred meters before coming to an abrupt termination, where some ancient attack, probably by berserkers, had blasted an enormous crater into the outer surface of the Fortress. Looking in that direction, the same direction that was so faintly down, the Prince could see the stars.

Harivarman thought that the discovery he was making, or was on the verge of making, had no parallel in human history.

The original berserkers had been constructed by a race now known only as the Builders, as their last, all-out, desperate bid to win an ancient interstellar war, a war they were fighting against living opponents who were now remembered only as the Red Race. Little information was now available about that war, because it had been fought at about the same time that humanity on Earth was beginning to chip flint and perhaps make arrows. The berserkers' Builders had been arrogant and powerful without a doubt. But they had long since vanished from the stage of Galactic time and space, following the Red Race into oblivion, more than likely victims of their own hideous creations.

The metal war-machines that humans called berserkers were the ultimate enemy of everything that lived. The creators of those inanimate weapons were gone, but the weapons themselves raged on across the Galaxy, endlessly repairing and replicating themselves, improving their own design, and refining their killing capabilities in an eternal effort to accomplish their basic programmed task, the elimination of all life, wherever and whenever they could find it.

Throughout the centuries since Earth-descended humanity had found itself locked in a struggle against the berserkers for survival, human intelligence had postulated and continually sought one great key to victory. Theory held that at least at the beginning of the Builders' ill-starred creative effort, there must have existed some sort of control system by which the Builders could turn the berserkers on and off. A safety code, perhaps. Some means by which the metal monsters could have been handled and tested in reasonable safety by mortal if unearthly flesh and blood.

As far as Harivarman in his earlier studies had discovered, no trace of any such control system or code had ever been found, by Earth-descended humanity or any other living race. Possibly no such code or system had ever existed. If the Earth-descended Dardanians were now a mystery to their cousins who had spread to other worlds, the unknown Builders, eighty or a hundredfold more distant in time, and not of Earth at all, were that much more difficult to understand.

But it seemed now to Prince Harivarman, with neither his own skepticism nor his computer yet able to fault the truth of his discovery, that the answer to the riddle of the berserker control systems might be within his grasp—one answer to it, anyway. The control sequence that appeared to be revealing itself to him might, he supposed, work for only a certain model of berserker, or perhaps it might work only on machines that had been built in one particular factory or base . . . Harivarman supposed that this piece of hardware before him could hardly be one of the original machines, still largely intact even if not functioning after fifty thousand years or so . . . but he really had no way to judge.

Of course the first question he had to face was whether the controlling code he thought he saw—a relatively simple sequence of radio-frequency signals—was really what it seemed to be. As far as he could tell with the equipment and knowledge he had available, it was. Thank all the gods of space and time, he was not faced with the opportunity for a full practical test.

But if the code was genuine, why should it have been left here? Left here still intact, fifty thousand years after its intended usefulness to the Builders had ended, exposed to the possibility that enemies might someday capture and examine it?

Harivarman couldn't guess why, except that the Builders were demonstrably capable of making gross mistakes. Even colossal blunders. And he knew from experience that even berserkers could sometimes simply malfunction.

As part of his intensive study of the enemy during his years of fighting berserkers, the Prince had taught himself the Builders' ancient language too, or almost as much of it as any living human being knew. That was not much; it included the little that had been picked up from rarely captured records of the Builders and what little more had been deduced from that. The audible form of the language was all clicks and whistles, beyond any Earth-descended throat and vocal apparatus. But the written symbols could be manipulated. And the electronic signals of this code he was now uncovering ought to be easy to reproduce.

Never before, to Harivarman's knowledge, had anything like this seeming control code been found by any human seeker. Had such a discovery ever taken place, it would have been of tremendous importance for all humanity, for all Galactic life, and the news of it must have been spread rapidly. Of course, the only reasonable place to look for such a control code would be in a berserker device that had been captured more or less intact. The Prince knew that the total number of captured intact berserkers in the whole war had been no more than ten or twelve, an amazingly small number considering that the human war against them had raged through thousands of battles, fought across millions of cubic parsecs of the Galaxy, and had dragged on over a span of many centuries. The machines as a rule destroyed themselves when they could fight no more. Or they destroyed at least their own inner secrets. And if the ten or twelve other berserkers known to have been captured had ever carried similar controlling information in their memory banks, they had erased it before they fell into human hands.

But it had not been erased from this one. . . .

Harivarman at length had to force himself to lay down his tools for the day. He had to avoid rousing suspicions of any kind by an unusually prolonged absence from the City. He packed some of his equipment back into his flyer and commanded the machine to take him back into the City. And he was even more thoughtful on this return flight than he had been on the last one. But this time he immediately programmed the flyer to head for his own garage; all thought of announcing his discovery to the Templars had been abandoned for the time being. The realization that he had done this crossed his mind, and he told himself vaguely that he would make that announcement eventually, but in his own way, and in his own good time.

He had left his temporary workshop erected in the distant chamber, with the berserker drive and part of the control system inside it, open to discovery and inspection by anyone who might happen to come along. Doing so would save him time when he came back for the next work session, and time was all-important now. He would just have to risk discovery of his work site. If anyone should stumble on it or seek it out, there would be no doubt anyway as to what sort of work was going on, or who was doing it.

But no one, it appeared, was interested in his remote archaeological research. Harivarman spent the rest of the day unmolested, thinking and resting part of the time, and quietly obtaining a few more tools and materials.

Next morning Beatrix called him early.

"Harry. Am I going to see you? Or did I waste my time and effort completely in coming back here?"

"I . . . you'll see me, I promise you." He was known for not making promises lightly. "But not just yet. I appreciate your coming back."

"Do you? I wonder. I suppose I thought that perhaps at last you would."

He did his best to be brilliantly convincing. They talked a little longer. But what it came down to was that he put off seeing her, as tersely as he could—let her think that he was afraid of being spied on. He put off Lescar, too, by ordering him to remain in the City to gather information.

Harivarman was soon back at his lonely task.

By the end of his second long session of work on the berserker's drive-controlling circuits, the Prince considered that he had done all that was possible, under the conditions, to confirm his discovery. He had actually recorded a version of the basic control signal, and had loaded the recording into a handheld radio transmitter. His next experimental investigations, if he were ever able to conduct them, would necessarily be much more daring.

But it was time now to forsake science and get back to engineering, specifically to the driving necessity for escape. Periodically the Prince's memory, like some nagging robotic secretary, reminded him that any day now, any hour, another ship would arrive at the Fortress, a ship of his enemies, and he would almost certainly be arrested. A rational, conservative part of his mind was starting to argue that he should go to the Templars now, before that happened, go to them this hour, this minute, with what he had discovered.

The rational argument with which he tried to convince himself went like this: No human authority would allow the agent of such a discovery, an achievement of such great and glorious consequence for all life in the Galaxy, to be arrested for some crime committed in a place far from where he was, to be taken away and quietly murdered. But Harivarman had been involved in politics too long to allow mere rational argument to determine his decisions. Maybe the widely beloved Empress had come to believe that she could never be murdered either.

And there was still another reason why Harivarman held stubbornly to his secret. In his mind faint nagging doubts about the truth of his discovery persisted. Those doubts in themselves might have been enough to hold him back from making an announcement. Instinct whispered to him that something was not right, something about what he thought he had discovered . . . maybe it was only because the revelation seemed too perfectly well-timed, coming as it had.

But there it was. The interstellar drive was real and right enough. Not only the control circuits but the whole drive unit was functional, or ought to be, as far as Harivarman's rough tests could tell.

If the Prince was not going to be able to depend on the great value of his discovery to save his life, then escape, using the berserker's drive, appeared to be as much of a necessity as ever. For his third work session on the berserker the Prince brought Lescar out to the job site with him. He told Lescar very little more than he had told him at the start, and showed him only the room in which the innocent-looking drive unit now reposed, and got him started working on it. Lescar's first assigned task was to dissect the control system of the drive further, in preparation for its installation in a different kind of vehicle.

As Harivarman had expected, Lescar's only open reaction to this assignment was to signify his understanding of it and immediately take up a probe and get to work. The servant's willingness to take on any task the Prince assigned him was understood by both.

But the Prince was frowning, even as his assistant

took his tools energetically in hand. To Harivarman
himself, the necessity of explaining some of the technical details of the escape project to a helper, putting the
whole idea into plain words, had been enough to make it
begin to seem impossible.

And the more fiercely Harivarman tried now to recon-
vince himself, the more unlikely the whole scheme of
using the drive unit began to appear in his thoughts. It
was an *interstellar drive* they were concerned with here,
and not the motor of a groundcar. It was even a drive of
a largely unfamiliar type.

For a few moments the Prince hovered on the brink of
changing his mind suddenly, of telling Lescar to aban-
don the project and go back to the house and forget what
he had seen. But the Prince did not do so. Instinct
forbade that too. The trouble was, thought Harivarman,
that they had no choice. The more time he had in which
to consider the political situation, the more firmly he
became convinced that now, with the Empress gone, his
enemies were soon going to attempt to finish him off,
one way or another.

A day of intensive effort passed, and then another,
with the two men working busily—most of the time not
really side by side, but just out of each other's sight.
Lescar's job in its present stage could rarely benefit
from two pairs of hands, and the Prince was still keeping his own work secret even from Lescar. Harivarman
labored in the adjoining room, now tracing the paths of
control signals through the body and the main brain of
the berserker, seeking additional memory banks, looking for more confirmation of his find. The indications

that he found were intriguing, but still somewhat ambiguous. A large part of the thing's brain was evidently inaccessible, inside an inner seal of armor impervious to any of the tools he had on hand. In there, if anywhere, he thought, would also be a destructor device, a booby-trap.

The Prince had contrived to keep the berserker covered most of the time with a sheet of opaque plastic, material he sometimes used as a background or light-reflector when making photographs. Lescar, on the couple of occasions when he happened to glance into the room where the Prince was working, saw nothing that startled him particularly. Harivarman had implied that he was trying to get the astrogation system of a Dardanian lifeboat working.

Throughout these days of hard work the Prince actually grew increasingly skeptical regarding his world-shaking discovery. Or perhaps he was not so much skeptical of the discovery itself as of its immediate value to him. To announce a revelation of such magnitude now—especially if it were quickly challenged, as any such claim would be—would lay him open to charges of making up wild lies in an effort to save himself. And there was no way his claim could be quickly proven.

But, if he had not discovered what he thought he had—then what had he found?

He badly needed to talk to someone, and he could not talk to anyone. Not yet. Not even to Lescar.

And doubt still whispered to him that *something* was not right. A kernel of unease still nagged at him. Perhaps it was only because he had to bear his knowledge all alone.

Harivarman found himself continually being struck by the fact that his discovered control code, if such it truly was, appeared to be so easy to use. There was even a fairly wide choice of frequency and modulation of the signal. The signal itself, suitably compressed, could be transmitted in a fraction of a second, complex though the code-sequence was and virtually impossible to arrive at by accident or through trial and error.

Of course, ease of use, if you thought about it, was really logical enough. If you had a control code for berserkers at all, you'd certainly want it to be easily and quickly usable.

All very logical, but yet something about it nagged.

By the second day after Lescar had been added to the work force, something like a routine had been established, and the two men put in several hours of effort without anything out of the way happening. By this time Harivarman was ready for a break, and he had left his own job for the moment, as he did periodically, to confer with Lescar. The Prince was standing, almost drifting, in the room where his assistant labored, though he had not joined Lescar inside the inflated shelter. With the transparent wall of the shelter between them, the two men were discussing, in the private code of gestures they had worked out, the length of time a flyer might have to be immobilized to fit it for escape.

Suddenly through the stone around them there came a faint vibration, frightening because it was unexpected and at first inexplicable. Harivarman could feel it through the one hand with which he was gripping the wall, holding himself in position.

Simultaneously Harivarman observed an odd change, as of a moving shadow, in the light that shone through the imperfectly closed doorway from the next room. That shadow would move in his nightmares for the remainder of his life.

In the next moment, before Harivarman could speak or move, the connecting door between the rooms burst fully open. That intrusion was accompanied in vacuum-silence by some destruction of the adjacent wall, as a large object that was too wide for the doorway came through it anyway on six long mechanical legs, stone bursting and erupting around it. The berserker's half-gutted belly still hung open, a cable or two trailing from the site of Harivarman's surgery. The legs were all unfolded now and at least four of them working, performing at least well enough to propel the huge berserker at the speed of a walking man.

If Lescar cried out, the sound was not broadcast on radio and Harivarman did not hear it. Harivarman did not spare a moment to look at his helper, but instead took one look at what was coming through the doorway and sprang for the doorway leading out to the corridor. It was an instinctive effort to reach . . . no, not the flyer. Nothing in the flyer would be useful to him now. It was a prisoners' vehicle, weaponless.

Even as the Prince sprang to escape, he saw from the corner of his eye how the thing turned after him; it might still be powerful enough to brush stone walls aside, but this first real sight of it in unimpeded motion suggested that it was crippled, and terribly slow for a berserker. Now Lescar in his shelter might be given time to get his helmet on, before the plastic was ripped away from around him.

The Prince scrambled through the door and leaped from its outer sill. He flew across the corridor, caromed off the far wall, and in another practiced low-g dive spun back again directly for the doorway of the berserker's original room. He had left his recording of the supposed control signal in there.

Meanwhile the berserker, perhaps only belatedly recognizing the presence of another life-unit, had turned back after Lescar. Reaching out one of its limbs it tore the shelter down, the ruptured plastic exploding in a puff of briefly visible atmospheric fog. Harivarman, reentering the room at top speed, holding what he hoped was a control device in hand, was just in time to catch the faint wavefront of that puffy blast, and to see that Lescar had indeed managed to somehow close up his helmet.

In both hands the Prince raised like a gun the small recorder-transmitter that held what he had deduced was the control code. He transmitted the signal.

The machine, just on the point of seizing Lescar, halted. It had actually caught him by one arm before the signal reached it, but the movement of the berserker's arm that would have crushed the man if it had been followed through was instead aborted. The slowed effort of the metal arm only launched Lescar gently into a harmless hurtling flight, a flight that ended when his master caught him in midspace as he went by.

That last aborted movement of the berserker had left its own body spinning gently. It brought itself to a neat and almost gentle halt, a giant spider hanging against the big room's opposite wall. It clung there, obviously still in control of itself, no doubt still alert, but making no further demonstration of hostility.

The Prince clutched his servant in his powerful arms, damping the desperate struggles that the smaller man was making in his blind panic. Eventually, talking on radio, wrestling, soothing, Harivarman got Lescar under control, held back from crazy flight.

According to Harivarman's elementary understanding of how the code should work, the berserker might now be susceptible to spoken orders transmitted on the same frequency as the first disabling code had been.

Lescar had frozen in terror and shock. Still gripping him cautiously with one hand, the Prince managed to turn on his own helmet microphone to that frequency. Then, pointing with his free arm at the machine, Harivarman said: "Remain there. Do not move until I order you to move." It scarcely occurred to him as a possibility that the machine might not be able to understand his speech. His language was, he knew, not greatly changed from one of the human tongues that had been in common use on a number of worlds in the days of Dardanian greatness; berserkers, like humans, made an effort to learn the languages of the enemy.

The machine remained.

The Prince still held on to Lescar, who was still in pitiable shape though not seriously injured physically. The man was cowering, and his face seen through the helmet glass looked stunned; Harivarman could feel the tremors in the other's body even through their two suits and his own gloves. "You're safe now, Lescar. It's not going to move."

Harivarman was not yet trembling himself. He thought that he might, later, when he could afford the luxury. Now, dragging his servant with him, not taking his eyes from the inert berserker, Harivarman backed from the room out into the corridor. Lescar did not resist, or try to help.

His master had him inside the flyer, both their helmets off in breathable air, before the servant spoke. "Your Honor, I will go and get weapons. Somehow. Then we must destroy it."

"Later, my old friend. Later. For now, this moment, do nothing. Just wait here and rest. Will you promise me?"

It took the Prince a few more minutes of talking, persuading, calming, before he was sure that Lescar was going to follow orders strictly.

Then Harivarman resealed his own helmet, and went back to face the thing that he had found, and the thing that he had done.

Chapter 9

In the process of soothing and coaxing Lescar out of his near-catatonic state the Prince had gained time himself to recover from the ghastly initial shock. He saw Lescar settled safely into the flyer. Then, feeling himself more intensely alive than he had felt for years, he returned to the room where he had left the berserker, to again confront the deadly thing that he had evidently been able to bring under his control.

Looking through the doorway from the corridor, he saw that the machine was exactly where he had left it a few minutes earlier, clinging like a spider against the opposite wall of the big room.

The Prince stood in the doorway. He keyed in his suit radio's transmitter on absolute minimum power, carefully choosing the same frequency at which he had sent the immobilizing code. It was not a frequency in common use within the Fortress, and with the low power he was using it was unlikely that Lescar in the flyer, or any other living listener, was going to pick up this transmission.

Speaking softly, again raising one arm to point at the machine, he demanded of it: "Do you understand me?"

The answer in his helmet was low, but clearly, slowly spoken. "I do." The tones of that voice were strange, fragmented and uneven. The Prince had heard the like often enough in his years of warfare. That voice had been put together as the berserkers in the old days had fashioned human voices for themselves, electronically melding words and syllables together from the recorded speech, the preserved emotions, of some of their multitudes of human prisoners.

Harivarman felt a faint shudder go through him. It was as if something in the space around him had sucked heat out of his suit. He said: "Use the minimum effective power in your transmissions, please." Then, marveling at that last word he had just used, he added: "That is an order."

"Order acknowledged," the berserker answered. Then it paused for two seconds before it asked him bluntly: "Are you goodlife?"

Somehow that shook the Prince, and turned his fear to anger. He felt a wild impulse to deny the accusation, to clear up any misunderstanding that the berserker might have on that point. But he was only talking to a machine.

Before he could speak to the damned thing at all he had to clear his throat. It had been a long time, he thought, a decade or two at least, since he, Prince Harivarman, had been so affected by nervousness.

When his throat was clear he demanded of the berserker: "Are you ready to receive further orders now?"

"I am standing by for orders." It was not going to press him, then, to respond to the question about his goodlife status. Harivarman felt relieved, and at the same time somehow guilty for the feeling.

He said: "I order that from now on you do nothing harmful to me or any other human." His throat felt dry again, and again he had to pause before he added: "Unless or until I specifically order otherwise."

"Order acknowledged." The broken-sounding syllables came out eerily, possibly the words of human prisoners that it had killed a thousand years ago. Its voice-tones chimed and changed, as if in mockery.

"And it will be obeyed? You will obey that order?"

"That was my meaning. I will obey. I must. I am constrained to do so."

Harivarman relaxed slightly, clinging with both gauntleted hands to the stone frame of his doorway. Now his suit was too hot, and he could feel himself sweating inside it.

So, what was he going to do now? He felt exhausted. And Lescar needed to be taken back to the house, to have a chance to pull himself together. And it was necessary to find out what was happening in the City, to know if those who would be coming to arrange his death had yet arrived. . . .

And now, the berserker. It appeared that Harivarman

was simply going to have to go away and leave it here, as it was, still essentially functional.

"I order you," he said, "to remain in this room until I return. I order you also to transmit no signals of any kind till I come back."

"Orders acknowledged."

"And harm no one. No unit of human life."

"Order acknowledged."

"Good," he said, and closed the door on the damned thing, and wished that there were gravity enough for him to lean and sag against the door.

Anyway, he reassured himself, the chance of anyone else stumbling on it out here was astronomically remote. If no one had found it here in two hundred years . . . He reminded himself to emphasize that point to Lescar.

Still, Harivarman found himself almost unable to simply leave. He was tempted to weld shut both doors of the room. Only the vivid memory of the death machine breaking its way through the stone-walled doorway between rooms kept him from wasting time on that.

Leaving the doors of both rooms closed, all traces of his investigation, as far as possible, removed from the corridor, Harivarman rejoined his servant in the flyer. When he climbed into the vehicle's cabin, Lescar looked at him in silence. On the little man's face was a haunted expression the Prince had never seen there before.

The Prince sighed to himself. Managing Lescar in the immediate future was not going to be easy. Still, at the moment, Harivarman felt oddly confident and happy. It was his usual response when there was a real and immediate challenge to be faced.

He raised a hand to the control panel, to start the flyer, then let his hand fall without touching the controls. "Well, Lescar? Speak, tell me all of your objections."

Lescar only shook his head, a slow, slight movement.

The Prince, making his voice urgent, full of soft energy, said: "You see, don't you, what a monumental discovery I have made? I found a way to stop the thing in its tracks—to make it obey my orders."

Lescar's lips moved; the words were so low that Harivarman could not make them out. His eyes still stared at the Prince hopelessly.

Harivarman, gripping him by the arm, giving him a little shake, persisted. "Do you see what this could mean?"

The servant's eyes turned away, and he was silent. And now Harivarman was distracted from his task of management. There was a faint new illumination growing in the corridor around their flyer. It signaled the imminent arrival of another flyer, or at least a vehicle of some kind.

The two men looked at each other. Lescar with a slight head motion indicated mutely: *I'll be all right.* Harivarman left him at once, closed his helmet and cycled himself out through the flyer's small airlock. In a long, gently curving dive he projected himself to where the approaching Templar staff car had just drifted to a stop. He wanted to meet its occupants, whoever they were, before they got out and started nosing around, noticing nearby doors and rooms and other things. Only one vehicle had arrived. If they were coming to arrest me, thought Harivarman hurriedly, there'd be more of them . . . but he wasn't really sure of that. He supposed it might depend on whether the new arrest warrant from Salutai or the Council message addressed him as Prince or only General. All a matter of status.

Commander Blenheim, wearing a spacesuit marked with the insignia of her authority, her helmet open, was seated in the rear of the newly arrived staff car. He could see her watching his approach. When Harivarman appeared just outside her window, she motioned for him to use the airlock and join her. Already sitting beside her in the back seat was a young man, unknown to Harivarman, and also wearing a spacesuit, though without insignia of rank. Like the commander he was wearing his helmet open. Up front in the driver's position, separated from the rear by a glass panel, sat a driver-bodyguard with sergeant's stripes on the shoulders of his suit, looking dutifully straight ahead.

The Prince cycled himself in through the airlock. This staff car was a somewhat larger vehicle than his own flyer, and notably more luxurious as well, with a touch of artificial gravity laid on in the interior. *Down,* as Harivarman entered, was suddenly toward the tiny cabin's deck.

"I've been rather curious about what you do out here," was Commander Anne Blenheim's greeting.

"I'll gladly include some of these sites in the next tour," the Prince replied almost absently, easing himself into a seat facing her. He realized that he must sound and look happier than the last time this woman had seen him, and he wondered what she, who probably had a good grasp of the political situation, might make of that.

From the seat beside hers, the spacesuited youth whose name he thought he could guess was gazing back at Prince Harivarman, favoring the eminent man with a muted stare. It appeared to be an attempt to disguise sheer awe. The Prince had been the subject of enough awed glances in his time to know. But it was impossible for him to tell whether the young man was wearing a uniform or civilian clothing inside his spacesuit. At least he was not a Templar officer, Harivarman was sure of that.

The Prince said: "Commander, if your companion here is who I think he is, well, I've looked forward to meeting him."

"Good," Commander Anne answered dryly. "That's why he's here now." She paused. "Also, I wanted rather urgently to have a talk with you, General Harivarman. To confront you with certain—facts. I wanted to make up my mind about certain things, as much as possible, before I am called on to make decisions."

"If you mean your approaching decision as to whether to hand me over, when someone who hates my guts comes to the Radiant and demands that you do so—yes, I think you're right to give that one a lot of thought."

Anne Blenheim's blue eyes, trying to conceal their own strain, studied him carefully. "What makes you so sure that someone is coming to arrest you?"

He only looked at her.

She looked away at last. "Yes . . . well, I may as well tell you, General. We've had radio contact within the past hour from another unscheduled ship; it'll be the third to arrive here in two days. It was reluctant to identify itself very precisely. But it's from Salutai, and it will of course be here in a matter of a few hours.''

Harivarman was once more looking at the young man, who still gazed back at him with starry eyes.

The commander sighed. "General, this is Chen Shizuoka. From Salutai.''

The two men touched hands in traditional greeting.

The youth said: "Prince . . . I feel honored to meet you.'' It was obviously a considerable understatement.

The Prince was unable to see either a mad assassin or a crafty schemer in this young enthusiast before him. But something odd was going on. Harivarman said coolly: "I hear that you arranged a demonstration in my favor.''

"It was an honor to be able to do so, sir.'' Now Chen's face and voice grew quickly troubled. "But then . . . a few days later—only after I had been brought here to the Radiant—I found out that Her Imperial Majesty had been killed. Even while the demonstration was going on. As I say, I was already here before I found that out. But even before I left Salutai, someone had tried to kill me too. They fired at me in the street.''

"Aha. I hadn't heard about that.'' Harivarman glanced at the commander, who evidently had.

She gently prodded young Chen. "But you said nothing about anyone having shot at you when you enlisted?'' It sounded like she had been over this ground with the youth before, and doubtless more than once, but she was going to do it once more for Harivarman's benefit.

"No ma'am, I didn't. I wanted to get offworld, to save my life. I thought then that it was Security shooting at me. Now I think it must have been someone connected with the Empress's real assassins." Chen, without further prompting, now related his whole version of the events on Salutai, beginning with the secret preparations he and his friends had carried out for their impressive demonstration. It sounded like about the hundredth time he'd told the story, so that by now it had a rehearsed tone.

Harivarman found himself inclined to believe it anyway. He said to the young man: "If all that's true, it seems to me that you have been used."

Chen nodded, miserably, reluctantly. "I still can't believe that my friends—the ones who helped me organize the demonstration—were mixed up in an assassination."

"Perhaps not all of them were." Harivarman looked into the blue eyes of Anne Blenheim, and there saw himself being weighed, even as he had just weighed Chen and his story. The Prince hoped she was as perceptive as he was himself.

Harivarman said to her: "The young man here may be as innocent in this matter as I am, you see. But I shall be very much surprised if accusations, indictments, are not soon brought in from Salutai against me."

She shook her head. "I suppose we may know more about that when this third ship arrives. But your guilt or innocence is not up to me to determine, General."

"Theoretically that is so. But in practice you may very well have to decide my future. You will be the highest Templar authority here on the Fortress when that ship gets here. If they're coming to get me, as I assume they are, you will have to decide whether to turn me over to them or not."

She regarded him silently.

He pressed her. "Isn't that what you meant just now when you spoke of having to make up your mind about certain things? And in bringing the young man out here to see me? Do you really think I've been spending my spare time in captivity trying to arrange an assassination of the Empress? When you can see what peril that puts me in?"

Commander Blenheim shook her head. "How am I supposed to know that? I've only been here a few days myself."

"You're going to have to know it."

She didn't like to be told, by her prisoner, what she had to do. "I repeat, that is not my decision, General. We'll talk of this again. Very soon, I suspect." She keyed a circuit, and spoke to her driver: "The general is getting out now. Then take us right back to the base."

Harivarman closed up his helmet that he had opened on entering the vehicle; and shortly he was drifting in the corridor's near-weightlessness again, watching the staff car depart. He had distracted the commander neatly from taking much interest in what he was doing out here.

When Harivarman reboarded the other flyer, he found Lescar hunched in the same seat as before. The little man had apparently not moved at all, though his face now looked a little more normal. Impassively he heard his master's description of the encounter with their chief jailer, and with Chen.

At last Lescar commented: "A close call, Your Honor."

"Yes." The Prince was being determinedly calm and regal. Close calls didn't count. "Now, where were we? How far did you get with your job, before we were interrupted?"

Lescar dared to give his master a severe glance. "Forgive me, Your Honor, but we had reached a point where no humans should ever be."

"Lescar, Lescar, listen to me! Do you think I enjoy this, working secretly on a berserker? I thought that it was dead, when I brought you out here; obviously I was wrong about that. I'm sorry."

The apology made Lescar uncomfortable, as the Prince had expected it would; the little man fidgeted, and muttered something.

Harivarman went on. "I'm no real engineer or scientist, obviously. All I can tell you is that now I'm reasonably sure that the machine is under my control. It's following my commands. It's not attacking us. And I'm also sure that it offers us our only chance of saving our lives. That last judgment does fall within my field of competence, and on that point I'm very sure indeed."

Lescar moved at last. Not much. Only, as if he were cold, to huddle within his folded arms. "But . . . if it's as you say, Your Honor, and someone's already coming from Salutai to arrest us . . . well, isn't it too late now for us to start trying to put together a starship?"

"It may be too late. Or it may not. When Roquelaure's people get here I may be able to . . . well, to stall them for a time. For a few days. If I can get the commander to see the truth. I have a few ideas about that now. They can't take us away unless she turns us over to them. To get that drive installed in one of our two flyers is still our only chance, I think.''

Lescar had made a good start toward recovery from his savage shock. Harivarman judged it safe to leave him alone now. But it was only against his servant's advice, and even pleading, that the Prince himself now returned once more to the berserker chamber, intending to resume his cautious dialogue with his chained beast.

At the last moment, Lescar, aghast, actually got out of the flyer too and followed him; whatever else might happen, he was unable to allow his Prince to face a berserker alone.

As the two of them drifted in their sealed suits along the airless corridor, the radio whisper of his servant's minimally powered voice came to Harivarman: ''But why must you talk to it again, Your Honor? We have the drive extracted, we don't need the rest. For a chance to escape, of course it's worth the risk of continuing our work on the drive. But the other thing . . . why take the chance? What do we gain? At best we'll just get ourselves arrested. Sooner or later it'll be found out, what we're doing.''

''Lescar, I spoke a moment ago of creating a delay, to give us time to modify our ship . . . I think I now see a possible way to manage that.''

Lescar was stubbornly silent.

His master continued inflexibly along the corridor, with the other following, until they were just outside the deadly room. There Harivarman halted. "If I can control it, talk to it—"

"No sir! No!"

"—that should solve our control problems for the escape. And perhaps for other things as well . . . now I want you to go back to the flyer. I think I can manage this particular job better and more safely alone."

Lescar sighed. He was obviously far from convinced. But he had long ago made his decision as to whom to devote his life. He went as ordered.

Then the Prince alone went once more into the room where the berserker waited, to see what he might be able to learn from his new metal slave.

As before, the thing did not appear to have moved so much as a centimeter while he was gone. It was still against the wall where its last aborted action against Lescar had left it, clinging to the stone with its six long insect-legs outspread, each leg as long as a man's body.

But now the lenses on the thing's head turned, smoothly, to focus on Harivarman as he entered. That was all, but it was enough to bring a weakness to his knees.

Once more making sure that he was using the proper radio frequency, and at a minimum of power, the Prince demanded of it: "Are there any other machines—allied with you—still functional on the Fortress? You understand what I mean by the Fortress?"

The tinny, squeaky, disjointed whisper came back into his helmet: "I understand. The answer to your question is affirmative."

Harivarman paused. He had not really expected that.

He had thought he was only eliminating a remote possibility. But now . . .

"How many such machines exist? Where are they?"

"Forty-seven such machines exist. All of them are gathered in a single chamber, approximately two hundred and fifty meters from this one."

"*Forty-seven.*" He couldn't help whispering it aloud. Could berserkers lie? Of course they could. But presumably not while under the constraints of the controlling code.

Harivarman had to clear his throat again before he asked another question. "How do you know that they are there?"

"They were and still are under my command."

"But they are not—active." Otherwise, surely, they would have come out killing, a hundred years ago or more.

"No more than I have been active, or am now. They were all in a slave mode when I was damaged, and have been inert, as I have, ever since. They depend on me for activation."

Presently, moving as the machine instructed him, while it in obedience to his orders remained behind, Harivarman went out into the corridor again. On the regular communication channel he exchanged a few words with Lescar, reassuring his servant and reiterating his orders that Lescar wait for him in the flyer. Then the Prince went on, as the machine's radio whisper directed him. He traversed another nearby corridor, one that as far as he knew had also been unexplored for centuries. From this passage he broke his way into another room whose doors had been sealed by binding time. This chamber was even larger than the one where he had left the berserker controller, and even closer to the cratered outer surface of the Fortress.

This was certainly a room full of machinery. The Prince moved quickly and boldly to make a closer examination of the contents. Considering the risks he was already facing, it seemed a waste of time to try to take precautions now.

Here was evidence that the thing in the other room had told him the truth. Here were a whole fighting company of its inanimate brothers, slaved to it in sleep. Death machines were crammed in here cheek by jowl until they reminded the Prince of so many terrified human infantry, stupefied with the strain of waiting for the order to go on an assault. There were a variety of types: Here were awkward, inhuman-looking androids. And here were a few transporters, some of them strongly resembling the flyers that humans used to move about the Fortress. Others looked like little more than quasi-intelligent missiles. Here was a nuclear pile on caterpillar treads, ready to roll itself wherever it was told, then melt itself down on command; the Prince had encountered the type before. Other types of berserkers, even more rare, including some that Harivarman could not at once identify, filled out the roster.

It was a whole assault force, the equivalent perhaps in fighting power of a small human army, waiting to be awakened by the orders of some evil robotic general. The Prince counted twoscore of the sinister metal shapes before he stopped. Then he made himself go on.

He counted forty-seven in all, just as the controlling berserker had told him there would be. All of them were as inert, faintly filmed with dust, as the first had been when he had discovered it.

There was at least one important difference—as far as Harivarman could see, none of these machines were damaged in the least. They must have made their landing on the Radiant Fortress at the time of the great battles, and then have been gathered here in this room as a ready reserve. And then—or else humanity might not have won those battles—they had been immobilized by the fortuitous damage to their controller in the other chamber.

So they should be, they must be, as it had said, still under its control. It had never been able to unleash them because of its paralysis. And it could not do so now, because the Prince had ordered it to hurt no one.

Harivarman had seen the death machines at close range a few times before, in several shapes and sizes. But never before had he seen them in such perfectly preserved variety. Perhaps no human being until now had ever seen the like, and lived. A vast treasure trove of knowledge of the enemy waited for human research-ers here.

That treasure would be used, eventually. He would see to it that it was used, and properly. He certainly would.

But first . . .

The Prince closed the doors on the assault force.

He made his way back to the flyer, hardly conscious of what he was doing.

Heading back to the City in the flyer with silent Lescar, the Prince laughed suddenly, and quoted something:

"I can call spirits from the vast deep . . .

"Why, so can I, or so can any man . . . but will they come when you do call for them?"

"Should I have understood that, Your Honor?"

"Don't wish so, Lescar. Don't wish so."

Chapter 10

Young Chen was still riding with Commander Blenheim in the back seat of her staff car when it rolled to a stop at dockside. She had come directly from her chat with General Harivarman to witness the arrival of the latest unexpected ship from Salutai. This was the third such arrival in two days, and she was thinking to herself that it might have been years since this port had seen such a burst of unplanned activity.

Had she wanted to, she might have tuned in one of the car's remote viewers while being chauffeured to the docks, and got a look at the stranger while it was coming down the entrance channel, or even caught a glimpse of it telescopically imaged as it approached in space. But the commander's thoughts were still concentrated on Harivarman, and she waited for her first look at the arriving ship until it appeared directly before her eyes.

As soon as the hull of the vessel, approximately spherical and a hundred meters in diameter, rose into view through the forcegate she recognized it as an advanced type of battlecraft, bearing the insignia of the planetary defense forces of Salutai. As such, it would be under the direct command of that world's controversial prime minister, Roquelaure. Commander Blenheim for the most part studiously avoided taking an interest in politics, at least outside that which went on within the Templar organization itself. But Harivarman had once or twice mentioned the prime minister to her as one of his bitterest enemies.

The commander in passing remembered hearing someone say that Prime Minister Roquelaure, one of the Imperial officials who had been closest to the Empress, was now also one of the most likely candidates to replace her. And Roquelaure would almost certainly represent Salutai when the Council of Eight met, as they must meet in the near future, to decide who would now occupy the Imperial Throne.

She got her driver's attention, tapping on the staff car's window. "Sergeant, I'm getting out here. Call for an escort, and see to it that Recruit Shizuoka is taken back to his quarters and confined as before." The young man sitting in the rear with her looked at her silently, hopelessly. The commander said nothing to him; there did not appear to be anything to say.

Now Anne Blenheim got out of her car, for a better look at the warship. The insignia on the hull, a mythical beast rampant with upraised claws, gave the whole ship an arrogant look, she thought. The ship now emerged completely from the gate, and at that point ceased its rising. Most of the top half of the hull was now in view, the bottom half cradled invisibly in more fields and in massive pads that had come into position smoothly as the traveler cut power on its engines. Now moving passively, under harbor power and control, the great hull was being eased slowly sideways through the broad channel that would guide it into dock. The commander's educated eye took the opportunity to study the warship's armament; the variations in hull shape that defined a battlecraft were unmistakable to the experienced eye. The exterior weapon projections were under hatches now, but there was no doubt that they were there.

As soon as the docking was completed, the visitor's main personnel hatch opened, and some military people in sharply designed uniforms began trotting out of it onto the dock. They continued to come out, pair after pair of them like mirror images, until the watching commander could count sixteen sharp military uniforms in all, in two rows leading from the hatch. They were actually bearing arms, the commander noticed with surprise and disapproval, as they took up their positions for what was evidently to be some kind of a guard-of-honor show.

The deployment of these troops had the incidental effect of providing a pretty effective occupation and coverage of dockside space, as if they were on the lookout for snipers, or ready to repel a boarding rush. Whether intentionally or not, these armed people—dragoons, she thought Roquelaure called the little army she had heard he was so proud of—were confronting the

two or three Templar guards, who were always posted
in positions overlooking the docks on what really
amounted to no more than ceremonial duty. The dragoons stared up at their outnumbered cousins-in-arms
belligerently, while the young Templars goggled back in
sheer surprise, for which their commander could hardly
blame them. The invaders'—well, that was the impression that they gave—uniforms looked sharper than the
Templars', too.

Motioning her driver to follow with the car, the commander had begun walking briskly toward the visitor's
main hatch even before it opened, and by now she had
come down a flight of stairs and was on the same level
as that hatch, ready to greet or confront whoever had
sent out all these guards as they emerged.

And now in the ship's open hatchway appeared the
man who had to be the object of this belligerent-looking
guard of honor. Commander Anne recognized him as
soon as he appeared, though she had never seen him
before in person, and had certainly not been expecting
to see him now; almost anyone in the Eight Worlds
would know that gaunt, aging face on sight, trade-
marked as it was with long, curled mustaches. It belonged to Grand Marshall Beraton, a Niteroi native and
a legendary hero to all the Eight Worlds. His career in
anti-berserker warfare went back long before General
Harivarman's in that ancient and apparently endless field
of endeavor. The grand marshall, Anne Blenheim thought
to herself, must now be at least a couple of hundred
years old, and if anyone had recently asked her about
him she would have said that he must have retired long

ago. In passing, she wondered suddenly if the grand marshall might have been on the Fortress during or before the last berserker attack against it, and whether he might therefore be able to advise her on some points of historical restoration.

The grand marshall stalked out of his ship and stood looking rather fiercely about him, ignoring the two ranks of his guards. Then his stern expression altered as his gaze lighted on Commander Blenheim's approaching figure. It was a subtle change, in keeping with his dignity. So was his bearing as he advanced toward her now on his long legs. Of course her uniform and her insignia made her quickly recognizable by rank and status if not by her personal identity.

Coming in that ceremonial pace to meet her, the impressive old man halted four paces away, and granted Anne Blenheim the salute that was her due here as commanding officer; elsewhere, of course, his own rank would be far greater.

She returned his salute sharply.

"Press coverage?" Those were the grand marshall's first words of greeting. At least that was how Anne Blenheim understood them. They had been delivered in an aristocratic accent with which she was not overly familiar, and the question was asked in a low, almost conspiratorial tone, as the grand marshall looked alertly to right and left.

"I beg your pardon, Grand Marshall?"

Beraton's great age was even more obvious at this close range, but by all appearances age was still treating him very kindly. Bending near, smiling faintly as he towered over Anne Blenheim's own modest height, he said, this time not quite so softly: "Thought there might be press on hand. Not sure that it's a good idea at this stage. Just as well there's not." She got the impression that the grand marshall was enjoying himself, that he would have enjoyed some press on hand even more. The old man's expression was just suitably tinged with sadness, in keeping with the gravity of what she supposed must be his mission.

It was one of those occasions, Anne Blenheim decided, when it might be better not to push immediately to clarify the meaning of what someone had just said.

She had hardly begun her formal welcome, offering the hospitality of the base, before another officer, this one a much shorter and younger man, came marching out of the open hatch and approached them with short-legged, energetic strides. Behind him, well inside the ship, a man in civilian clothes appeared momentarily, and retreated out of sight before Anne Blenheim was able to get a good look at him.

"Captain Lergov," the short, energetic officer introduced himself, at the last moment breaking off what was almost a charge to toss her a quick salute.

"My second-in-command," Beraton amplified.

"Commander Anne Blenheim," she told them, looking from one to the other. "Welcome to you both, gentlemen, and to your crew." She was a little surprised, not at the coolness in her own voice—she thought the visitors' behavior so far had earned that—but that she did not regret that there was cause for coolness. "Is this a duty call?"

"Afraid so," said the grand marshall. Looking a trifle sadder and keener than ever, he fell silent at that point, as if the subject were too painful for him to continue. Lergov meanwhile muttered something about seeing to his people, and turned away to give his honor guard a quick looking-over; Anne Blenheim observed how the sixteen young women and men who composed it stiffened visibly, fearfully, under his inspection.

The seeing-to did not take long. Lergov turned back, able now to spare a few more moments, it appeared, for a mere Templar colonel. But no, he was ignoring her. "Grand Marshall?" he asked, in a tone of deferential prodding.

"Humf, yes." And from an attache case that had heretofore been tucked under one of his arms, looking like part of his elegant uniform, Beraton now produced a folded document of what looked like genuine heavy paper. This, with a gesture conveying understatement, he now presented to the base commander.

She examined the document. It was indeed real, heavy paper, as far as she could tell. Unfolding it she saw that it came in both electronic and statparchment forms—the electronic in the form of a small black tab attached to the paper—and it was from the Council themselves. Or at least, though this was not explicitly noted, from a quorum of the Council's members. As many of them as possible must have been convened in an extraordinary session as soon as possible after the shock wave of the Empress's death struck through the Eight Worlds.

To Commander Blenheim at first inspection, the order seemed undoubtedly authentic, legal, and official. As such it would seem to require that the base commander of the Templar Fortress at the Radiant turn her famous prisoner over to these people at once.

So, he was right, was Anne Blenheim's first thought after reading the sense of the message, seeing in her mind's eye the general's impassioned face. She felt angry with Harivarman for being right. *Then why has he been hiding out there in the empty regions, occupying himself with archaeology? Why wasn't he—doing something? Of course, he might have seen that there was nothing to be done.*

"Can you please order him brought here at once?" the grand marshall was inquiring of her. It sounded rather as if he were asking some junior officer to have his car sent round. Evidently the old man, impetuous as any youth, was ready to turn in his tracks, undock his ship again, and depart in a matter of minutes.

The commander continued to study the printed order in her hands. She felt glad that she had already had some time, a few days, in which to anticipate this moment, and ponder the several choices that it might pose.

She said: "I'm afraid, sir, the business mentioned here can't possibly be concluded that quickly. This paragraph calls on me to hand over other people to you as well . . . offhand I don't know that I have a right to do anything like that."

"No right? No right?" The old man looked her up and down, in a way that gave the impression that he was revising his opinion of her downward. "I understood that I was speaking to the commanding Templar officer."

"And so you are, Grand Marshall. But civilians here are only very tenuously under my jurisdiction. At a minimum I'm going to have to talk to the judge advocate first on the subject of those people. As for General Harivarman himself, I've already sent courier relays out to inform the Superior General of my order—inform him of the assassination of the Empress, and the possible implications—and I hope to have some reply from the SG in a few days.

"Meanwhile, won't you come aboard? We may be a little short of completely finished quarters for a crew the size that yours must be"—she glanced at the two armed ranks, letting a touch of disapproval show—"but we can offer you all some hospitality."

Actually, prodded by Harivarman's warnings, she had several hours ago ordered such legal staff as she had available to get busy researching the situation. So far there had been no report. The commander suspected that no one was going to be eager to stick his or her neck out and advise her firmly as to what to do—no one of course but General Harivarman himself, and now these people who had come here to arrest him.

But the order looked damnably authentic. And, at least regarding the general himself, it looked convincing too.

It looks like I'm going to have to give him up to these people. And I don't want to do that. And Anne Blenheim's own silent words surprised her, for they suggested an uncomfortable and unwelcome personal attachment.

For the moment, the commander was politely adamant with her visitors, assuring them that all the people

named in the arrest order were on hand, but that she
needed to hear from her superiors, or her advisers at
least, before any of them could be simply handed over.

Beraton, his feelings perhaps wounded by his failure
to overawe her instantly, seemed to withdraw uncom-
municatively inside a protective shell, perhaps to heal
them. Lergov became rather ominously silent. The grand
marshall formally accepted hospitality for them all, but
he informed the base commander that most of his ship's
crew would probably remain aboard his ship. One impli-
cation was that their stay was going to be quite brief.

Five minutes after ordering the arrangements for
hospitality, Commander Blenheim, the Council's formal
document still in hand, was conferring in her office with
her judge advocate. Major Nurnberg was a rather short,
stout woman who took her usually dull job quite seriously.

The commander complained: "They want Shizuoka,
too, and not only him. The way this thing is worded, it
seems to be telling me that they can arrest anyone on the
Radiant Fortress with whom Harivarman has become
closely associated during his stay. If they discover someone who they think fits that category, they can just
direct me to hand that person over. I frankly can't see
myself giving them that, or anything like it. Not without
some clear directive from the Superior General himself.
Or some equivalent authority."

"You may have a point, ma'am." Major Nurnberg
was evidently going to play it cautiously, for which her
boss could hardly blame her. "Looks to me like they're
just fishing to see how much they can get. This is our
territory. As to the general, of course he's not a Templar.

I don't see that you have any possible grounds to refuse them in his case. As for Recruit Chen Shizuoka . . . maybe we can wait for word from the SG.''

''And the civilians they're demanding I hand over to them?''

''Well . . . I'd like to do some more research, ma'am, before I say yes or no definitely on that.''

''Thank you, Major. I'll keep putting our visitors off for a few days, then.''

''That seems like a good plan, ma'am.''

Anne Blenheim could only hope that word from the SG came soon.

Chapter 11

Within a few minutes after Harivarman had concluded his talk with the base commander in her staff car, he had arrived back at his house with Lescar. And as soon as he entered the house he found that now, in a kind of apparent time-reversal, the long-awaited summons to a conference with the commander had finally arrived.

The communication waiting for the Prince in the memory of his holostage was couched in the form of a courteous invitation: *If the general would visit Commander Blenheim's personal office at his earliest convenience . . .* He didn't bother to check the time the message had been received to see if she had sent it before she spoke to him. At least she hadn't called back to cancel it afterwards.

Approximately an hour after receiving the message,

Prince Harivarman was standing in the commander's drab office—it was a temporary facility, for the wave of remodeling had evidently reached here too. The room was much more spartan than even a temporary base commander's office would have been in the ascendancy of Colonel Phocion. There were only two or three pieces of furniture, and the craggy face of the current Superior General of the Order glowering down from a holographic portrait on the wall. Harivarman had met the current SG several times, and there had been mutual respect.

As Harivarman entered, Anne Blenheim got up from behind what must also be her temporary desk, and came around it as if to meet him at close range. But there was hesitancy in her movement, and it stopped altogether before she had left the desk completely behind her.

Neither of them said anything until the door had been closed behind him, by the clerk who had shown him in.

With one hand still on her desk Anne Blenheim said: "They've come for you. As you predicted."

"And you've made your decision." He smiled; that she had hesitated just now made him confident as to what that decision was.

"And they want your man Lescar, too."

The Prince nodded. "Of course."

"And the recruit Chen Shizuoka—"

"My co-conspirator. Yes, of course."

"—and some other people too. All of them civilians."

"I see. And out of this list you are going to give them—?" Then, struck by a thought, he interrupted himself. "I suppose the list includes my wife as well?"

"It does now. They were somewhat surprised to find her here, but they put her on the list as soon as they learned she had come back to the Fortress."

Harivarman nodded. The yacht that Beatrix had come in was conspicuously visible, and naturally his enemies would have managed to find out who had been on it when it arrived.

Anne Blenheim drew a deep breath. "I hope to hear from the SG before I have to give them any final answer. It should really be his decision."

"But, as we know, it's quite likely that you are going to have to make it."

"Perhaps. Quite probably I will."

"Having made some difficult decisions of my own in my time, I sympathize." Harivarman paused again. "So, who else do they have down on their list? I suppose it's fairly elastic, so they can open it up again any time they want and stuff more people in."

They were both still standing in the middle of the room, facing each other. The commander said: "I'm afraid your friend Gabrielle Chou is on it too."

"Ah."

"And you're right, the Council order does contain a vague, blanket clause: Any other person intimately associated, and so forth, with the aforesaid General Harivarman can be arrested. I should have no trouble in finding legal precedent for refusing to go along with that one. Unless of course the SG should show up and give me a direct order to the contrary, which seems unlikely."

The Prince was silent for a little time. "The bastards are worse than I thought, really. More arrogant, I mean.

But I suppose I should have expected nothing better of them.''

Commander Blenheim said: "Of course I haven't agreed to anything as yet, except that they can see you. There's a Captain Lergov who insists that he must see immediately with his own eyes that you're really still here.''

"Lergov.'' Harivarman could hear the change in his own voice. He raised both hands in an aborted gesture.

Anne Blenheim asked: "You know him?''

"I know of him. To know him that way's bad enough. If the two of us had ever met, I suppose one of us might not have survived the encounter.''

"But he's not the one in command.''

"I thought his rank was a bit low for that. Who's in charge, then?''

"Come along. You can see for yourself.'' The commander moved to open a door at one side of the room.

The Prince did not know who he expected to see. But a moment later he found himself surprised, almost as if some ancient news recording had come to life before his eyes. He was confronting Grand Marshall Beraton. Harivarman had met the old man once or twice before, briefly, on ceremonial occasions, and held him in contempt, for several reasons. The Prince had no reason to doubt that the feeling was reciprocated.

There was a long moment of silence as the two men faced each other. Their mutual contempt on the grounds of philosophy and politics was tempered by a certain grudging mutual respect. Each man would have agreed that the other had in the past done well fighting against berserkers.

It was the tall old man who spoke first. "I must say, Prince, I am greatly surprised and saddened to behold you here before me, under such circumstances."

Harivarman was in no mood to suffer fools gladly. "Grand Marshall, I must say that I am not really surprised to see you. Roquelaure has a well-known knack for choosing the proper tool."

A flush mounted in Beraton's aged cheeks. "I should have expected better from one of your rank," he murmured.

"You don't really think that I conspired to kill her—? But I suppose you have been made to believe just that, or you wouldn't be here. That's why the prime minister picked you, isn't it, after all?"

A short man who had been standing at one side of this room, by his uniform a junior officer in the armed forces of Salutai, approached them in an arrogant manner. "I am Captain Lergov." He gave Harivarman an impassive look, and a perfunctory salute.

"Ah. I have heard of you, Lergov." The Prince scarcely glanced at Lergov, but kept his gaze fixed on the grand marshall.

"Prince Harivarman." Evidently the old man had forgotten, or nobody had told him, or he had chosen to ignore, the rule about calling the exile *General*. "Prince Harivarman, you are under arrest, for high treason to the Imperial Throne, and for regicide."

Harivarman only looked at him coldly.

Commander Anne, standing at one side, said: "I have

informed the general that I have not formally transferred him into your custody as yet. As base commander here I am still responsible for him.''

Beraton protested to her: ''I would say your authority over the prisoner has now become a mere formality. You don't contest the legality of the Council's order, surely?''

''I have not yet accepted it, Grand Marshall. For one thing, the order as written involves other people besides General Harivarman. You seem to intend to implement the provision for the arrest of his wife, his friends, and even some people who are only vaguely associated with him.''

''The Imperial Council in emergency session has authority to issue such orders.''

''That may be for all I know, Grand Marshall Beraton, or it may not. But here I have the authority, and the responsibility as well.''

The tall old man stared at her frostily. ''Yes, madam. Responsibility. Indeed you do.''

Commander Anne continued: ''And the arrest order you have presented me specifically includes Cadet Chen, who is on the Templar rolls.''

Beraton repeated: ''When the Imperial Throne is vacant, as now, the Council, in a case of high treason to the Throne, has supreme authority.''

''Perhaps, sir. Though in the case of arresting a Templar, on Templar territory, I doubt it very much. But in any case I am still responsible to some degree for all of these people on your list, and I must be sure. Before making any formal response at all to the Council's

document I want to clear the whole matter with my
legal staff.''

Captain Lergov, who had been hovering at a little
distance to one side, demonstrated impatience. ''How
long is that going to take, ma'am?''

Anne Blenheim looked at him; her almost-plump face
was capable of surprising hardness. ''These are difficult
questions. It may well take several days, Captain.''

The grand marshall made a small well-bred noise in
his throat. ''A simple search for legal precedents? Come,
now, Commander.''

''Perhaps not simple, Grand Marshall. I'll let you
know when I have reached a decision.''

Harivarman said suddenly: ''I presume that this meeting is being recorded.''

''It is,'' Commander Blenheim assured him.

''Good. I want to put it formally on record that I
protest the terms of this arrest order. If the base commander here turns me over to these people, I will be
murdered by them, or my mental faculties will somehow
be destroyed while I am in their custody, probably
before I arrive at Salutai.''

That was enough to set the grand marshall quivering
faintly with rage. ''And I would like the record to
show my own formal protest, that the prisoner's remarks
are a damned lie, and that this man, the prisoner, knows
it.''

The Prince said: ''You had better check with Captain
Lergov first.''

Beraton glared at him but said nothing. Nor did Lergov,
who only gazed back stolidly.

There was little more to be said. In a few moments, both grand marshall and captain were gone.

Harivarman stood gazing at the base commander. Some of her aides had reentered the room and were waiting, as if now they expected Harivarman to leave too.

The commander dismissed them with a look. "General, I would like to see you briefly back in my private office."

When the two of them were alone again, she sat behind her desk and touched a control. "We are no longer being recorded," she said, and hesitated briefly. "In your wife's case, and the others, I don't know yet what my final decision will have to be."

The Prince stared at her. His right arm that had started to rise in a confident gesture dropped back at his side. "Well. Like most final decisions, it will have to be whatever you make it. I assume you're not going to—"

"Let me finish, please. I'm afraid I may have misled you somehow. In your case, there's really no doubt, I'm afraid, what I must do."

"*—what—?*"

"I am saying that in the case of you personally, General, it appears to me more and more certain that I have no grounds for refusing the Council's order, or even delaying compliance."

Stunned, he stared at the uniformed woman. He could find no words to say to her. It was all too obvious that she was deadly serious.

"I am sorry, General, if you failed to understand that point clearly from the beginning. I thought—"

At last he found his tongue. "I see I must tell you again. Perhaps you're the one who has failed to understand. I am not speaking rhetorically, or fancifully, or for some political effect. Once they have me on that ship, I'll be murdered."

"I have no evidence of that, General Harivarman."

So, she'd do it to him. She really would. There were a thousand words of protest, of outrage, to be said, but he could say nothing. Rage, of unexpected intensity, choked him. He wanted to hit her, smash her in the face.

She went on, with cold control: "As a favor, I am telling you now, privately, ahead of time, what I am shortly going to have to tell the grand marshall. I really have no choice. You must soon be transferred into his custody."

"*His* custody. As if the old fart were capable of . . ." Somehow Harivarman had mastered himself, at least enough to speak coherently. "I am very grateful for the favor, Commander. And your responsibility for my welfare, as your prisoner?"

"The Council's order is clear, and my responsibility is to obey it. You are to be returned to Salutai for trial on these charges of—"

"I see why you need no recording in here. You turn into a recording yourself. Yet once more I'll say it. Beraton would not willfully murder a prisoner, but he's too great a fool to have any real control over what happens on that ship. If you hand me over to Lergov, and his political crew, I'll never see Salutai alive. Or at least not with my brain intact. Does that mean nothing to you? I had thought, in my foolishness, that we had even come to mean something to each other on a more—''

''General Harivarman, I have been aware that from our first meeting you have been trying to—establish some such relationship. Foolish though it would have been, as you say. Fortunately none has been established.''

There was a little silence. Her eyes challenged him to find a trace of weakness in them.

''I see,'' he said at last. His throat again was growing tighter and tighter, so that it was hard now to get even those two words out.

There was more tense silence. At last the commander began to repeat: ''I have no evidence to indicate that—''

''I was right about them coming for me. I'm right also about their intentions. Once more I tell you if you put me on that ship with them, I'll never see Salutai alive. I can easily think of several ways by which they'll be able to destroy me en route and get away with it. Do you believe me?''

''Even if you were right—''

''I am.''

''I'll recite my speech one more time, General.'' Now it was as if she were exasperated with some dull recruit. ''I must act on facts, evidence, not political opinions. And even if you were right about their intentions, *I have no evidence*. Can you show me any?''

''The past record of these people stands as evidence. Fatuity in the case of the grand marshall, a fiendish propensity for evil in the case of Lergov, and of those who sent them both. Specifically Prime Minister Roquelaure.''

She hesitated marginally. "There are strong differences of opinion about the history and the politics of the Eight Worlds. Your own record is perhaps not spotless."

"And yours is."

"My record is irrelevant."

"I would have thought mine was too, now that I am helplessly in Templar custody and someone wants to murder me."

She said: "My orders, and the Compact of Exile, leave me no choice."

"You're just doing your duty."

"That is the truth."

"I hearby volunteer to enlist in the Templars."

"Are you speaking seriously? You can't be, you must know that that's absurd."

And even as she spoke, she was hoping in a way that he would keep on with this futile argument; if he had faced the inevitable with dignity it would have been much harder for her to go through with what she had to do, and it was hard enough to do so anyway.

But the general's arguments ceased abruptly. He let out a long sigh. A remoteness suddenly came into his manner. It seemed to Commander Blenheim, watching closely, that his anger had not dissipated, but had hardened.

At last he asked, in an altered voice: "Can you at least stretch your concept of duty enough to give me this much—a little time to myself? A couple of hours of freedom, before they take me away and kill me? There are a few farewells that I would like to say."

It seemed to her that he was posing, trying to arouse

her pity, not really concerned about saying farewell to anyone. "You are lowering yourself in my estimation, General." Then she wished she had not said that. But she, too, was very angry now. As if in some effort to be fair, to make amends, she added: "Will two hours be sufficient?"

Harivarman sighed again. "Two hours should give me the chance to take care of everything," he answered softly.

Commander Blenheim started to turn away, then swung back, wondering. He hadn't seemed to her at all the suicidal type . . . although under present circumstances, if he believed what he was saying about being murdered . . . "You will report back here to me at the end of that time?"

Calm now, his rage certainly controlled, the general gazed back at her solemnly. "I'll be here, or at my house. You needn't worry."

"Then you can go. Two hours."

"You have my word."

Lergov was waiting in the outer office when Harivarman came out. She saw him give the Prince another impassive glance as the two men passed each other.

Harivarman glared back, at both of them, one after the other, and departed.

Anne Blenheim faced Lergov, and demanded: "Is there anything else I can do for you, Captain?"

"When you are ready, hand over the prisoners to us, ma'am. We don't necessarily need to have them all at once." Lergov sounded more courteous than he had before.

"I'll let you know, Captain."

"I'd like to remind the colonel, if I may, that General Harivarman is now under Council authority, and it would not be well received by the Council if you should allow anything to happen to him before—"

"I said, Captain, that I am still responsible for the general. I'm about to order guards posted at his quarters. As soon as the situation changes, I will let you know."

"Yes ma'am." This time Lergov's salute was closer to the proper military form.

Chapter 12

Very rarely, no more than two or three times in all the years of his association with the Prince, had Lescar seen his master as angry as he was now. The little man cringed away from this fury, even though he knew that it was not directed at himself, and hesitated even to speak to try to calm it. Prince Harivarman, coming back from the meeting with the base commander, went stalking through the exiles' house as if he sought some object for his wrath, and came as close to raving as Lescar had ever heard him come.

To Lescar's great relief, this unproductive phase of behavior lasted only for a minute or two. After that the Prince, regaining control of himself, went to his room and started to change clothes, donning utility garments as if he were going back to his secret work. Lescar understood, or thought he did. Some last attempt at concealment or destruction of the berserker must be made. Though whether such an attempt could succeed or not . . . At the same time the Prince, now giving the impression of being very much in control of himself and of the situation, began to issue orders. Lescar was to see to certain arrangements, and to make very sure that they were carried out. The chief task assigned him was to summon both Gabrielle and Beatrix to the house, telling the women whatever seemed likely to get them there.

"Here, to this house, Your Honor? Both of them here at the same time?"

"That's right. They must come here. Call them as soon as I leave. I probably won't be back yet when they arrive. But see that they stay here, no matter what happens, till I get back. And stay here yourself, unless you hear otherwise from me."

"Yes sir. I will do my best."

"I know you will." The Prince's tone softened slightly. He had now, moving with great speed, got himself dressed and ready, for all the world appearing as if he were only going out for another afternoon of archaeology. At the door he turned back. "The bastards are out to get us, my friend; but they'll find it's not going to be that easy. We'll see them all in the ninth hell yet!"

"The lawyers on Salutai will help us, I'm sure. Your Honor. When we get there—"

The Prince came a step back into the house. "The lawyers on Salutai? We'd never reach there alive. Haven't you been listening to anything I've told you over the past few days?"

"Yes sir. I just thought that perhaps now—"

"Lescar. Did you think I'd let them argue me into that? Going to the slaughter peacefully, and bringing you along?" If there were secret listening devices in the house, the Prince had evidently given up trying to evade them.

"Whatever Your Honor wishes." Then, suddenly, Lescar thought he understood his master's new plan; the Prince was not about to destroy his discovered berserker, but to reveal it to the world, claim it boldly as a great discovery. "You said, Your Honor, that you had some plan for arranging a delay?"

The Prince looked at him in an odd way. "Yes, Lescar, that's it. I think I have. A good long delay. I'm going to see about it now."

"The commander is not—altogether convinced, then? I mean, still not convinced that our enemies are right?"

The Prince smiled; Lescar had seen that particular smile on his master's face before, and knew it probably boded ill for someone. But right now he was glad to see it. When the Prince fought he generally won, whereas his giving up meekly would have led them all into totally unknown territory. And a shade of worry had even crossed Lescar's mind that the Prince when brought to this kind of an extremity might even kill himself. Thank all the Powers that was not to be.

The Prince said: "I think perhaps Commander Blenheim can yet be made to see the justice of my cause."

"That will be excellent, sir. Excellent."

"I am glad to be able to offer you—a certain hope."

"And sir, of course . . ." Lescar let his eyes move sideways, in what might have been the direction of the last archaeological site.

"I am going to take care of that too. Right now. It all fits in. Don't worry." And the Prince seized his servant's hand and shook it. That also had happened only two or three times in the past, at moments of great crisis. The Prince went out. A moment later Lescar heard the faint sound of a flyer departing the garage.

Left alone, the little man hastened to put through the two calls as he had been ordered.

The first was to the former Princess—she had had to relinquish the title on separation—Beatrix, in her lodgings at one of the City's more luxurious tourist facilities. Beatrix, without asking questions, without appearing to be particularly surprised, agreed to come to Harivarman's house at once. Lescar said nothing to the Princess about who else he was supposed to summon.

Next Lescar called the City apartment of Gabrielle Chou, where the answering robot said that its mistress was not in, and insisted that there was absolutely no way that she could be reached at present.

"I repeat, this is an emergency."

"I am sorry, sir, but—"

"Then I must leave a message. Tell her," said Lescar, "that it is vitally important to—to her own future welfare, that she come to Prince Harivarman's lodgings as soon as she can."

He broke off, wondering and worrying. He had never really liked Miss Gabrielle. But he meant her no harm, and of course he had done his best. Her own future welfare. That was what his master had told him: provide whatever reason would get them there.

*   *   *

It took the Prince only minutes in his swift flyer to reach the room in which the berserker controller unit awaited him. There were moments on the way in which he imagined himself finding it gone; but it seemed that he had already had enough bad luck for one day. The thing was there, just as he had left it.

It took him only a few minutes more, standing in the doorway of that remote room, with his suit's lights shining on the metallic and deadly beauty across from him, to issue the machine his orders. He discovered that, as in his old days of military planning, when the moment came to issue orders the details lay ready in his mind. Some part of him must have known that he was going to do this, must have been at work on the details already, perhaps for days.

"Orders acknowledged," the controller said. The tones of its voice sounded like, and no doubt were, the exact same tones that it had used with those words before.

Trembling a little, the Prince got out of the way of his new slave as soon as it began to move again on its six legs. As far as he could tell from watching these first ordered movements, the great belly wound that his experimenting had inflicted on it did not inconvenience it at all, no more than the old wound whose trauma had now evidently been somehow bypassed. He retreated farther as it came past him, through the doorway into the corridor. This doorway was wide enough for it to get through without knocking more bits out of the walls. He drifted near it as it hovered in the corridor, and he tried without success to pick up its radio signals as it called in its extra bodies from the deep.

But the signals certainly were sent. Only seconds had passed before the Prince saw the forty-seven fighting units come swarming in wraith-like silence around the corner of the nearby corridor intersection. Almost instantly they had roused themselves from the inanimacy of centuries. They were coming toward Harivarman now, and toward the controller that had summoned them.

In the weak gravity the android types among them moved almost like suited expert humans, shoving themselves in graceful trajectories from corridor wall to corridor wall. The miniature flyers hovered on the invisible forces of their drives. The self-propelled guns, the crushers and the gammalasers escorted one another in loose formations calculated to allow for mutual support.

Still the Prince, using his comparatively simple suit radio, could manage to detect nothing of the complex communications traffic that must be passing between them and the controller.

He was reassured when all but one of the silent assembly shambled to a harmless halt some meters away from him. That one, a tall, three-legged thing, came to drift harmlessly close beside him, in evident obedience to one section of his detailed orders. There was a certain voice recording that he wanted to make now, a recording that this particular machine would be assigned to carry on a certain mission.

It was all working, or it was going to work. A great feeling of triumph arose in Harivarman. His nagging feeling of something not quite right, something faulty in his perception of events, had been almost swept away.

Almost, but not entirely.

After the recording had been completed to his satisfaction, he placed himself directly in front of the controller once more. The vague feeling nagged him still. He supposed it was unnecessary guilt. "My orders are understood? And they will be obeyed, in every particular?"

"Orders understood. And will be obeyed." It had already told him so, but it would patiently tell him again and again, however often it was ordered. Impatience was no part of its programming. He was truly in control, as far as he could tell. Again the man felt reassured.

Harivarman reentered his flyer, and gave the final signal. This command too was promptly relayed and obeyed. He let the wave of his assault troops get under way ahead of him. First he followed the limping controller in its progress toward the City, while the other machines swept on ahead and were soon out of sight. Just to keep up with the controller he had to drive the flyer faster than he had expected. He had almost forgotten how swiftly and effectively berserkers of any type could move, what good machines, considered purely as machines, they were.

Suddenly the Prince found himself talking aloud. "Now if only the Templars don't fight . . ." Of course there never had been any Templars who would not fight. But perhaps this time, if everything went as he had planned, this time they might see, they might be convinced, that they had no chance.

Impatient, exultant, and fearful all at the same time, Harivarman accelerated his flyer's progress, passing the controller, leaving it behind. The thought crossed his mind that he should perhaps have made more recordings, and sent one or two machines ahead, warning the Templars to surrender. But he could remember that a day ago, two days ago perhaps, he had already considered that plan and rejected it. To have warned the Templars would only have made combat and killing certain.

The Prince set his radio to scanning the communications bands again, this time trying to pick up the first human reactions broadcast from the City ahead. So far there were none, none that he could receive here anyway. Damn the Fortress and its ancient peculiarities. . . .

So far he had passed no traffic coming out of the City. That was not necessarily significant. Traffic here in these remote ways was never heavy, and frequently it was nonexistent.

At last Harivarman's flyer emerged through a forcefield gate at the end of the ship passage, and came up into atmosphere. These inner gates had no real automated defenses, and he thought that the berserker machines had probably been able to come through them without fuss or difficulty.

Above him now there shone the familiar fiery sunpoint of the Radiant, centered within the great interior curve of distant surface that here answered for a sky.

The first change from normality that Harivarman noticed was smoke, over on the other side of the Fortress's vast central space. Smoke mottled the comparatively thin, concave layer of the atmosphere there, spreading grayly across the distant curve of surface. And mixed in with the film of smoke, pocking it and disappearing, there were detonating flashes, silent at this distance.

Harivarman swore, wearily. It had perhaps been inevitable that not all the Templars could be caught completely off guard; nor even, perhaps, had all of the dragoons been taken unawares.

The second change was much closer. He passed a wrecked flyer, a fairly sizable machine, that lay against one of the roadway's sloping edges, crushed and flattened there as if a human being had hurled a berry or a nut against a wall. There were no outward signs of the flyer's occupants, living or dead. He did not stop to look for them.

The Prince drove his flyer on quickly, past the silent wreck to which, he noted, no emergency vehicles had yet responded. He kept his vehicle under manual control, to be able to react intelligently to any sudden emergency, relying on his reflexes to slide it safely through tight corners. He had to get over to the other side of the inner surface, where the fighting seemed to be.

Only now did the Prince come in full view of the City, which occupied only a relatively small part of the rounded and self-mapping world that was the inner habitable surface of the Fortress. Now there was suddenly plenty of radio traffic for Harivarman to listen to, and now he beheld ahead of him a nightmare scene. More smoke, more detonations—he could hear the sounds now, delayed by distance—the sky-tracks of berserkers and their projectiles twisting and dodging through the light counter-fire that was still going up from a site near the Templar base.

Harivarman accelerated again, turning down a new street. He had always seen vehicular traffic here, but there was none now.

Heading for his house, fearful now of what he was going to find there, he passed several damaged houses, pocked with flying fragments, debris of some kind hailing from above. Now he saw smoldering parts scattered in the street, fragments of what looked to Harivarman like the remains of a wrecked berserker. The fighting had not been totally one-sided, then, surprise or not.

Looking into his rearview screen, he saw the controller pacing after him, much faster than any human could have run, keeping his speeding flyer in sight. He had the flyer still in offground mode, wheels retracted, for greater speed and maneuverability, but he was keeping within a meter of the road surface, not wanting to draw fire from either side.

Now he slowed just enough to let the controller catch up with him. Pulling beside it, Harivarman shouted questions and orders at it, demanded a report.

It focused lenses on him as it paced tirelessly beside his speeding vehicle. In the same half-human-sounding tones that it had used before, it reported that his orders had been obeyed, were still being obeyed, that its units were killing only when they met resistance. It reminded him that he had authorized them to do that.

He glared at the machine, mumbled something, and drove on rapidly. He had to get to his house. Each scene of violence encountered on the way made him more fearful of what he was going to find when he arrived there.

A minute later he was passing within fairly easy sight of the docks. He could see quite plainly that all of the ships in dock had been smashed, immobilized. One of them was still exploding, one flare and shock after another, and something in it burning. Smoke went up to foul the air, but the automated damage control devices at dockside had been allowed to operate, and the air was being cleaned, the destruction so far contained.

Rage returned to Harivarman, as sick and bitter as before, but this time never to be satisfied. What was done, was done. Even if it had been against his orders, though how that would be possible . . . perhaps not against his orders, after all. Perhaps the docks, the ships, had been a center of resistance. He had given the berserkers authorization to kill, to shoot back when necessary to achieve their objective. He had said to the controller that they could crush human resistance whenever and wherever it threatened to hold them up.

He had never expected that there would be resistance on this scale.

But it was all on their own heads, on the heads of those who would have gone calmly on, satisfied to do their duty, watching as he and Lescar and Bea and others were taken away to pre-judicial murder.

Harivarman's flyer passed the wreckage of still more human-built machines. There was the first human casualty he had seen clearly, a Templar body lying in the street. There had been more fighting then, more killing than he had planned for. Well, so be it. He had hoped for a greater surprise, for Templars taken totally unaware, made prisoners, rendered ineffective without bloodshed. He glanced back toward the docks. Above all he had hoped for the berserkers to be able to capture an intact ship for him, one in which he would be able to get away. He should have known that no attack would be likely to achieve such a measure of surprise. Not here, and not against Templars.

Everywhere the Prince looked now, his determination, and what was left of his self-possession, received another shock. He simply hadn't expected that there'd be this much physical destruction. But the whole City was certainly not in ruins; there had been no wholesale massacre, such as uncontrolled berserkers would surely have accomplished with the advantage of surprise. At least the Prince could be sure now, with considerable relief, that the entire civilian section of the Fortress, with the exception of the civilian area immediately around the docks, appeared to have been spared any general attack. On the whole, the berserkers appeared to have carried out the detailed, complicated orders from their new human master at least as well as could have been expected.

He had had no choice. He had had no choice. *He had had no choice*.

He had pulled ahead of the controller again, and now when he stopped his vehicle to look around, it caught up with him once more. As it did so he commanded it to stay near him, ready to receive his further orders. But at the moment he could think of no more to give it. When he drove on again, it maintained its position near his flyer, pacing swiftly on its six giant legs, still apparently untroubled by the severed cables and other loose ends that trailed from his dissection of its belly.

When the Prince arrived at his exile's house he found two dead Templars lying outside his door.

He could see that one of the Templars had drawn a pistol, and he could see how the weapon had been crushed, along with the hand that held it, and for a moment Harivarman thought that he could feel his heart stop, wondering what he was going to find inside. Bea was in there, or he had done his best to arrange it so. Then he saw that one of the fallen figures outside the door was still alive, and he stopped, feeling the impulse to try to help the wounded young woman. He could do nothing at the moment. Maybe there would be help for her inside.

He gave the front door his voice and his handprint to identify, and it opened for him immediately. Inside, Lescar, of course unarmed, came running in ecstasy to see his master still alive. But the servant was also in an agony of terror. He blurted out the story of how the house had already been visited by berserkers, but somehow, inexplicably, the machines had left without killing them all.

Beatrix was there too, and to Harivarman's vast relief she was unhurt. At first she was simply overjoyed to see him. But it took Bea only a moment, even less time than Lescar needed, to realize that something had changed in the Prince's situation, something besides the mere fact of the attack.

Harivarman shunted aside the first tentative questions of her terrible suspicion. He demanded: "Where's Gabrielle?"

Beatrix only fell silent, staring at him. Lescar said: "Miss Gabrielle did not answer my call, Your Honor, or return it."

The Prince was silent for a moment. "All right. Can't be helped. Give me a hand with this girl out here." Then he and Lescar carried the wounded Templar into the house and put her on a bed, and Lescar summoned the household first aid robot. The machine immediately began calling the base hospital, which did not respond. It kept trying.

Beatrix was still staring, silently, at her husband.

Harivarman looked around for the controller, but could not see it anywhere. It could have entered the house, he thought, and be in the next room now. All the doorways were probably too small for it, but small doorways had not troubled it before.

Beatrix demanded of him tensely: "What are you looking for?"

"Never mind."

Now there were sudden sounds outside the house, a woman's voice screaming, and pounding. Harivarman dashed to open the front door that he had closed and locked again when they brought in the girl. Gabrielle, her appearance transformed by terror and some slight physical damage, fell into his arms.

Gabrielle reported, as soon as she could speak coherently, that she had tried to reach the Templar base quarters as soon as she realized that an attack had started. But there was fighting, destruction and smoke all around that area, and she had been forced to run away from it. She had been able to think of no other place to turn for protection except to Harivarman.

She looked back over her shoulder and began to scream again. The Prince raised his eyes and saw that the controller had arrived.

Harivarman took a step toward it. "Come no closer," he called out. "None of these people with me now are offering resistance."

"Order acknowledged."

Bea and Lescar were both staring at him now, in a way that he had never seen either of them look at anyone or anything before. Obviously they were each realizing in their respective ways some portion of the truth. Gabrielle's face as yet showed nothing but animal relief, as the berserker obediently stopped its approach.

He was not going to take the time to try explaining or justifying himself now. Instead he issued orders. With Lescar's and Bea's help the Prince got Gabrielle and the still-breathing Templar guard into his flyer. Taking the driver's seat himself, on manual control, he set off at once for Sabel's old laboratory. Some of the machines should be there already, in accordance with Harivarman's earlier orders, setting up a command post for him.

The three women were in the back seat, Bea working efficiently at being a nurse. To Lescar, sitting beside him, the Prince explained en route why he was moving out of the house so quickly. Besides avoiding the presumed electronic bugging there, the transfer should make it harder for the Templars or dragoons to zero in on him with any missiles or other deadly tricks.

Lescar agreed mechanically, as if he might not really know or care what he was agreeing to. Meanwhile he stared out his window at the controller that paced beside the flyer, keeping up with it. Only now, Harivarman thought, was the little man really beginning to understand just what his master had done. Explanations were in order, of course, but they would have to wait.

When Harivarman eased the vehicle to a stop near Sabel's old lab, a berserker unit was already on guard outside. And the controller, stopping beside the car, reported that in accordance with the Prince's orders the place had already been given a security check.

The controller stayed right behind him as he went inside; here the doorway happened to be large enough. Bea came after it, giving it a wide berth but looking as if she might already have accepted its presence.

She spoke for almost the first time since he had rejoined her. "I want to send that vehicle to the base hospital, with that girl in it. She might live then. Will it be shot down if I do?"

The Prince opened his mouth, closed it, then looked at the controller. "See that it's not," he ordered.

"Order acknowledged."

"That takes care of half the problem. Program the pilot not to fly, Bea. Maybe it can drive into the base on the ground without the Templars shooting it up . . . are you going with it?"

Beatrix moistened her lips. "I'm staying with you," she said.

Harivarman turned a little shakily to look at Lescar— but of course, in Lescar's case there was no need to ask.

He turned to the controller, and demanded from it a report concerning the machine that was sent to extricate Chen Shizuoka from his house arrest.

"It has proven impossible to locate the life-unit Chen Shizuoka as ordered. Efforts continue."

"Damn. I thought they had him in confinement, near the base."

"A search of the designated area failed to locate the life-unit Chen Shizuoka. A wider search is proceeding, as rapidly as possible under the constraints that you have placed upon my operations."

"Those constraints must be observed. Carry on." The Prince turned away from the thing, and went to Beatrix where she was sitting on the floor in one corner of the large and almost empty room. Maybe he thought, trying to rouse her from her shock, he should have sent her off with the wounded Templar girl. But Harivarman had mental reservations about the flyer's being allowed into the base, whether it stayed on the ground or not. Most likely the Templars would shoot it up.

"Life-unit Harivarman." The Prince turned, slowly. He had never ordered the controller to call him sir.

"What is it?" He had the feeling that it was about to tell him that the game it had been playing was over now, that he and those with him were about to die.

"Why," it asked him, "are you especially interested in the life-unit Chen?"

He stared at it. What next? "What do you care why? If it makes any difference, I think he may have information that I'm going to need."

"It is only that I must allocate resources and set priorities among the various commands that you have given."

"Carry on as best you can. Right now I have yet another job for you. Setting up some communications."

And presently, through a juggled communications relay that he hoped would be impossible to trace, the Prince, sitting in his new command post, managed to make contact with the base commander in her headquarters.

"I'm back at my post somewhat early. I keep my word, you see."

"Harivarman, where are you?"

"In a safe place, for the time being, Commander. As you are."

"What do you mean by that?"

"That you won't be hurt, and that no more of your people will be hurt, as long as you follow my orders from now on. But you're good at following orders, so you should survive."

Realization grew on her only slowly. "You've done this, then. Somehow. Damn you."

"It became necessary, Commander. You see, I really had no choice. I understand that necessity, a lack of choice, excuses anything." It gave him great pleasure to throw some of her own words back at her.

It came as no surprise to find that the pleasure did not last.

Chapter 13

"I never got to go to a university," Olga Khazar was saying, almost wistfully.

"I'm not sure you missed much," Chen Shizuoka said. His feeling at the moment was that his own efforts to obtain an advanced education had never done him any particular good.

He was into practical learning now. He had discovered that if he set one chair on top of another and then leaned the tall double mass of them against the control of the door-intercom of the hotel room that was his prison cell, he could keep the intercom unit turned on steadily. Olga Khazar had again been left on duty outside, and she was willing to talk to him almost continuously. None of the other guards who had so far taken their turns watching over him in his various rooms of confinement had been anywhere near as communicative as Olga was, and she was not going to stay on guard forever. He wanted to benefit from her presence while he could. For Chen, having some kind of regular contact with the world was practically a necessity.

"Looks quiet out there in the hall now," he commented. "Where's everybody?" He had been locked up in this room for several hours now, and had already realized that at least some of his fellow recruits from the transport were being housed in nearby rooms; Chen had been able to hear some of their voices, half-familiar, passing his door from time to time.

Olga, trim-looking as usual in her uniform, mean-looking pistol on her hip to show that she was on guard duty, was leaning against the wall outside. Through the intercom Chen could see her little image complete from head to toe, along with a little bit of wall on either side. Her posture was unmilitary, he supposed, but right now probably no one could see her but himself. She said: "Right now I think they're all out on the firing range."

"Already? They've only been here a couple of days. I thought that kind of thing came later."

"It's three days now since your ship got here. We like to start people early with weapons. It's a big part of being a Templar. What were you studying at the university?"

"I thought I was going to be a lawyer."

"I wish I had a chance like that. I come from Torbas."

"Aren't there any lawyers on Torbas?" Chen knew it was perhaps the poorest of the Eight Worlds. Olga only shrugged and looked sad. Chen tried to think of what he might say to Olga to console her for being born in poverty and missing out on a university education, but at the moment he felt too envious of her to be able to come up with anything useful along that line.

He was the one who needed consolation. She, after all, was not locked up. Nor was she suspected of some insane crime that she would never have committed. Nor—no, he *wasn't* paranoid—was she the victim of an involved and ominous plot.

Chen was still trying to think of the best thing to say next when conversation was interrupted by a distant blast, a faint vibration racing through the floor. In the little intercom screen, Olga's image turned its head away, distracted by the noise.

"More remodeling," Chen decided. "Clearing the slums."

"I don't know. It didn't sound . . ."

"Didn't sound what?"

"I don't know." Then she surprised him. "Wait, I'll be right back."

"Leaving your post? Oh, I'll wait, all right."

She was back in about five seconds, properly at her post again, standing up straight in a military way and using her communicator. "Post Seven here. Officer of the day?"

Olga repeated the call. Apparently she was having trouble getting anyone's attention. She called again, several times, but Chen could tell that no one was answering.

She paused to look into the intercom at Chen. "I don't think that was blasting," she said, and then went back to trying the communicator on her wrist to hail her superiors. But still nobody responded.

Her manner remained calm, but something about it was alarming. It didn't take much to alarm someone who was already locked up, Chen realized. He demanded: "What's wrong? What is it, then?"

And even as he spoke, there were more faint blasting sounds, this time accompanied by faint distant screams.

"I think it's berserkers," said Olga Khazar, in a remote, taut voice. She had paused, holding the communicator a few centimeters from her lips. Her head was turned away from him again.

"Berserkers. *Berserkers?*" It couldn't be, not really. Not here on the Templar Fortress. And yet, somehow, he already knew it was.

She didn't answer, she was busy.

"You've got to let me out!"

Her dark eyes in the screen turned toward him. "I don't have a key."

"I don't care! You've got to—"

For ten long seconds they argued back and forth.

Abruptly she gave in. In a way that scared him all the more, making the whole threat real. She said: "All right, all right. Stand back away from the door, way back. Better go into the latrine."

Her image was drawing its sidearm.

Going all the way into the toilet was unnecessary, thought Chen. He didn't want to lose a second getting out of the room once the door was open. He retreated into the middle of the room, looked about wildly, and dove behind a sofa just in time. There was a ripping, shattering noise, and he heard small pieces of something fly against the walls.

Olga's voice, heard directly now, yelled at him: "Come on!"

Chen burst from concealment, and ran for the room's door, which now hung open, amid aerial dust and the smell of something scorched. Fragments of metal and stone powder were strewn everywhere, and Olga Khazar had her firearm in hand. Chen moved forward, through more dust, out of the room. The corridor was empty except for Olga and himself, but in the distance he could hear people yelling.

"Thanks!"

She looked grim. "I figured it was part of my duty, to keep you alive. Come on, follow me."

Chen followed. He thought he knew where they were headed, or the first stop at least. Yesterday he'd already been taken, under heavy guard, through one practice drill with the spacesuits, and he'd had to wear one on his little drive with Commander Blenheim. He now knew enough about the suits to use one in an emergency, which this certainly seemed to be. He followed Olga at a run down one corridor and then another to where their assigned emergency suits were stored.

Olga holstered her pistol, then took the belt and holster off and laid them down. She opened two of a row of lockers and dragged out two suits.

Chen said: "I could use a gun, too."

"I don't have one of those to give you. Get that suit on quick." She knew the tone for giving orders, all right, even if she was at or near bottom rank herself.

Probably, Chen thought, she had listened to enough of them to master the technique.

He asked: "Where are we going now?"

She had her own spacesuit on already, over her regular uniform, and was clipping the holstered pistol on at her hip. "I'm going to rejoin my unit, and you're coming with me."

That was all right. The young lady sounded as if she knew what she was doing, and Chen was not about to try going anywhere alone just now if he could help it.

Suits on, helmets closed, they moved again. The suits were so light and well designed that they hardly slowed one down. As they trotted, Chen keeping up with Olga, there was more blasting, mixed with other sounds of weaponry, to their right and left. And now a large detonation ahead of them as well. Berserkers, streaking units in the sky, were intermittently visible. Fast as missiles, some of the assault units projected themselves in streaking curves that bent around the Radiant's distorted core of space, picking up speed again as they neared their intended spots of impact or landing.

Gun in hand now, Olga slowed down, then stopped, then peered around a corner. "I don't know how much farther in this direction we can go . . ." She moved to a different corner. "Let's try down here instead. Some of my squad should be around . . ." She stopped abruptly.

Chen peered over her suited shoulder. Ahead, part of a wall had been demolished, along with something else. The mangled body looked unreal to Chen, a dummy in a Templar uniform.

But Olga recognized the dead young man, and called him by name. Chen could see that she was almost sick.

Chen, feeling only numb (*this isn't really happening*), spoke to her—later he could never remember what words he had used—trying to comfort her somehow. Then he bent and picked up the fallen Templar's weapon, a kind of short rifle. He thought it was what they called a carbine.

Looking as pale as her dark skin would allow, Olga muttered: "I'll show you how to use that when we have a chance."

"Better show me now."

"Aim it. Get an approximate aim first. Look at your target through the scope sight, here, if you have the chance." Her eyes were distracted, searching for terror and death around them, but her fingers moved surely on the carbine. She was repeating a lesson that she could have given in her sleep. "Here's the locking sight control. Touch it when you're looking at your target; the sight reads your eyeball and locks on. Your trigger is here, your safety here."

Chen rose to his feet, the weapon cradled in his arms. He looked up. He saw an enemy machine passing swiftly in the distance. He tried to aim, knew he was mishandling the sight somehow, but blasted off some rounds anyway, without noticeable effect.

Olga struck his arm down violently. "Don't draw them down on us, you damned fool! Don't shoot unless you have to. I don't know how much good a carbine's going to do us."

"All right."

"We can't get through to the base this way. We'll try the docks. Come on." They started in another direction.

They were now coming into a different part of the City from any that Chen had visited before; soon he would be hopelessly disoriented. But that worry dropped from his mind almost at once, replaced by something more immediate.

Looking back across a plaza, he started and then grabbed Olga by the arm. "One of them . . . one of th-them's coming after us."

At a distance of a couple of hundred meters it looked tall, and it was walking on three legs, a relatively slow-moving machine. Maybe it was a primitive type, but there was little comfort in the thought.

"Let's move!" Olga ordered. It had been moving directly toward them, and there was no reason to doubt that it had seen them; no reason at all, except for the fact that it had not killed them yet. Maybe it was out of ammunition, and would have to get within reach to do that. . . .

They pounded around a few corners, and then on the edge of a plaza, behind a screen of masonry, they tried to hide from it.

A few seconds passed before the machine came into sight again, in the middle of an otherwise deserted street. It was approaching their location, but not directly, and it might not have spotted them yet.

Presently Chen heard the berserker calling his name, in the tones of a human voice, a voice he thought he could recognize. It boomed out loudly through the streets, uttering words in a world gone mad.

"Chen Shizuoka. Come with this machine and it will guide you to a place of safety. Chen Shizuoka, this is Prince Harivarman speaking. Come with this machine—"

Chen looked into the eyes of Olga, who was standing close beside him. The only answer he could see there was that she was as frightened as he was himself.

Chapter 14

Serving as defensive bunkers for the high command on the Radiant Fortress were chambers cut or built like other rooms out of the mass of stone, but hardened with thicknesses of special armor, and equipped with shielded communications conduits leading to what were considered key defensive points in various other sections of the Fortress. Commander Blenheim's bunker was directly underneath her ordinary office—not her temporary one—and it had taken her two full minutes to reach the bunker after the attack started.

Grand Marshall Beraton had not visited the Radiant Fortress for well over a century, but he still remembered perfectly where the bunkers were. He and Captain Lergov were taking shelter in their own assigned hardened chamber within a minute after the commander had reached hers.

Before the grand marshall had gone underground, he had dutifully tried to find out what had happened to the crew of the Salutai ship on which he had arrived, but that information proved at least temporarily impossible to obtain. All around the docks was devastation, and at Lergov's continuous urging the grand marshall soon came away. The bunkers, as Lergov kept repeating, would offer the best communication facilities, the best chance to try to get a line on what had happened to their troops.

Their bunker connected through a hardened, sealed passage with that of Commander Blenheim. They joined her presently, and listened with her while reports outlining the situation kept coming in.

There was no question that a real beserker attack was in progress, though where the machines could have come from was beyond anyone's ability to guess. The automated outer defenses and alarms were not what they had been in the old days, but it was hardly possible that they had permitted a landing force to get by them without at least sounding the alarm. Another mystery was that although the enemy had seized a commanding position, they were not pressing their advantage.

That was fortunate. There were only a few hundred Templars on the Fortress, most of them a cadre preparing for the cadets' school that was to have opened here in the near future. And here on the inner surface of the Fortress they had little, almost nothing, in the way of heavy weaponry with which to defend themselves. And what little the Templar base had of such armament had already been knocked out. More such ordnance, a lot more, was available out on the outer surface of the Fortress, and a little more at the interior firing range. But none of the strongpoints on the outer surface had been manned by humans for a long time, and as far as the commander could recall, no one at all had been at the interior firing range.

One bright spot in the situation, though it was of no immediate benefit to the now-besieged garrison of the base, was that one ship, a message courier that had been standing by to receive messages in one of the small outer docks, had managed to get away when the attack struck. At least the available evidence indicated that the courier had escaped successfully. Of course if there were spacegoing berserkers in the area, it would seem there must have been to effect a landing, then the courier's fate was problematical at best.

Once inside the commander's bunker, Captain Lergov retreated into the background, where he was presently joined by a civilian man as short and impassive as himself. This newcomer was introduced to Commander Blenheim as Mr. Abo, a cultural representative, whatever that was, from Prime Minister Roquelaure's office. Captain Lergov in a few words to the commander explained who this man was, and that he had remained on the Salutai ship up until the attack.

Commander Blenheim, who had other things to think about, was not greatly interested. Neither was Grand Marshall Beraton, she could tell. He was hovering, acutely conscious of the fact that he was not really in command here, yet aching, as a veteran, as a grand marshall, to take over

Well, she was a veteran too. There were her combat decorations on her jacket if he wanted to see them. The garment, taken off when she got into her spacesuit and combat gear, hung on the wall behind her now.

Sparing no time for discussion with her visitors, she was busy trying to stiffen the nerves of some of her junior officers when the call came in from Prince Harivarman.

His face, looking almost unruffled, appeared on the screen, and his voice was almost calm: "I'm back at my post somewhat early. I keep my word, you see."

"Harivarman, where are you?"

"In a safe place, for the time being, Commander. As you are."

Whatever she had been about to say to him was suddenly forgotten. Something in his face, his voice, made her catch her breath. "What do you mean by that?"

"That you won't be hurt, and that no more of your people will be hurt, as long as you follow my orders from now on. But you're good at following orders, so you should survive."

Beraton and Lergov looked at each other. The commander sat back in her chair, realization growing on her slowly. She said to the image in the screen: "You've done this, then. Somehow. Damn you."

"It became necessary, Commander. You see, I really had no choice." Harivarman's image paused; it seemed to be smiling. "I understand that necessity, a lack of choice, excuses anything."

"You had better get here, to the base, if you can."

"Oh no. No. You are coming to see me instead."

"To see you! Where are you?"

He ignored the question. "I suppose you're down in your bunker now. I want you to go up to the inner surface and get in one of your staff cars; you won't be blasted. Come unarmed and alone; that'll save time and argument at this end. I'll give you directions, once I get a report from one of my lookouts that your staff car is under way."

"You must be mad."

"Not in the least."

"If you're able to move about freely, Harivarman, come here."

The image shook its head. "I just said I was not insane. You're coming here. You have half an hour to get here, and I promise you an explanation of all this when you arrive. Unless, of course, you prefer another attack. If so, just stay where you are. This time I'll tell my machines not to be so gentle. And one more thing. Be sure to bring with you the original Council order for my arrest." And Harivarman broke the connection.

"Goodlife." Beraton, watching over Anne Blenheim's shoulder, breathed the word unbelievingly. He drew himself up to his full height. "I will go and talk to him, the madman. Your post is here, Commander."

"You will obey orders, Grand Marshall, and I order you to remain here. I'm going to talk to him. I expect I can handle him. But if I don't return in two hours—" She hesitated. "I want you to take command of the Fortress." Anyone else she left in command, she thought, would be incapable of arguing successfully with a legend anyway.

Perhaps the grand marshall was surprised; at any rate, he gave her a salute, and ceased to argue.

On the way out of her bunker, Commander Blenheim glanced into the adjoining one. Lergov was back in there now, with his civilian aide. They were on a communicator there, trying to reach some of his people; the radio space in the Fortress seemed to be filled with berserker-induced noise, jamming everything but their own signals.

Arriving in her surface office again, Anne Blenheim issued a few final orders to Major Nurnberg and others who had come up, it seemed only to argue with her, out of their own protective holes. She would not argue, but issued orders instead. Everyone was to hold their fire, unless fired upon by the berserker enemy. They agreed, and tried yet again to argue her out of going to the meeting with the lunatic Prince. But she squelched them quickly. Instinct, feeling, something, had told her at once to go, despite the obvious danger. Not going would hardly be safe either. Her staff car was ready now, and as she climbed into it, shedding her gunbelt on the way, she reviewed the situation as it now stood in her own mind.

The Templar compound was surrounded by the enemy in three dimensions. The fighting in and around the base, against perhaps three dozen berserkers, had been sporadically fierce since the first lightning onslaught. But the sounds of fighting had died away.

Everything she saw as she began to drive indicated that her earlier assessment of the situation had been correct. If the berserkers launched an all-out attack they would almost certainly win, overrunning her handful of surviving Templars in a short time. But as yet no such attack had come, and it seemed to Commander Blenheim of overriding importance to find out why. Harivarman had promised her an explanation if she came to confer with him, and at the moment she could think of nothing that she needed more.

As she cruised slowly away from the base in the staff car, she suddenly recalled something about the firing range. Colonel Phocion was out there today, with the new recruits, or some of them. Phocion had wanted to fill in time until his new orders came, someone had informed her, by taking a hand in the training of the small group of raw enlistees who had arrived on the ill-starred transport ship along with Chen Shizuoka. There might also have been, the commander supposed, a few non-coms out there at the range with them when the attack hit. But there had as yet been no word received in the command bunker from those people. The communications with the firing range, as with several other areas of the Fortress, had been disrupted by the berserkers' pulse technology.

Should she call back to the command bunker now, from her car, and remind Nurnberg or one of the others about the people at the firing range . . . but no, the enemy would most likely intercept the message. No, the people at the firing range would have to cope as best they could.

Harivarman's voice, so suddenly and unmistakable that it made her jump, came clearly over her car's speakers. "Turn left at the next corner, Commander."

She acknowledged the instruction with what she thought was admirable calm, and then presently realized that she was headed in the general direction of Sabel's old laboratory.

"Stop the car where you are," the general's voice ordered presently.

She obeyed. The street here looked familiar. Was this the very route that they had taken on that first outing with Harivarman?

"Get out," said the speaker in front of her. "Walk down the alley to your right, please."

Commander Blenheim got out, expecting to feel a weakness in her knees. She was not disappointed. She started walking in the indicated direction. Around the first corner, a berserker was waiting for her. It was a tall thing, standing motionless, rather like a metallic scorpion balancing on its hind legs.

Her stomach clenching suddenly, she slowed her steps. She could no longer make herself walk forward. Then she saw and recognized Lescar, the general's driver, who was beckoning to her. The little servant was standing within a few meters of the machine, but not looking at it, as if he were able to pretend it was not there.

Lescar's manner was apologetic, but determined. "This way, please, madam. The Prince is waiting."

The general, Anne Blenheim thought, with what she acknowledged as lunatic determination. But she did not utter her correction aloud. Instead she followed him down a deserted street and into the laboratory, by a different doorway than the one she had used before. The tall berserker escort came with them, following her silently.

In a room inside the small lab complex Lescar came to a halt, indicating the door that she should enter. Inside the door, she found herself looking at the Prince, who was seated behind a built-in table, alone except for two more machines that flanked him, like huge and metallic bodyguards, on either side.

She said: "It's really true, then. But I can't believe it. Not of you. I really can't believe it." Her voice was only a whisper, and it seemed to come from her almost involuntarily. "How could you . . . ?"

He flared back at her bitterly: "All right, I'm goodlife, then! What good did it ever do me *not* to be goodlife? The everlasting gratitude of humanity for my victories over the berserkers? Of course. We've seen how long that lasted. These machines are now tools in my hands, no more, like any other tools. A saw to cut my prison bars. If Templar guards stand in my way, I can't help that. They're wrong to be there." He paused. "I see you came unarmed. Good. You brought the document?"

"*They're* wrong? Harivarman, how could you?"

"How could I discover evil out in the dark corridors, evil that the Templars managed to miss for two hundred years? Why, I suppose I have a unique affinity for evil."

"Then you are really in control of them. However it happened. You really are."

"I am indeed. But don't be a fool and think me

goodlife. Do you suppose *I* serve and worship *these?*"
And he swung out an arm and rapped his knuckles
contemptuously against the carapace of one of the tower-
ing things beside him, the one on his right with cables
hanging from its opened belly. He said to it: "Send this
other unit out. Surely you can deploy it to better purpose
somewhere else. Make sure the Templars prepare no
tricks while I'm distracted here in conference."

In a moment, moving silently in obedience to some
silent order, the other unit left the room.

Anne Blenheim had to do something to keep from
screaming. She approached the table and threw the parch-
ment document down on it. "You wanted to see this.
What else do you want?"

"Right to the point, as usual." Harivarman took up
the Council's order, glanced at it for a moment, and
tossed it aside. "All right, I'm sure that right to the
point is best. I now have information indicating that a
ship, a message courier, was standing by in an outer
dock when the attack hit. I want that ship, for myself
and whoever wants to join me."

"Every ship in dock has been destroyed, the message
courier included." She wished herself a more practiced
liar. The courier was already gone, taking news of the
attack to the Eight Worlds. A fleet would be here in a
matter of a few days at most. If only it were possible to
somehow stall, to maintain until then whatever mad
precarious balance was holding the berserkers back from
slaughter.

He studied her. "Or, one way or another, it's gone."

She nodded. "And I have a better plan to suggest to you."

"Aha? And it is?"

"Surrender."

That got a quietly scornful reception. "If I were the type to surrender I needn't have gone to all this trouble. I have no taste for allowing myself to be quietly murdered. No thank you."

Somewhat to her own surprise and anger, she found that she was still really halfway concerned for this man's welfare. "I'm curious. Where would you go, if you did get away? Where could you go?"

"There are places."

"As goodlife you won't be allowed to exist in any decent human society. Not even in most of the societies that most of us would call indecent. Only the other goodlife and the berserkers themselves will have you."

Sounds as of fighting flared up somewhere outside. Perhaps, thought Anne Blenheim, they were from as far away as the Templar compound.

Harivarman turned almost casually to the monster remaining beside him, a six-legged giant that looked as if it had been badly damaged itself, with cables and lasered-off loose ends hanging from a cavity in its belly. With this thing he almost calmly exchanged some words. In a voice that to Anne Blenheim had the nightmare flavor of old training tapes, the killer machine assured him that the situation outside was still essentially calm.

It struck the commander that the man sounded not at all servile, as she had heard that goodlife always were before their hideous gods and masters. He sounded like a man giving orders to a robot—except that Earth-descended humans, with the frightening example of the berserkers always before them, had never dared to build robots as independently powerful as these.

He turned back to her. "Well?"

"I can't believe it," she murmured again, as if to herself.

"Oh? Just what is it that you can't believe, exactly? That I want to go on living, and not as a perpetual prisoner? Probably with my behavior so modified that I spend a great deal of my time smiling?"

"Things like that aren't done any—"

"Don't tell me that. I've seen some of the people that Lergov's worked on. I've talked to some of those who could still talk. You couldn't believe that I would take steps to protect myself? That's not what the individual is supposed to do, is it? You might recall that I tried appealing to law and justice—yes, and to mercy, too. I tried with my best eloquence, at our last meeting. As usual in the real world, eloquence and a just cause were not enough."

"Where is your just cause now?" she asked him.

"Where you put it. But it's still surviving. It will survive."

"I see . . . and what are you going to demand of me now? A ship is impossible, even if I were willing to give you one. As you can see for yourself, after what your allies have done, there are no ships."

"All right. Forget for the moment what I demand. First I'd like someone to understand what's really at issue here. Do you realize what I've discovered?" He raised one hand, holding what appeared to be a small electronic device. "The controlling code of the berserkers. Even if the code I have here only works for some of them, it also tells us the type of code that's likely to control the others. There's at least a chance now that we, that all humanity, can be freed of the damned machines at last."

The berserker he had spoken to, evidently one of their controller units, emotionless and uncaring as they always were, looked over his shoulder. And undoubtedly it listened to his words.

"The controlling code . . ."

"Would you like to sit down? Sit on the edge of my table here, we'll be informal. I'm afraid your Guardians unfurnished this room some time ago, and we have a certain shortage of chairs."

"The controlling code," Anne Blenheim repeated, in a whisper. No Templar officer would need more than a moment to grasp the implications of that. "If you really have . . ."

"Aha. I have, I really have. And that puts a slightly different face on the whole matter, hey?"

"Yes." She said the word reluctantly, but she had to say it. "If you're telling me the truth. What greater advantage than that could anyone have over an enemy?"

"Indeed, yes," said Harivarman. "Now . . ."

His words drifted to a halt. Commander Blenheim, looking closely, saw that something had just happened to General Harivarman. He still sat in the same position as before. His expression had altered—not by much. But now he was staring at the control device in his hand, as if something about that small object had suddenly struck him, something he himself had been unaware of until this moment.

The commander stared at him, waiting. Some new madness . . . ?

At last the general looked up at her. It was a strange, unreadable glance, and perhaps it was mad indeed. But his voice, as before, still sounded quite sane and calm. He asked her: "What did you just say, exactly?"

"I said, what greater advantage . . ."

"Yes. Of course you did." Waving her to silence with an imperious gesture, he stood up from the desk. "Now, as to my demands . . ." But, having said that much, the general once more fell silent, regarding her with the same odd look.

Anne Blenheim drew a deep breath. All she could think at the moment was that maybe this man had truly gone insane at last; at least this conversation seemed to be tending toward madness. She would take it over, then, if she could, and try to dominate.

She began: "If you can truly control the berserkers completely, as you say . . ."

Again it seemed to take the general a great effort to bring his attention back from the small device in his hand, to what his visitor was saying. "Yes?"

"Then order them to stop their attack."

This time the pause was shorter. He was coming back from whatever borderland he had been roaming for the past few moments. "Stop their attack? I have already done so. They are no longer attacking. They are maintaining their controlling positions.''

"Render them totally inert, then, if you can do it. Do that now, and in turn I'll see what I can do for you.''

He had by now regained something of his original bitter manner. "I suppose I should really have expected nothing better. You're not going to give me your solemn promise that I won't be prosecuted?''

"Would you believe me if I did? I'm no politician, no courtier, no . . .''

"What you're trying to say is that you're no experienced liar.''

"Harry.'' The name came out suddenly, as if she really hadn't meant to say it. "That's what your friends call you, isn't it?'' That wasn't leading anywhere, and she tried again. "Sorry, that was inadvertent. General, I will tell you only the truth, since I am not an accomplished liar, and I will make only promises that I intend to keep.''

There was a long silent pause between them. Then Harivarman said: "Unfortunately, none of the promises you have made so far are of the least use to me. Even though I do believe you mean them. So . . . as soon as I let your Templars up off the floor, you're going to arrest me. If you can keep Lergov or Beraton from shooting me down on sight.''

"You are going to have to let us up off the floor, as you put it, sooner or later, aren't you?'' She drew a breath. "Either that or you'll have to slaughter us all.''

He looked at his control device again. "We'll see. I

think I'll not necessarily have to follow either course of action.''

"What else?"

He considered carefully before he answered. "Sooner or later another ship is going to dock here. It probably won't be very many days until one comes along."

"Ah."

For a moment the idea of attacking him physically passed through the commander's mind. She was better than most women at hand-to-hand combat, better by far than most men, looking at her, would expect her to be. Still it was far from certain, very far, that she would succeed if she tried attacking this man now. And if the berserker that was still with them did not squash her when she tried, and she did succeed, and the control device came into her hands, what exactly would she do with it? She had no idea whether the controller would then obey her automatically or not. What controls on the device to press? How might her actions upset the delicate forces that at the moment were holding the enemy back from wholesale slaughter?

Rejecting that plan, at least for the moment, the commander said: "There's a point you might want to consider. Goodlife activity makes you subject to a Templar trial, right here and now. The people who have come from Salutai to arrest you would not have jurisdiction. They could not murder you as you fear."

"And what outcome could I expect from the Templar trial?"

She was silent.

"On the other hand, what if I were found innocent?

Why, then, I suppose I'd be free. No longer under Templar jurisdiction. Therefore quite free to be arrested by Lergov and carted off to Salutai, as soon as a functioning ship became available. Not that I'd ever reach that world alive—but we've been through that, haven't we? My being murdered would not affect your legal position in the least. An acceptable outcome to you, as no one could accuse you of breaking regulations. No, I intend to have the next available ship for myself.'

"All right, forget that suggestion. It wasn't well thought out." She hesitated, then took a plunge. "But I don't think your plan is well considered either."

"What do you mean?"

"Suppose I were to agree to it." The commander had to force herself to speak those words. "Suppose you did obtain a ship somehow, captured the next one to try to dock, and you got away. How would we be any better off here? We'd still be facing an overwhelming force of berserkers."

"But no, not at all. I would leave them on a timer, as it were. They would deny you access to the docks for a time, simply to prevent any quick repairs of the remaining ships, and use of them for hot pursuit of me, assuming such were possible. After the set time had elapsed, they would disable themselves or allow themselves to be disabled. A treasury of knowledge, such as the Templars have always sought. And you would have obtained it for them. I'm making you an offer that no real goodlife would make, and you know it."

"But at what price?" Commander Blenheim whispered. "At what price? You've helped them to kill human beings here, people under my command, Templars. No one but a goodlife would have—''

There was another outburst of noise, of fighting, somewhere outside the echoing empty room in which they were talking. Again the general turned to the controller at his side. ''What was that?''

''As before,'' the machine-voice answered him. ''It was necessary to take action against a local instance of aggression by the badlife.''

''Are you sure? Your communications must be imperfect too.''

''The probability is more than eighty percent.''

''Not good enough, for me.'' Harivarman waved a hand at the berserker. ''Go out and see for yourself, about that fighting. Report back to me directly.''

''It is not necessary—''

The general thumbed something on his control device. ''This is an order. Go out and see to the matter yourself.''

There was no more hesitation. The machine moved away, pacing with silent elegance, despite its damaged appearance.

Now the two humans were alone. Now, thought Commander Blenheim, I could risk everything, attack him with my bare hands. . . .

Across the table from her, Harivarman, looking almost absentminded, was again picking up the Council's order for his arrest. ''There are some changes I would like to see made in this,'' he announced, surprising her when she thought that she was beyond surprise. ''Before I'd even want to start negotiating with the Council.''

And, looking at her meaningfully, he pulled a writing tool out of his pocket.

It was half an hour later when the base commander left the man who had once been her prisoner. Her head was whirling as she departed, with relief at her own survival thus far, and with fear. And with a new and twisted hope.

Chapter 15

The berserker machine that had called to Chen Shizuoka in Prince Harivarman's voice was now calling to him again, as it advanced along an otherwise deserted street that led obliquely toward the plaza where Chen and Olga were trying to hide:

"Chen Shizuoka. Come with this machine to safety. Chen Shizuoka, this is Prince Harivarman. Come—" And even as the Prince's voice boomed forth from the berserker, it kept walking closer to where Chen and Olga were holding their breath, afraid to move.

Chen was peering out at the approaching monster through small chinks in a decorative screen of masonry. The tall screen separated the small plaza where he was standing from the nearby street down which the murderous thing was walking toward him on its three legs. His carbine, probably useless against this foe, was in his hands, the muzzle pointing up into the air. He was afraid to move a muscle, even the minimal movement necessary to aim the weapon, because aiming it would probably be a waste of time anyway.

His eyes moved again to his companion. Olga Khazar, standing pressed against the screen beside him, appeared to be on the verge of fainting, leaning on the screen, her hand that held the pistol pale-knuckled with the tightness of her grip.

The machine coming toward them down the otherwise deserted street was less than fifty meters distant now. It stopped briefly after every one or two of its triangular steps, turning its head from side to side at every pause, as if to sweep the area with its multitude of senses. The thing was almost twice as tall as a man, and pot-bellied as if its central torso might contain some kind of a cargo compartment. Now and then it raised its head even higher on an elongating metal neck, peering over stalled, abandoned vehicles and into upper-story windows.

Just behind the two people who were holding their breath and trying to hide from the berserker was the flat expanse of the small plaza, much like a hundred other plazas scattered around the City, and behind the plaza in turn there were some three- and four-story civilian buildings. In one of those buildings people were clamoring, oblivious to the approaching terror. It sounded like some stupid argument about what to bring and what to leave, as if there were someplace available for City people to flee. Chen could only hope that maybe the noise and movement behind himself and Olga, together with the screen in front of them, might be enough to mask their presence. The chinks in the decorative screen were very small.

For whatever reason, the prowling machine did not discover them. At the last intersection before the plaza it turned down a side street, and in another moment it was out of sight.

As soon as it was gone, Olga gestured, silently, urgently, for Chen to follow her. Then she turned and fled, moving as quietly as possible, crossing the plaza, going in the opposite direction from the machine.

Chen ran after her.

After a couple hundred meters she paused, and pulled him into a recess between buildings. Panting with the effort of the run, she whispered: "These weapons we've got aren't doing us any good."

"I've figured that," said Chen, nodding. His helmet and Olga's were both open; they could talk in low voices without breaking radio silence.

"If we could only get into the base . . ." She broke off, gesturing frustration; the base was where most of the fighting was going on.

"All right, so we can't get in there. We tried. Where do we try next?"

Olga only shook her head. Presently, when they had both caught their breath, she moved on, gesturing to Chen to follow. Chen didn't ask where they were going; he was anxious to go anywhere. He didn't want to sit in one place and do nothing.

Now they began to encounter a few other people, all of them civilians, on the streets. Most of the civilians appeared to be in flight, headed out away from the center of the City toward the relatively remote areas of the Fortress. Those among the refugees who took notice of the two spacesuited Templars at all looked at them more in fear than in reassurance.

Olga was setting a more moderate pace now, sometimes walking, sometimes moving at a jogging run. Chen, thankful that he had tried to keep to a program of running at home, kept up with her fairly easily. They had traveled more than a kilometer from where they had last seen the berserker before Olga stopped. When she spoke again, it was in something like a normal tone. "Maybe from here we can get a better look at what's going on."

She led Chen into another small plaza, and mounted the broad steps of its elevated central section. It offered them something of a vantage point, almost as if they had climbed a hill. This elevation, like every other on the interior surface, gave a fine view, as from above, of the surrounding territory at a distance of a kilometer or more. They had now made more than that much distance from the base, and from here it appeared to Chen at first that the conflict around the docks and the Templar base had cooled. The smoke in the air there had largely dissipated. But no, the fighting was not over; the sight and sound of it flared up again, and flared yet once more even as they watched.

"Look out!"

Chen turned quickly at Olga's warning. On a rooftop, several hundred meters back in the direction they had come from, he could again see the berserker that had called to them in Prince Harivarman's voice. As far as he could tell, the machine was facing almost directly toward him. Whether it could see him or not he did not know. But it called his name again, in an amplified bellow, and simultaneously it dropped from the rooftop out of sight, as if it were hurrying toward him again.

Olga was already running, fleeing in the opposite direction. Terrified, Chen followed her at the best speed that he could manage.

They rounded several corners, running hard. When Olga next stopped for breath, in a twisted alley, she demanded, almost accusingly: "What's it want *you* for?"

He had to gasp twice more before he could get out words. "How the hell should I know?"

His injured innocence was apparently convincing. Olga led the way again, this time at a mere walking pace, into a street where there were several abandoned flyers. She halted at one of these. "Let's take this one. We'll never be able to outrun that bloody thing on foot."

"Why didn't we try this sooner?"

This, Chen soon decided, must be some kind of service vehicle, for it appeared to need no special key or code to start. Olga took the driver's seat, and they were off. Under her control the flyer left the ground and swooped away, staying near ground level as it hurtled through streets and alleys. The thing pursuing them would never be able to travel this fast on the ground, thought Chen. But he could not imagine it giving up, and so it was probably still coming after him. If she separated from him . . . he was too scared to suggest that.

Olga's thoughts were evidently on other tactics. Driving, she mused aloud: "If we only had some heavier weapons . . . maybe I know where there are some."

"Where?"

"Out on the firing range. We've never used 'em much, since I've been on the Fortress, but I think they're there."

There was little traffic in these streets. Fortunately so, for Olga was taking blind corners under manual control at high speed. Chen wondered if the civilians knew something that he and Olga didn't, if it had already been demonstrated that large moving targets got shot at by either side, or both.

They rounded a corner swiftly and almost crashed into an oncoming flyer, a vehicle airborne and hurrying recklessly like their own. Chen opened his mouth to yell a warning, but it was already too late for that. Olga had barely avoided the head-on crash, but in the process their flyer had brushed a building. Damage alarms sounded aboard. The vehicle came down heavily, pancaking on the street with an ear-numbing roar, and skidded roughly to a broken halt.

Seat restraints held. Chen saw objects flying at him, but nothing hit him hard enough to do him damage through the tough spacesuit.

Olga was unhurt too, and already she was jumping out of the wreck. "Come on!"

Again, without discussion, she led the way. Moving as if she knew what she was doing, she opened a door in a wall and charged through it, down a ramp leading to some lower, relatively outer level. There might have been a sign to indicate where they were going, but if so it had gone past Chen too fast for him to read it. Through one sublevel passage after another their flight continued.

At last Olga changed course again, climbing a narrow spiral service stairway to the street. When they had regained the surface level, Chen immediately tried to scan the great map that the interior surface of the Fortress made of itself, to determine their location. But he was too unfamiliar with the Fortress to be able to tell where they were in relation to where they had started. All he felt sure of was that they had been fleeing for a number of kilometers.

Olga realized what he was doing, and pointed out to him the Templar base and its immediate area, which were now almost overhead, partially obscured behind the miniature solar brightness of the Radiant itself.

Chen was about to try to insist that it was time for conscious planning of their next move, when their conversation was interrupted. Chen's suit radio suddenly whispered some kind of gabble in his ear.

Olga waved him to silence; something was evidently coming in on her radio too. "Wait," she whispered, waving at Chen again.

The voice came again. It sounded to Chen like someone was operating a radio without being properly familiar with it.

Olga cautiously responded, at low power, asking for identification.

The voice replied, indistinctly. Chen couldn't make

out any of the words, until it asked: "Any more survivors out there?"

Olga said crisply: "Just tell me where you are, and then get off this channel."

"We're close to what looks like a firing range."

Her head swiveled, looking up at another portion of the self-mapping surface. "Stay put. We'll join you."

The firing range, as Chen was able to see for himself an hour later, was like a giant pit dug diagonally into the surface of the inner Fortress, with the targets at the outer, lower end of the pit, a hundred meters or more below the lines of firing positions. These positions were arranged in a series of semicircular terraces, each recessed and shielded to be out of the line of fire from the terraces above it.

As Chen and Olga came over the lip of the pit, people in uniforms strange to Chen appeared on the next terrace down, emerging from various shelters and hiding places and waving cautious greetings.

"What are those uniforms?" he asked Olga quietly. They reminded him somewhat of the security people who had chased him through the streets of the capital of Salutai.

"Dragoons. The people who came on the ship to arrest your Prince."

There were more than a dozen dragoons, Chen estimated, looking bedraggled and lacking spacesuits. Chen had seen nothing of the dragoon force until now, though Olga had earlier mentioned their arrival. These were not the proud imperialists she had depicted, but only a haggard, wounded, nerve-shattered remnant of that force.

There were two Templars among them, both wounded but walking.

"Where're your officers?" Olga asked the first dragoon to approach, coming wearily up a stair. The pits and revetments and shelters built around the terraces of the range at least gave the illusion of somewhat greater security than you felt when standing around out in the open, and the meeting quickly moved to a relatively indoor location.

The young man shrugged. "They were at some kind of a meeting, I guess, when the attack came; I think most of them made it into a shelter, back there near the docks. We were still aboard our ship when it was hit, and we had to get ashore; then we just lit out running." He spoke in the accents of Salutai, which sounded like home to Chen. "We ran into a couple of your people, and they said there might be heavy weapons out this way. If there were, somebody must have beat us to 'em."

"Looks like you've got some kind of communicator set up down there." Chen pointed. In one of the revetments on the next lower level, the dragoon troops had brought from somewhere a portable screen communicator with scrambler set up or, for all that Chen could tell, what they were using might have been a part of the built-in intercom between the command bunkers and this control center of the firing range.

"Come on down and join us."

"We'll stay up here on the rim," said Olga. "It's easier to keep an eye out from up here."

"Okay. Right. Suit yourselves. I'll report that you're here. Be back in a minute." The young man went down to rejoin the others, who were still milling about in a purposeless, disorganized fashion.

There was a man's face, rather blurry, on the communicator screen they had down there, and a conversation going on between the face and one or two of the dragoons. Chen stared at it absently, then recalled himself with a start to watch the interior sky again.

But his eye returned to the man's face on the communications screen. Something about that face, and the half-audible voice that issued from it, struck Chen as disturbingly familiar. Yes, he certainly ought to recognize that face; did it belong to some Templar officer he had seen on the transport, or near the docks right after landing? But in that case, it wouldn't be a dragoon uniform that the man was wearing now. Yet the man on the screen was uniformed as a dragoon, certainly—the picture wasn't that blurry—and wasn't that a captain's rank insignia on the collar? If dragoons used the same insignia as the security police . . . But somehow the appearance in dragoon uniform was jarring, it brought the face out of its expected context.

It took Chen a moment more. But then he had it. That face belonged to Mr. Segovia. Hana's friend, the man Chen had met just once or twice, a million years ago, back in the university library on Salutai. There was probably some logical reason for Segovia's presence here, some reason that he, Chen, was too shocked by events to grasp just now.

But yes, it was certainly odd. How could it have happened that Mr. Segovia was here, and wearing . . . ?

He was distracted by the problem, and ignored the sound of human feet approaching along a winding catwalk. Then someone spoke to him, in another familiar voice.

"Hello, Chen."

He looked up to see Hana Calderon.

Chapter 16

"I'm sorry now that you came back here, Bea."

"At this moment," Bea replied to her husband in controlled tones, "I am too."

It hurt Harivarman to hear his wife say that, and for the moment he had no answer to give her. It hurt more than he would have expected since for a long time he had thought that things were totally over between them.

The two of them were sitting in simple, brightly colored chairs, on opposite sides of a small patio table. Leafy trellises overhead shaded them from much of the direct light of the Radiant, and blurred the bright distant curve of inner surface, so that the fragments of it that were visible might almost be taken for bits of a real sky. The Prince and his wife were in one of the "outdoor" patio rooms of a large and elaborate house, of the type that the old Fortress inhabitants liked to call a villa. It was located about half a kilometer from Sabel's old laboratory. Someone had been living here quite recently, someone who had evidently abandoned the dwelling on short notice when the berserker attack hit—there were complete household furnishings, clothing in the several closets, food in the kitchen. There was even a jug of wine still on the table in front of Prince Harivarman.

"So, why did we move here?" Bea asked him. Her voice was so bright and interested, a media interviewer's or perhaps even a psychologist's voice, that he wondered if she thought him mad. Bea was sitting with her feet tucked under her in a deep chair. She had answered Lescar's summons wearing a coverall, a practical garment, as if she fully expected that visiting her husband again was going to involve some physical risk.

Leaning back in his own chair with his eyes closed in weariness, her husband answered. "I thought that moving might be prudent, once Commander Blenheim had gone back to the base with the knowledge that I was occupying the other place."

"You just told me you thought you had an arrangement with her now. After that private talk you had with her in the lab."

"I do think so. But still . . ."

"I see. And what kind of arrangement do you think you have?" Beatrix the interviewer wanted to know.

The Prince tried to think of some way to explain things to his wife, here in the controller's presence. He couldn't think of any way. His mind felt wearied, exhausted, as if he had been in battle for hours on end. As in a sense, of course, he had. At last he said: "A tacit understanding. You know, Bea, I didn't plan things to work out this way."

"How did you plan them, then?" Still not accusing; interested. He wondered enviously how she managed such control.

Yes, the controller was with them. It was out of the Prince's field of vision just now, but he didn't have to look directly toward it to make sure. For the past few hours, ever since it had returned to him following the commander's visit, the machine had hardly been out of sight and hearing of Harivarman for a moment. At present the machine was standing more or less behind him, on one side of the patio, listening to the Prince's every word and waiting for more orders. Not caring what the orders were.

In a sudden spasm of anger, Harivarman jumped to his feet and whirled around and threw the wine jug at it. The ceramic smashed on metal, and the red pungent liquid spattered. The target of his anger, the metal thing, did not move or react.

Harivarman turned his back on it and sat down heavily. He knew that he was going to have to take action, real action of some kind, soon, or risk cracking under the strain if he did not. This waiting was already becoming impossible.

How did you plan them, then?

The question was still hanging in the air, along with the smell of wine from the smashed jug. It was not a question that Harivarman wanted to attempt to answer. He got up and without looking at the berserker again went to find Lescar, wanting to get the mess from the broken wine jug on the patio cleaned up. If Lescar caught him trying to do such a menial job himself there'd be hell to pay, and Bea had not stirred from her chair.

The Prince had to look in three other well-furnished rooms before he found the little man, and the finding was not immediately helpful. Lescar was sitting alone in silence, face buried in his hands as if he were slowly going catatonic. Harivarman hesitated, and then left him as he was.

When the Prince came back to the patio to face Bea again, she asked him interestedly: "Why did you have Lescar call me, and tell me to come to your house?"

He made an almost helpless gesture. "I thought it might save your life, since you were already back on the Fortress. I didn't ask you to come back to the Fortress. Do you want to go back to your hotel now?"

"I was wondering," said Bea, "why you didn't make the call yourself. Where were you when . . ."

The last word rather trailed away, as Beatrix raised her eyes past the Prince's shoulder. He turned. Gabrielle was slowly descending an open, fragile-looking stair that curved gracefully down to the patio from enclosed rooms on the upper floor. She was still wearing the once-fancy gown in which she had come to him seeking safety. Her clothes, like her face and body, now showed ravages of rough usage in recent hours.

When Gabrielle saw the two of them looking up at her, she paused on the stair and said: "I heard a crash." She surveyed the splashed berserker and the fragments of pottery, and sniffed the wine-tinged air without making any direct comment. But when Gabrielle spoke again her voice was different, as if fear were entirely gone. "I thought for a moment that you had *done* something." The dominant look in her delicate face was no longer fear, but contempt, as she gazed down at Harivarman.

"What *are* you doing now, Harry?" Bea asked, speaking from behind him.

He turned to face her. "Waiting."

"Waiting for what?"

He was silent for a moment. "For three things," he said then.

"And they are?"

"The first two are reports from my machines."

"Your machines," said Gabrielle contemptuously. Now it was her turn to tackle him from behind. The Prince ignored her, and continued speaking to Beatrix. "Primarily," he said, "a report from the machine that I sent after Chen Shizuoka."

"The supposed assassin," said Bea, still sounding brightly interested.

"No—" He had been about to say, *no more than I am*. "Chen's not an assassin."

"Well. Whether he is or not, I'd like you to fill me in on what importance he has to us now. Why are we waiting for a report about him?"

"Do something!" This was Gabrielle again. She was now starting to scream hoarsely at Harivarman from above. "You just stand there like . . . do something, do something, do something!" It was as if she were emboldened by the inertness of the splashed berserker. She turned and ran back up the stairs as if she were going to her newly adopted room.

The Prince faced Beatrix again. "There's a second report I'm expecting at any time," he said. "It will have to do with more arrivals, landings on the outer surface of the Fortress."

Bea swallowed. "Human landings?"

"Yes, of course, that's what I had in mind. If you ask me who's going to land—that's what I'm interested in finding out. Bea, I'm trying to work out a way to get away from here in one piece. With my friends, with you, now that you're committed to me. And without any more fighting, if it can be done that way."

"And the third thing?"

"Some equipment I'm having them gather for me. I want to do some serious research on berserker communications."

"Can't that wait?"

"I don't think so."

Bea's control was suddenly slipping. She was shrinking down, huddling in her chair involuntarily. Her head turned, as if she could no longer keep from staring at the controller. She said: "Harry, I don't want to walk out on you again. But if you're doing this now in any sense for me . . . I don't know if I can stay here any longer . . . Harry, whatever it is you're doing with the damned machines, for God's sake stop it!"

"Bea. I—"

"Quit! Just give up, let Lergov arrest you! Whatever happens would be better than this!"

But then, having heard herself say that, she couldn't

stand by it. "Harry, I don't know what I'm saying. The problem is I don't know what's going on, and you won't tell me! I can't believe, I can't believe, that you're just—just—"

He found himself crossing the patio, pulling Bea out of her chair, and taking her in his arms. He said, close to her ear, knowing that the machines would hear him anyway: "If only I could just quit and give up, at this moment. If only I could."

She gripped his arms, ready again to persist. "You don't have to be arrested, Harry. You could make a deal. Let Roquelaure and his people have the damned control code, or whatever they want from you. Just so they'll let us get away together. Harry, I found I couldn't live without you: I thought I could come back and live with you, this time. I could have, too, but . . ." Bea's voice died away. Once more her eyes were staring upward past his shoulder.

Gabrielle was coming down the stair again, and this time she had a gun in her slender, pale, entertainer's hand, a tiny weight that still made her thin fingers shake. It was a little pistol, jeweled and almost ladylike. She must, the Prince thought numbly, irrelevantly, have had the gun with her since she arrived, brought it with her from her apartment. Unless she had just found it here in her adopted room, which seemed unlikely. Somehow it seemed to suit her, though he had never thought of her as bearing arms.

"Damn you," Gabrielle said to him, her eyes crazed. "I'm going to kill you, Harry." And she waved the gun. And then she started to level it at him with intent.

Most of the shock of fear felt by the Prince was not directly for himself. "Gabby, no! Put it—"

He had no time to get any farther than that, no time to do more than raise one hand in a useless gesture. Gabby was not listening anyway. She might or might not have actually fired on him. But what she might or might not have done did not matter. A tenth of a second before the pistol's muzzle came actually to bear on Harivarman, his life was saved.

The controller had been ordered to protect him. In this case it had probably no need to move its body or its limbs to do the job. He wasn't looking at it and he couldn't tell for sure; perhaps it turned its head. Harivarman knew that somewhere on its upper body a small weapons port had opened. A bolt of energy, instantaneous and almost invisible, stabbed past him, directed upward toward the woman on the stair. A bright flash filled the patio, accompanied by a dull throb of a sound. Gabrielle virtually disappeared. The Prince's only clear visual impression was of red hair bursting into flame. He heard the small bejeweled gun clatter on the stair, bouncing endlessly toward the bottom. A smell of singed flesh spread out to mingle with that of pungent, splattered wine.

Now Beatrix, combat veteran that she was, huddled deeper in her chair, hands covering her face. Lescar, no longer catatonic, came running into the patio where a moment later he veered to a helpless halt.

"We'll move again," was all the Prince could think of to say, when he could speak again.

*   *   *

Grand Marshall Beraton had now installed himself as a more or less permanent fixture in Commander Blenheim's bunker. She had never invited him to do so, but neither had she thrown him out as yet. The commander found the old man continually underfoot there, but she kept expecting that at any moment some real use for him was likely to come up, some problem or decision in which his experience might be invaluable. With this in mind she kept putting off the all-out effort it would doubtless take to shunt the grand marshall off permanently to an adjoining chamber.

Right now Beraton was pushing his luck, though. Now he was starting to argue that she ought to try to take out Sabel's old lab with some kind of missile, now that they were certain that the Prince—the general—was holed up there.

"I'm not really sure he's still there in the lab, Grand Marshall. Are you?"

"I'd say he's damned sure to be. Fellow with that kind of arrogance." The grand marshall paused, then added with sudden bitterness: "Should have clapped him in irons as soon as I laid eyes on him. *You* should have, if I may say so, Commander, long before that. Well, can't be helped now."

Still, Anne Blenheim refused to use a small missile on the old laboratory, giving as her reason that any such try would quite likely unleash a full berserker attack, or at least another punishing bombardment. And anyway, she told the grand marshall, she thought there might be antimissile weapons emplaced around the laboratory.

She could see that she was getting some strange looks

from those of her subordinates who were present. Quite likely they were wondering, not only at her refusal, but at the odd way she talked around the subject. Well, there was no help for getting odd looks just now.

Beraton, balked in his effort to take over her command more or less completely, his advice about a missile attack rejected, now came up with a new idea. He had to do that, she supposed, because it must gripe him that a mere young woman had gone out to meet the enemy face to face while he sat here in a shelter.

Now he wanted to at least duplicate the commander's bravery. He didn't put it that way, of course. Beraton's proposal was that he go and talk to Harivarman face to face. "We fought together once, he and I, you know. Or at least in the same theater. We met . . . I can't really believe that a fellow who fought so well once could—I'm going to go and face him with it. Do what I can to talk him into a surrender. I lecture you about your duty—hm? And here I'm not really doing my own."

The old man looked visibly older than he had only a few hours ago, she thought. "No, Grand Marshall. I . . ." Anne Blenheim paused momentarily, struck by a new idea. "Why not? Very well. Go and talk to him, if you like." She would at least get the old man out of her own hair, at least for a time. What would Harivarman think? Well, he could always send his visitor back.

Then, having second—or third—thoughts, she quickly qualified her approval: "But we'll have to call General Harivarman first, and see if he'll agree to another conference."

*　　*　　*

Sitting between her husband and Lescar in the slowly-moving groundcar, halfway through the process of moving to yet another villa, Beatrix announced that she was leaving Harivarman. "I can't do you any good staying with you, Harry. Not like this."

To Harivarman it was a door closing, with his life cut off behind it. But he couldn't say that he was surprised. Nor did he even know if he was truly sorry. It was as he supposed the final approach of death might be: a relief. He could handle it well, with a steady voice. "Where do you want to go, Bea? I'll send an escort with you."

Beatrix reacted almost violently to that suggestion. "No! No escort. Not of . . . them." Two tall machines, one of them the controller, paced beside the groundcar, one on either side. "Just let Lescar come with me for a little way. No more than that."

When they arrived at the newly chosen villa, one that scouting berserkers had reported as abandoned, Bea would not enter the house, or delay the separation.

A few minutes later, two blocks away, for the moment at least out of sight of berserkers, Beatrix was getting into an abandoned flyer, and tearfully saying goodbye to Lescar. The little man in his own odd way had always loved her, and now he was weeping too.

"I don't know what he's really doing, Lescar. He won't trust me with the knowledge, or I'd stay. Whatever it is."

"I don't know either, My Lady. But I must stay with him."

"Of course, of course." She started to add something else, and choked it back.

"Where will you go, My Lady?"

"To the base, eventually. I'll have to work my way there slowly. I can manage, I'll be all right. I know the Fortress, and I know my way around in a battle. Go back to him. You can help him, perhaps, and I can't. I never really could."

Grand Marshall Beraton was standing beside a small defensive outpost at the aboveground level of the base headquarters, trying his best to think through the problem of where his duty really lay. The job had been simple and clearcut at the start—simply arrest the wretched fellow and take him back to Salutai—but questions of rank, jurisdiction, and command had started to tangle things, as such questions usually did when they arose.

As now. The three enlisted people in the small half-shelter of the outpost were all too aware of him standing close behind them. Perhaps they thought he had come up here to conduct some kind of an inspection . . . it reminded the grand marshall of the time when . . .

He went off into some of the pleasanter rooms of memory, reviewing some of the happier events of his long, long life and long career. This process went on for some time, with no loss of enjoyment. Grand Marshall Beraton had to bring himself back sharply from mere reminiscing. He hadn't come up here to be effectively alone just to do that. He had to concentrate sternly on duty, for the situation was perhaps grimmer than almost any that he had ever seen. Thousands of innocent civil-

ian lives, not to mention military, hung in the balance
. . . all because of the evil of one man.

The grand marshall's meditations on Prince Harivarman's treachery were threatening to lead him into rev-
erie again, when they were violently interrupted. A
berserker flying device, probably on some kind of a
recon mission, came skimming in low over the base,
then arrogantly hovered almost directly above the surface headquarters building.

It seemed a direct challenge. It was too great an
outrage, coming on top of strains and stresses old and
new, some of them going back two hundred years. It
was unendurable. The grand marshall snapped out an
order to the three enlisted Templars who were gaping at
the enemy beside him.

The young non-com's voice was quakey, but he got
the words out. "Sir, our orders are not to fire, unless
they fire first."

Beraton leaned forward, a century and more of deci-
sive command telling him what to do. He seized the
small control unit of the launcher himself, and took a
blast at the foe. He saw the fiery dart of the small
missile spring up from the launcher itself, some forty or
fifty meters from the half-sheltered position where he
and the Templars crouched. Saw the dart fly up, only to
be deflected, hurled aside by some invisible force like a
ray of light reflected from a mirror.

Then the berserker blasted back.

Beraton was flung down on his face; the young men
around him, better protected in their suits and helmets
than he was, were less affected. The next thing he

knew, the berserker was gone, flown away, and people in combat armor were turning him on his back, arguing among themselves whether he should be moved.

Where the launcher itself had been, some fifty meters distant atop a low building, there was now only a smoking crater.

Grunting imperiously, clutching at their arms, he pulled himself to his feet.

"Sir, you'd better wait. We'll call a medic—"

"I need no medics, dammit. Back to your post."

He had needed that shock, it seemed, or something like it, to clear his mind. As his mind cleared from the concussion, it seemed to go on clearing, until hours, days, perhaps years of cobwebs had been swept away. He saw truth now in glaring daylight. The truth about the goodlife villain, that made him no longer fearful of the swarming evil in the sky. Duty called. Seldom if ever in his life before had that call, that message, come so clearly and unequivocally to Grand Marshall Beraton.

It took him less time than he had expected to locate Captain Lergov. So things usually went when one's duty had been understood clearly, when worries about nonessential difficulties had been abandoned.

Lergov was just coming up a stair from the third underground level to the second when Beraton intercepted him. The grand marshall guessed that the near miss on the surface had sent the timid captain down temporarily to a shelter still deeper, if one not necessarily really safer.

Well, there would be no more of that.

"Captain, I require your assistance."

The stocky man, who had once seemed to Beraton to possess a kind of impassive courage, but now seemed only secretive, replied: "Certainly, sir. What can I do?"

"Come this way. We can discuss it as we walk."

"In a moment, sir." And the captain turned away briefly. It was a way he had of putting off a grand marshall's requests and even orders: finishing some detail of his own. This insolent habit had never really struck Beraton as forcibly before this moment as it did now. This moment's delay was used by Lergov to leave his precious subordinate, Mr. Abo—the grand marshall had never had much use for most politicians—in charge of his precious and utterly useless communicator. But Beraton let the irritation pass now. He had something much more vast on his mind.

Lergov looked about apprehensively when the two of them had reached the surface, and took note of the newly devastated building nearby. But for the moment things were quiet again, and the captain only asked: "Where are we going, Grand Marshall Beraton?"

Beraton was already leading the way toward some nearby staff cars, all of them apparently so far undamaged. He spoke crisply over his shoulder: "We are going to arrest the traitor. You and I were sent here to do that. It is our duty, and we should have faced up to our duty long before this moment."

Captain Lergov stopped. It was a dull dead stop. His eyes had a stunned look, as if he were the one who had an aching head.

"Arrest the traitor, sir?"

"To arrest General Harivarman. Yes. He is the man we have come here to arrest. We are going to obey our orders and take him into custody."

Lergov said: "Grand Marshall, he is . . ."

"He is what? Speak up, man, if you have anything to the point to say."

"He is, he is *protected*, sir. It doesn't seem likely we can just, just . . ."

"Well, we are not protected, whether we sit here like cowards or go about our duty like men. When in doubt, Captain, proceed to do your duty. There's an axiom that will carry you through." Beraton's head had suddenly begun to hurt abominably, and for a moment he could see at least two Lergovs in front of him. But willpower helped him straighten his vision out.

"Sir. In my opinion we cannot simply go out there and . . . there is the matter of coordinating the dragoons' defense. Our soldiers are scattered . . ."

"Scattered in the face of the enemy, while you want to hide in a shelter. Captain, I am giving you a direct order. Get in this car. Take the driver's seat; I shall ride in the rear."

"Sir, you are tired, you are hurt."

"I am not hurt. I am perfectly capable."

"You are injured, wounded, sir. Grand Marshall, I must with all due respect refuse to . . ." There Lergov stopped again, staring with disbelief at the drawn pistol that had suddenly appeared in the grand marshall's fist.

That fist was trembling a little now, but only partially with age and weariness. "Mutinous scum!" Beraton roared. "Hand me your sidearm!" He snatched it from

he other's trembling hand, knowing proudly that the
eavy weapon in his own was staying level with murder-
us steadiness. "I'm placing you under . . . no. No, by
ll the gods, I'm not arresting you. You'll have one
hance yet to redeem yourself, and why should you sit
afe in a buried cell while better men and women die up
ere? Get in the car, and drive!"

Chapter 17

Chen stared at Hana. Even after the shocks of recent days and hours, her mere presence here at the Fortress still jolted and astonished him.

The implications of her presence began to come upon him only gradually, in the moments after the first shock.

His response to her greeting was not entirely happy. "What're you doing here?" he demanded.

While Olga stared at the two of them in silence, Hana looked around, then grabbed Chen by his spacesuited arm and pulled him aside, a few steps down a narrow catwalk nearby. It was a passage among exposed structural elements, where it seemed likely that they would be able to count on at least a few moments of relative privacy.

"I'm doing the same thing here that you are," Hana said to him then. "They had me locked up on the ship, but now I'm free."

"Locked up."

"Yes, of course." Hana gave her head a rapid little
shake, her usual way of expressing the opinion that
someone else was being unnecessarily slow. "The prime
minister's security people rounded me up near the capital shortly after the Empress was killed. Of course
didn't even know at the time that she was dead. Neither
did you. But now they think that we had some connection with it." And she favored Chen with her familiar
little conspiratorial smile.

Chen nodded. The gesture was not really a sign of
agreement or belief, only that he understood what she
was saying. A few days ago he would have taken at face
value just about anything that Hana might have said to
him. But no longer.

As if she sensed some change in him, Hana's own
manner now turned mildly accusing. "What've you been
doing since you got here, Chen? What're you up to
now?"

Olga, who was hovering near, was looking as if she
might at any moment remember that Chen was officially
still her prisoner. But before she intervened in the
conversation, one of the dragoons who had separated
himself from the main group that was still on the next
lower terrace came up a nearby stair to Hana. The
manner of this soldier's approach was not that of a
guard approaching a prisoner, but rather that of a private addressing an officer—in recent days Chen had
become familiar with both attitudes.

"Uhh," said the soldier. It was a tentative sound
made in his throat as he approached Hana hesitantly

Chen had the strong impression that his next word was going to be "Ma'am."

Hana turned to him with annoyance. "You guys figure it out, can't you? Let me alone for a minute."

The soldier nodded silently, turned and walked back toward his group, obediently leaving her alone. Hana, as soon as the young man was gone, turned back to Chen and saw how he was looking at her. Quickly she offered an explanation: "Some of them seem to think I'm someone important, just because I was kept locked up in a private cabin—but never mind about that. What's been going on here? Where did these berserkers come from?"

Chen studied her. Hana's clothes, the only civilian garments on anyone in sight, were worn and dirty-looking. She had evidently not had an easy time of it, traveling the kilometers between here and the Salutai ship at the docks. But the clothes Hana was wearing now had been expensive garments once, not the kind Chen was used to seeing her wear. She had no spacesuit. Neither did any of the dragoons in sight. Of course, so far the Fortress's life support systems were still working beautifully, and no one needed spacesuits. So far.

"I don't know where the berserkers came from," said Chen.

"And what've you been doing?"

He started to open his mouth to tell his old friend Hana about his meeting with the Prince, but the words died somewhere inside him before they could be spoken. "Surviving," he said instead. Definite suspicion had been born.

Olga, looking increasingly suspicious herself, and ill-at-ease at being so outnumbered by dragoons, was hovering nearer and nearer to Chen and Hana.

"This is Olga," said Chen, turning to make the belated introduction. "She and I came out here trying to find some heavy weapons."

"So did we," said one of the two other Templars who had been visible among the diffuse group. Evidently drawn by the sight of familiar uniforms, they had been approaching slowly. Both of them looked worn and shocked. The Templar who had just spoken went on: "But someone's already hauled it all away, what little heavy stuff there really was out here."

Chen turned back to Hana. "So, the security people grabbed you on Salutai and locked you up. But why did they bring you here?"

She accepted the question coolly. "They had some idea of confronting the Prince with me, evidently. Trying to make it look as if we had some deadly conspiracy going, and he was in on it—it's all really stupid." She paused. "Of course, now . . ."

"Now what?"

"Well. I hate to credit it, but it looks now as if the Prince may have turned goodlife."

"*Prince Harivarman?*"

Chen had been about to ask Hana about Mr. Segovia's face on the communicator screen, but the accusation against the Prince—and coming from Hana herself of all people—had temporarily blasted Mr. Segovia entirely out of Chen's thoughts. Before he could refocus, Hana was off in a different direction.

"Tell you what, Chen. Let me go down there and talk to these people for a few minutes. I'll see if I can get them to organize themselves a little better, so we can all do something constructive together. Don't you and your friend go away."

"We won't," said Chen mechanically.

With a parting smile Hana moved away from them, going down another stair to talk to the dragoons.

Olga stepped up beside Chen as the other young woman departed. Olga said: "She's supposed to be their prisoner? She doesn't act like one."

"No, she doesn't," agreed Chen.

Most of the dragoons were now gathering in one place, making a knot of people on the next terrace down. The two Templars, who appeared to be wandering around rather dazedly, had now rejoined the gathering there. Chen saw that the dragoons were now moving the communicator. Maybe they were hoping for better reception. Hana was embedded in the group, talking to them. At this distance Chen couldn't tell what she was saying, but a couple of the soldiers were now repositioning the communication device so its screen was no longer visible where Olga and Chen were standing.

"Where'd you meet her?" Olga muttered suspiciously.

Chen sighed. "On Salutai. Of course. It was a kind of a political club. We were supposed to be working to get Prince Harivarman recalled to power. And now she's trying to tell me that the Prince . . ."

Chen broke off. His memory had suddenly shown him the tall robot pacing in pursuit of him, with Prince Harivarman's voice calling him, booming from its speakers. The Prince, goodlife. *Goodlife*. But no, it couldn't possibly be.

"Huh." It sounded as if Olga disapproved of organization on Prince Harivarman's behalf. Or maybe she was only envious again, of people who had time and opportunity to make up things like political clubs.

Chen said suddenly: "Come on. Let's move over this way just a little. I want to try to see something."

The two of them, with Chen for once in the lead, did a little climbing, maneuvering around and behind some structural supports, the titanic bones of the Fortress, that stood exposed here in the immediate vicinity of the firing range. In a few moments Chen had reached a point from which it was possible to see the communicator screen once more.

"What is it?" Olga asked, hanging on his shoulder from behind. "What's wrong?"

Chen got one more good look at the communicator's screen, before someone in the group around it turned a control on the device and the screen went blank. But even after that the man's voice still issued from it. At this distance, most of the incoming words were indistinguishable, but the tones of the voice still came through. And Chen was more than ordinarily good at remembering voices.

"I think I know the man," said Chen, "that one they're talking to."

"So. Who is it?"

"His name's Segovia . . . Olga, I don't like this. I think we'd better move on."

"I'm not crazy about it either," Olga admitted.

"There're no weapons here anymore, and those people are all disorganized. They're going to get themselves wiped out, one way or another. All right, come on."

Olga sounded jumpy, which was natural enough after what they had been through already. She added, as they climbed back to the catwalk: "If I could signal to those two Templars—but maybe I can get them on their suit radios afterwards."

And she moved off at a quick pace, heading away from the firing pits, with Chen right on her heels. Hana must have been keeping half an eye on the two of them, or else she had someone else doing so, for they had gone only a little distance when Chen heard Hana's voice calling after him.

Chen said: "Ignore her. Let's keep going."

Three seconds later a sound, as of a struck gong, reverberated through the structural beam beside his head. It was not quite like any sound that Chen had ever heard before, yet there was something hideously familiar in it. For the second time in a few days, he knew that he was being fired on.

Less frightened than outraged at Hana's treachery, Chen turned and fired back, almost blindly, the carbine throbbing in his hands as it projected missiles. Olga's handgun blasted. Then the two of them ran again. When shots sounded around them they stopped again, crouching behind girders to return fire. Chen caught only quick glimpses of dragoons, and couldn't tell if he had damaged any of them or not. He saw Hana herself appear briefly, back near the pit, then drop out of sight as if she might have been hit.

Olga was running again and he turned and followed her, putting distance and angles and walls and more girders between themselves and the dragoons. There were shouts behind them, but no more shooting.

He fled on, following Olga's moving back. He counted the steps of his flight for a while, trying to estimate the distance they had come from the firing range, and then gave up. He had no idea where they were going now. All he was certain of was that now two sets of powerful enemies were after them.

The only faction that wanted to keep them alive—unless he was willing to trust what a berserker had said, calling his name in a Prince's voice—were the Templars, who were still holding out around the base. An intermittent thunder-rumble of fighting from that direction testified that the base was indeed still holding out, that it was the only place where they might find help, and also that trying to reach it might well be suicidal.

When they had put more than a kilometer between themselves and the range, Chen and Olga stopped for a brief rest, then drove themselves on. Chen worried and worried at the question of why the machine that had pursued him should have called on him in Prince Harivarman's voice. He could come up with nothing that seemed very satisfactory in the way of an explanation.

All the fountains were still running in the plazas that they passed, though the plazas were empty of people. Very few flyers or groundcars appeared to be in use anywhere in the City, and the temptation to borrow another one was correspondingly reduced. Olga and

Chen passed several wrecked vehicles, one of them in particular looking scorched, as if something other than a mere accident had brought it down.

Here and there people were starting to look out of their doors and windows. Some of the civilians called out questions when they saw Templars passing. Olga called back their ignorance, and advised the questioners to stay in shelter as much as possible. The drinking founts in the plazas and the streets still worked, the air remained normally breathable. For whatever reason, the berserkers were not attempting to destroy all life within the Fortress.

"He's made a pact with them, that's what he's done," Olga muttered. "A regular damned treaty, to save his neck."

Chen refused to believe it. Even if the Prince were willing to turn goodlife, why should berserkers care to make a treaty with him, a powerless exile?

But if they were here, as they were, with a military advantage, which they appeared to have, why were they not slaughtering the human population, expunging life from the Fortress down to the bacteria in the air and in the scattered gardens of imported soil? That was what berserkers did, whenever they had the chance.

Not this time, though. Something was different about this time.

Olga wanted to know more about the man on the communications screen. Why had Chen thought the presence of that particular man's face on the screen so important?

"Because now that man is one of Roquelaure's

dragoons, and when I saw him before, he wasn't."
Chen paused. It seemed to him that an interior light was
dawning. It was an ugly light. "Or at least he didn't
have his uniform on then."

Olga had no immediate reply. Chen wondered if the
look she gave him meant she thought that he was crazy.

Chen tried to explain. "I thought then that he was one
of us, our group. Or at least that he was sympathetic to
our cause, to get Prince Harivarman set free."

Olga had evidently given up trying to understand
about Segovia. But she had an opinion on the Prince:
"They should have kept that man locked up. Instead
they let him run around the Fortress wherever he wanted."

"I know." When Olga looked at him, Chen amplified.
"The commander took me along in her staff car to meet
him. I think she wanted to see, well, if we might have
been in any sort of plot together. We weren't, of course.
She took me way out in the boondocks to meet him, into
the airless area. Somewhere near the outer surface of the
Fortress, it must have been."

They hiked on, heading in the general direction of the
Templar base, but not hurrying to get there or taking the
most direct route. They paused to rest fairly often.

"Why'd you join the Templars, Olga?"

"Getting away from things." She didn't sound anxious to give details, and Chen didn't press for them. He
understood how that could be.

They had been under way again for only a few minutes when a civilian called to them from an apartment
window, wanting to know what news they had. The
man told them that the regular broadcast news channels

were useless due to some kind of sophisticated jamming, and a thousand rumors were circulating among the people. They gave the man what information they could, and were invited in for food. At that point both Olga and Chen discovered that they were ravenous. And despite their frequent rest stops, the hours of exertion and danger had taken their toll in exhaustion. Feeling like fugitives, the two of them took a welcome chance to sleep, one at a time, in the apartment, keeping their suits on and weapons ready. Like everyone around them, they were still breathing ambient air, which seemed as safe and as steady in pressure as ever.

Several hours later, Olga and Chen were on their way again, passing now through an area of the City that had so far been practically untouched by the fighting. Here the abandoned vehicles looked intact, but there was no use in tempting fate, no need for vehicular speed. During their last rest stop Olga had voiced a vague plan of trying to circle around to the other side of the base and get in that way. But she had had no answers to Chen's questions about details. If he thought about it, he realized they did not really know where they were going. He tried to think about it as infrequently as possible.

In a plaza larger than almost any other they had passed, they came upon an ancient monument that Olga explained was dedicated to the legendary Helen Dardan. Fountains played at the four corners of the plaza, and in the center the bronze statue of Ex. Helen stood. It was a statbronze statue dominating the plaza, from its place atop a monument with marble steps. Helen the Exemplar,

Helen of the Radiant. Helen Dardan, ruler and patron of the Dardanians during the time they had built the Fortress. Helen's time, as Olga explained, was centuries before Sabel's. But everybody knew that.

Shortly after leaving the plaza of Helen's monument, they came to what had to be the entertainment district. Here as elsewhere in the City most doors and windows were shut, and almost all businesses were closed. One that wasn't had a sign in front proclaiming it the *Contrat Rouge*. Recorded music wafted bravely out from the relative dimness of the shadowed interior.

Olga and Chen looked at each other. "Maybe they've got some information in here," she suggested.

Chen licked dry lips. "Sounds like a good idea. We can find out."

Inside, the dimly, romantically lighted place appeared at first to be completely empty of human beings. There were only the bartenders, squat, half-witted service robots devoid of any information aside from the service menu. These appeared ready to serve customers, but the humans could all too readily imagine the robots sullenly ready to revolt, to follow those other machines outside.

Chen suggested: "How about if we have a beer? I've got a little money."

"I can't see how it's going to do any harm."

They moved to settle in a booth. "Hey, Olga, look." The optics in the translucent walls produced their bizarre effects.

Then they both jumped to their feet, weapons at the ready. One other booth, a little distance from their own, was not empty. They moved down the aisle toward it.

The sole occupant of the other booth was a woman, hollow-cheeked, brown-haired, and well preserved for her age, which was obviously advanced when one looked at her closely. Her garments were considerably more flamboyant than the clothes most oldsters wore.

Chen lowered his carbine again. "Hello, ma'am? Are you all right?"

The lady did not appear greatly surprised to see them, though otherwise she appeared to be alone in the *Contrat Rouge*. Her smile gleamed up at Chen, easy perfection in a carefully made-up face. "Right enough. Time some customers came around." The voice was careful and clear, that of a performer, but the words ran into each other here and there; the lady, sitting with a glass of dark liquid in front of her, was pretty obviously not on her first drink. "Sit down, kids. Care to join me? I'm Greta Thamar."

The name meant nothing to either Olga or Chen. But they looked at each other, sat down, and ordered beer from a robot which had been following them since they entered.

Greta Thamar ordered another drink. The robot waiter looked into her eyes with careful lenses, and went away without acknowledging her order.

When the beer arrived, almost immediately, her ordered drink was not on the tray with it. Nor did the robot offer explanations.

The aging lady said: "I'm drinking more than is good for my worn mind." And she laughed. It was quite a young laugh, almost carefree, with something incongruous about it. Now she appeared to notice her companions' weapons and spacesuits for the first time. "You two are in the service, hey?"

"Yes ma'am," said Olga, and then asked deferentially: "Have there been any berserkers around here, ma'am?"

"They were here. Oh yes. But I never saw them." Greta Thamar looked vaguely into the distance. "The Guardians wouldn't believe me. But I knew nothing of what Sabel was doing with the berserkers."

"The Guardians, ma'am?" That was Olga, puzzled. She looked at Chen. Everyone knew that the Guardians had existed centuries ago.

And Sabel? Chen thought, lowering his beer stein with a grateful sigh. Was that supposed to be a joke, or what? It was his turn now to look at Olga, but he got no help from her.

"We meant just recently, ma'am," he offered. "Have you seen any berserkers near here today?" And then on impulse, Chen added another question: "Do you know where Prince Harivarman is, ma'am?"

"I've met the man. Can't say I was all that impressed. I met a Potentate once." Chen had some vague idea of what that meant: another ghost-name out of ancient history.

Olga, as if consulting some oracle, asked the elderly woman: "Do you know if the Prince is goodlife?"

Greta Thamar only looked at her, the perfect smile frozen on her face.

Olga, as if defensively, went on: "If the Prince is really working with the berserkers, then he's goodlife. If he's the one who found a way to let them get aboard the Fortress somehow."

Chen broke in. "Maybe they've been here ever since the last attack hundreds of years ago."

"It was here," said Greta Thamar. "Georgicus found it, out in the far corridors somewhere. There might still be more of them out there. He did all the things they said he did, but I was innocent."

Olga spoke, answering Chen. "Impossible. The way all those rooms and corridors were searched in Sabel's time?"

"You weren't here when all that happened."

She had to admit the truth of that. "Well, no. But I had to learn the history when I joined the Templars. And if the Prince is under arrest, it must be for something."

"Oh, really? What about me? Does that mean I'm guilty too?"

She looked at him. "I'm not entirely convinced you're not."

"Love is the answer," said Greta Thamar suddenly. That was a line from a song, Chen realized suddenly, as the lady began to sing the rest of it under her breath.

He was ready for another beer, and here were two, no, three bartender robots coming along the aisle in a row. Business must be looking up. The booth-optics showed them as three kinds of dancing animals.

And then he caught a clear glimpse of the moving figures, through lined-up openings in booth walls, when they were still two curving aisles away. More of them now. Not dancing animals at all but dragoon uniforms, men and women moving with weapons ready. As Chen gaped at them through the walls again, they turned into prancing nymphs and satyrs.

Chen wasn't waiting to see what might come next. Olga, alarmed at his alarm, was right beside him as he hit the deck. He started to cry a warning to Greta Thamar, but there was no time. The shooting had already started.

Olga was quicker with her pistol than Chen was with the more awkward carbine, and he admitted to himself that she was probably more effective too. Gunfire started and rose at once to a crescendo. Greta Thamar ducked under the table, crying her alarm.

The booth walls burst in at Chen, spattering him with bleeding images and melted plastic. He stayed on the floor, pinned down under heavy fire. He tried to use his carbine and it quit on him; out of ammo, he supposed, though he had earlier reloaded from a spare pack on Olga's gunbelt; fortunately most Templar small arms used the same load.

Crawling desperately from under one table to under another, under the sagging booth walls, he realized that he had lost sight of Olga now. Things looked very grim. He thought he heard Hana calling out, but with the firing there was no way to hear actual words.

He crawled under another booth, saw boots running in front of his face, and lay still. Then he crawled until an open door came into view, and he jumped up and ran for the door and tripped and fell before he reached it.

Someone shouted behind Chen, and he rolled onto his back. A dragoon only five meters off was leveling a rifle or weapon of some kind at him.

With a great crash, what looked like one whole side wall of the place burst in. The dragoon who had been on the verge of shooting Chen was gone, wiped away like a bad drawing. Something tall and metallic, something that moved three-legged through walls and space alike was coming on. Another dragoon, gun blazing, was flung out of its way.

In mad terror, Chen crawled away, got to his feet, and fled again. The Prince's recorded voice boomed after him in an appeal. Scrambling desperately, Chen made his way out over and through the rubble of the tavern's demolished outer wall. He could hear dragoons, or someone, still screaming behind him.

The familiar, three-legged shape was close behind. It followed Chen out into the street and there swooped down on him.

He scrambled and tried to run from it. Useless. He fell again. It closed in on him, loomed above him—reached out an arm for him. He saw it open the internal compartment of its torso, to tuck him into it, and he knew why it had been chosen for this job.

—and at the last moment, a blinding explosion in front of Chen. He saw the monster toppling, headless, and then for the second time in as many days he saw and heard no more.

Chapter 18

The Templar staff car came gracefully over the low patio wall and then, its gravitic engine gammalasered into little more than a lump of exotic lead isotope, it fell like a ton of scrap metal inside the barren courtyard of the building that had once been occupied by Georgicus Sabel.

The berserker whose beam had disabled the staff car did not bother to pursue it to final destruction.

Lescar, out doing a little scouting on behalf of his master, had been watching the vehicle suspiciously for the last minute, as it had moved erratically up one street and down another, hopping now and then over walls and buildings as if whoever controlled its movements were uncertain of his goal. Then a hovering berserker half a kilometer away had evidently become suspicious of the odd maneuvers also, and had fired. Lescar, his own inescapable berserker escort close at his heels, was at the wall of Sabel's old lab within a minute, and over the wall a few moments later. It had occurred to him that some of the Prince's friends might possibly be aboard that staff car, in which case they would certainly need help. Or on the other hand it might be, happily, some of the Prince's enemies who occupied the car, in which case there might be a good chance for equally appropriate action.

Lescar dropped over the wall and looked at the crashed vehicle. None of the occupants seemed yet to have stirred. For a few moments longer there was still no movement. Then one of the doors on the vehicle's undamaged side opened slowly, and a short man in the uniform of a captain of Prime Minister Roquelaure's dragoons emerged. He straightened up slowly and stood there dazed for a moment. Then he turned back to the car and dragged out an old man whose uniform was also military but of a different color. The chest of the old man's tunic was almost fully covered by a multitude of decorations, and there was blood on the uniform jacket now, among the ribbons. The old man could not support himself. It appeared to Lescar that he was still breathing, but not much more than that.

Carelessly the short man let the old one fall. Then he rummaged inside the disabled car again, and came up with a handgun. Then he started to aim the weapon at the collapsed old man. And only then—perhaps the dragoon captain had been a little dazed himself—did he at last catch sight of Lescar watching him. The captain's eyes widened, as if he recognized Lescar, though Lescar did not know him. And he started to change his pistol's aim, toward the small, gray, unarmed man.

"We are not alone," Lescar informed him almost calmly. Lescar's escort had not followed him over the wall directly, but it was now walking into the courtyard on its six legs, through a doorway almost behind the other man.

The eyes of the short captain almost twinkled: *You can't fool me like that*. And he was starting to aim his gun again.

"The Prince will want to talk to him!" said Lescar hastily to his escort; his master had deputized him—loathsome thought—to be able to give certain types of orders to the machines whenever the Prince himself was absent.

The dragoon captain was still aiming carefully, when the metal arm came over his right shoulder from behind and took him by the wrist.

Lescar on returning with his single prisoner to the Prince's new headquarters—a villa not unlike the last, though somewhat larger—found the Prince himself engaged in an electronic dialogue with the controller. A considerable amount of test equipment, more elaborate than anything the Prince had been able to use as a lonely field historian, had been set up in this new courtyard and was already in use.

Harivarman looked up when Lescar entered, walking behind a prisoner with his arm in a sling. When the Prince saw who the prisoner was, he silently put down his electronic tools and came forward, staring.

"He was riding in a staff car," Lescar reported succinctly, "with Grand Marshall Beraton. But the old man is dead."

The commuters' tube-car must be less crowded than usual this morning, thought Chen. It must be so, because how otherwise could he have dozed off, as he must have, sprawled out here on a pile of something or other aboard the train, lulled by its familiar swaying motion. And around him this morning his fellow students and other assorted travelers were being unusually silent. Because . . .

An approximation of full memory returned with a jolt, causing Chen to open his eyes quickly. He was lying on his back, indeed riding on some kind of a vehicle, jouncing faintly up and down on an improvised padding of what looked like household quilts and blankets. He had even been tied to his transportation, kept from falling off by a single strap around his waist.

The vehicle was something new to Chen's experience, a little too small to be a regular car. With considerable difficulty Chen finally recognized it as the carriage of a sizable self-propelled gun—the barrel would be retracted, somewhere under him, and he wondered what would happen if it had to be unlimbered suddenly.

He was being carried along a City street of the Fortress at a pace no swifter than a fast walk. Indeed, walking not far from Chen's side at the moment, keeping pace with his transport, was a coverall-clad woman whose face he felt he ought to recognize, though he had never seen her in person until this moment. Finally he identified the widely-known countenance of the Lady Beatrix. Well, he had never seen her depicted in a coverall.

He must have murmured something, for the former Princess turned to him. When she saw that Chen was awake, she came to walk closer at his side. Meanwhile the gun carriage, almost the size of a staff car, rolled on, as far as Chen could tell under the control of no one at all.

The lady said, matter-of-factly: "I see you've decided to be with us again. How do you feel?"

"I'm all—ow." Chen had tried to sit up, and felt evil reaction in several parts of his body at once. "What happened?"

"Colonel Phocion shot the head off a rather large berserker, just as it was about to pick you up and tuck you away into its cargo compartment. And you were stunned, either by the blast or when a lot of various parts fell on top of you. But we couldn't see that there was anything much damaged; I think you're going to be all right now."

"Colonel Phocion?" He'd heard the name somewhere; yes, someone who was supposedly gathering up heavy weapons.

"That's right. Using this seventy-five millimeter you're riding on now. That's the colonel walking up ahead of us. You'll get to talk to him presently; right now we're rather intent on getting to another part of the City. Shooting tends to draw berserkers." And the lady looked up and around warily; right now the sky immediately above them was empty, the street around them free of menace.

Squinting down past his feet, in the direction he was being carried, Chen could see a lone figure pacing about half a block ahead of the gun carriage. The figure was clad in what must be heavy combat armor, just as in the adventure stories.

Then Chen suddenly remembered something else. "Olga. Where's Olga?"

The lady looked at him. "I don't know any Olga. Where was she when you saw her last?"

"Back in that tavern. Oh. Ow."

"Then I'm afraid the outlook mightn't be too good for her."

"Oh." He loosened the strap that held him, and made himself sit up.

The lady walked closer, put a hand on Chen's arm. "We can't turn back now, I'm afraid. And we've already come quite a distance from that tavern. So, you're Chen Shizuoka. My name is Beatrix, if you haven't already recognized me."

At any other time, Chen would have been overwhelmed at meeting the former Princess. Now he could only ask: "Where're we going?"

"Following the colonel. He seems to know what he's about."

Chen looked ahead again, at the impressive figure in heavy combat armor. Chen supposed that anyone who put that on became impressive. Even from the back the striding figure was imposing, with portions of the armor's outer surface streaked and blackened, suggesting recent exchanges with berserkers.

The self-propelled gun that Chen was riding on had evidently been programmed to follow the colonel along the street, rather like a giant robotic bulldog. The colonel turned a corner now, and presently it followed.

Chen took a quick look back, then another. "Something's following us—"

The Lady Beatrix glanced back too. "That's only our robotic ammo trailer."

"Ah." It was maintaining a distance of about a half block behind.

The lady raised her voice a little and called out. The striding figure in heavy armor stopped at once and turned, then gestured the robotic gun carriage to catch up. It accelerated, then stopped itself when it had nearly reached him.

"Colonel Phocion," said Lady Beatrix, "this is Chen Shizuoka, as we thought. As you can see, he's awakened."

A flushed, almost chubby face and graying temples showed behind the colonel's heavy faceplate. "I want to talk to you," he told Chen grimly, his voice coming from a small speaker below the transparent plate. "But right now we have to keep moving." He glanced back, into the curving grayness of the sky. There were a few more berserkers to be seen swarming there, well to the rear of the three traveling people. "Our firing brought them out," the colonel added. "It's a little easier to fight them out near the outer surface. They're not there to interfere," he added with a brief grin.

With a stride forward, and a motion of his hand, the colonel set the gun carriage in motion again.

"The outer surface?" Chen asked. He was feeling somewhat better already; not quite ready to jump down off the carriage and walk, but improving.

"The colonel's been out there almost since the attack started," the Lady Beatrix explained. "I just joined him within the hour, when he came back into the interior."

"Sir, how do you fight them if they're not there? I mean—"

"Communications, young man," the colonel said. "There'll be a human fleet arriving here sooner or later. I've been knocking out communication channels. When the fleet comes, the berserkers won't necessarily be able to tell that it's arrived."

"I see, sir," said Chen.

"Do you? There's something I'd like to see, something that's made me very damned curious about you." He stopped again, stopped his following machine, and demanded: "Why was that damned berserker robot running all over the City bellowing your name? Did the Prince truly send it after you? If so, why?"

"I know he really sent it," said the Lady Beatrix. "I've told you that. And also that he wouldn't tell me anything."

"Yes, My Lady," said Phocion, and almost bowed. Then he glared at Chen. "Well?"

"I have no idea, sir. Ma'am. I've talked to the Prince but once, and that briefly. Very briefly. I think he believed me, that I had nothing to do with the Empress being killed."

Phocion glared at him some more, shook his head and muttered, and finally led on again. He turned off the street presently, and down a narrow alley through which the gun was barely able to pass. Then he stopped, kneeling beside a large but hardly conspicuous utility box. From somewhere Phocion's armored hand had produced a key, which he now used on the box to open it.

"Not supposed to still have this," he muttered, regarding the key. "Legacy of my tour as CO here. Looks like it's just as well I kept it."

From a tool box underneath the gun carriage, Phocion took out an optical device that he plugged into a communications nexus in the utility box. The small holostage on the device lit up, and a moment later Prince Harivarman's head was imaged in it. The Prince's face turned sharply toward them—apparently he was aware that at least a tenuous contact had been established. His image was streaked with noise. Its lips moved, but no sound was coming through.

Phocion swore. "Can see just about everywhere, except where I really want to—the Prince, and the base— damned berserkers still have a pretty effective communication curtain up around those areas."

"If he wants to communicate with us, he can order it opened, can't he?" The Lady Beatrix stared at her husband's image, as if she could not imagine what to make of it.

At last some words came through clearly. Harivarman, recognizing the colonel at least, shouted a question: "Do you plan to go on attacking the berserkers?"

"Of course I do."

"At your own risk. I can't give you immunity. I need the berserkers active to keep myself from being arrested. Do you mean to arrest me, Colonel, when you can?"

Phocion shouted back. "I've got myself in trouble, General. But I draw the line at being goodlife. Or tolerating them."

The Prince was speaking again, words that were now half-obscured by noise. ". . . real evidence, look in the outer regions. Around where I was working . . ." There was a little more; Chen thought he heard the word "surrender," but he couldn't tell the context now. Noise had increased.

Presently there was nothing left on the screen but noise. Colonel Phocion turned it off. He looked at the others.

"The outer regions," said Lady Beatrix.

Phocion turned to her. "What do you think of that? Now am I supposed to shoot him or try to help him?"

"He's still my husband, Colonel. If you're going to try to shoot him, you'd better start now, with me."

"I don't know if I am or not, blast-damn it all! Should I be out to get him? Is *he* out to get the rest of us? Has he told the berserkers not to shoot at me? Not so's I've noticed it!"

"Actually he might have, I suppose. They've not been pursuing us, though you did blast one of them."

Phocion sighed, a heavy sound on radio. "All right, the outer regions, then. At least there'll be fewer berserkers out there, I expect. A better chance for us to be picked up alive, if and when a human fleet arrives. But I don't know where he was working, and he expects us to find some kind of evidence there.''

"I know that," said Chen. "I've seen the place. I remember what the numbers were, the coordinates. They were on the screen in the staff car that we rode in.''

"Then we go there," said the lady. "I don't know what kind of evidence we'll find, but we can try.''

"I'm afraid I do know," said Phocion, in a low voice.

The others looked at him. He amplified: "I'm afraid I let them in.''

Phocion, having made that remark, was willing to explain it. Beatrix insisted that they keep moving, starting for their new goal at the outer surface, even as he spoke.

They found a twisting service ramp that went that way, wide enough to accommodate the heavy gun. They tramped downward through dim light, the weapon and the ammo trailer following. The colonel said: "A few months ago I was in something of a bad way. Knew I was going to have to leave my command here, being eased out—there comes a time in a man's career when he knows he has no more to look forward to. A point when he realizes that the rest is certain to be all downhill.

"However, not by way of excuse: explanation. I've hesitated to tell, naturally, but I've got to tell someone. I might cash in at any minute here, and no one would ever know. . . . What it comes down to is that about three standard months ago I accepted a bribe. Yes, in my capacity as base commander. Of course the idea of berserkers never entered my mind then. Didn't know who the people were, who talked to me. Never thought of goodlife. . . . This sector had been peaceful for so long—however, as I said, this is not meant as an excuse.

"Smuggling was what I thought I was selling myself out for. Supplying certain civilian needs—I even had the bastards' word for it that Templar people would not be involved at all . . . and I took their word . . . I don't know who they were. Shows you how far down I was. I was going to set myself up for a pleasant retirement . . . well.

"Point is, there was a time three months past when a landing—of anyone, or anything—could have taken place on the outer surface of the Fortress, and none of us in here any the wiser. For all I know now, it could have been berserkers."

"But if they arrived only a few months ago, that means—" The Lady Beatrix, Chen could see, was struggling agonizingly to think clearly. He could also see what she must be thinking. If Colonel Phocion's suspicions were correct, it meant that the Prince's claim of having discovered *ancient* berserkers was almost certainly false.

"I still believe him. I can't help it," the lady whispered finally.

At the lowest landing of the descending ramp that was still in atmosphere, the colonel brought them to a large locker containing spacesuits—it was, he told them, where he'd stashed his gear when he came in from his first raid on the outer part of the Fortress. Just beyond the airlock leading down, the vehicle that he had used then waited.

Presently the three of them, the self-propelled gun and ammo cart following as before, were traversing airless passages on the way back to the outer surface.

They were three quarters of the way there when Beatrix, driving, brought the flyer to a quick halt. She reported that she had sighted several mysterious figures in the distance. They had looked like a Templar or Templars, moving quickly.

Chen at once thought of Olga. But assuming she had survived the shootout in the tavern, how could she be here, ahead of him, already?

It seemed to Colonel Phocion, and he said so, that Commander Blenheim might have managed to get some people out of the base to carry out some unknown mission in these parts. "I expect she might have managed that. I could have, and she's a smart gal."

They waited for a few minutes, the flyer's lights out, in almost total darkness. There were no indications of Templars, berserkers, or any other entities being in the vicinity.

Cautiously, they proceeded.

Lescar, in one room of the latest villa—this one large and gloomy—was listening in surreptitiously as Harivarman and Lergov began a strained conference. The Prince had given Lescar other orders, meant to keep him out of the way, but as the servant had observed to himself on certain occasions in the past, there were some times when looking out for his master's welfare required him to do things even against his master's will.

Lergov was so far being allowed to sit at his ease. He

began the conversation by informing the Prince rather stoically that he was worried about his fate.

There was some Dardanian music playing, from some small part of the electronic equipment that was now strewn everywhere. Prince Harivarman liked to listen to it. He ignored Lergov's worries about fate, and took a more positive approach: "What do you *want*, Lergov?"

"What do I want, sir? I'll settle for very little at the moment. To get out of this with a whole skin."

The Prince nodded slowly. "I happen to want something too, Captain. I wish to be Emperor." (And Lescar, listening secretly, drew in his breath.) "And not only that, but to be Emperor with some security—something I fear would be hard to manage as long as Prime Minister Roquelaure is still a force to be reckoned with."

"All quite understandable, sir."

"I am glad you are easy to converse with, Lergov. And I am certain you have other talents. To arrange things as I want them, I could use the help of a dependable man like yourself."

There was a pause, in which Lergov swallowed. "What will Your Honor trust me to do?" he asked at last.

"Tell me a few things, to begin with."

"What do you want to know, sir?"

Here Lescar turned and looked around him, bothered by the feeling that perhaps someone else was also listening in. But there was only the house around him, as far as he could tell. And the scattered items of electronics. Of course, someone might be listening.

Prince Harivarman was saying to the captain: "Tell me about the prime minister's involvement in the

Empress's assassination. And what part you played. I know some of it already.''

Lergov told a strange and revealing story. Of his adoption, on Salutai, of the identity of a liberal protestor named Segovia, and of his role as liaison with a woman named Hana Calderon, also in the employ of the secret police. She had played the role of chief provocateur, making sure there would be a demonstration before the Empress by a pro-Harivarman protest group, who could then be blamed for her assassination, as could the exile himself.

Harivarman signaled to the controller, as always at his side. He gave some low-voiced orders. Lescar could not hear what they were, but he could see Captain Lergov turn pale.

Harivarman asked his prisoner: ''But it was Roquelaure who was really behind it all?''

''Oh, absolutely, sir.''

The Prince said, as another berserker entered, bearing tools: ''You will not be harmed here. The machines are only going to see to it that you stay where I can find you later, while we are—busy.''

Lergov said: ''I appreciate your consideration, sir.'' He sat still, quivering a little, as the machines began to weld together a steel cage surrounding him.

''Think nothing of it,'' said Prince Harivarman. Then he asked the captain: ''Aren't you afraid that I've been recording what you've told me?''

The captain looked as if he didn't know whether to take that seriously or not. ''Perhaps you have been too long in exile, Prince. I have in the past concocted a good many recordings of my own. Some of them were even truthful—perhaps I should say genuine. Truthful is a word that . . . but the point is that no one fears supposed secret recordings anymore, or even pays them much attention. Faking them indetectably, creating false images and voices, has become too easy . . . sir, if you don't mind my asking, when are you going to let me out?''

''An important message for you, life-unit Harivarman.'' It was of course the controller speaking.

Harivarman stood up. ''See that this little welding job is finished. I'll hear the message elsewhere.''

Chapter 19

The procession was a small one, moving first under the grayish interior sky that held the Radiant, and then turning down into the airless regions, out of sight of any sky at all. In consisted of two human beings, both garbed in heavy combat armor, who rode together in a commandeered flyer, and two berserker machines that alternately paced or glided beside the humans in their vehicle.

Lescar was occupying the right front seat of the flyer, riding beside the Prince who sat at the controls. For the first long minutes of the journey, neither man had anything to say.

When Lescar spoke at last, his voice was weary. It sounded even in his own ears like the voice of someone ready to give up, as if his body and his mind were numb. He didn't want to sound like that. It was a matter of pride, which sometimes seemed to be all he had left. "Where exactly are we going, Your Honor? Would it make any sense for us to be going now back to the place where you—performed your research?"

Harivarman sounded tired too, drained of emotion. "All I'm doing right now is following the controller. It says it'll take me directly to the people who have just landed. Sounds like more dragoons, from the description it gives of them."

It seemed odd to Lescar that his master would want to go directly to confront more dragoons, but the servant did not consider it his place to comment on anything so obvious. There were other points, though . . . "Your Honor? I dislike to bother you with questions."

"Go ahead."

"Our latest domicile. Even a bigger house than the last . . ."

". . . even though there are now only two of us. Yes, what about it?"

"Why, Your Honor, were there so many suits of heavy combat armor stored in a basement locker?" There were few enough other furnishings of any kind, and the house had not been occupied recently."

His master, face obscured by moving shadows, gave him a quick look. "The place was some old Templar officers' quarters, evidently, and lucky for us . . . what's that trying to come on the screen?"

The small communicator on the panel in front of them had lit up, and a moment later it presented the face of Commander Anne Blenheim. Somehow, for the moment, the channel was free of static.

"Harivarman. There you are." The commander paused for a moment, as if she were now uncertain what to say with the momentary chance to talk. "Have you any knowledge of what's happened to the grand marshall—?"

"Beraton is dead. Captain Lergov can be picked up when you get around to it." The Prince tersely specified the location. "Send some people with tools. He's welded into a sort of cage. I thought that would keep him out of trouble for a while."

Anne Blenheim was ready to say more, but the conversation was broken off, by blast after blast of recurrent noise.

"Your Honor, I recognize this corridor. We do appear to be going to your research site."

"So we do." And the Prince sounded uncharacteristically, fatalistically calm. They were already very close to the place, and the controller could hardly have brought them along this path by chance.

"Your old field workshop, Your Honor . . ." Then Lescar stiffened. "There's someone inside." There were lights glowing within the plastic bubble, though it was not inflated and the walls sagged limply. Through them a lone figure could be seen moving about.

"I think I can guess who it is."

The figure came now from inside the shelter to stand in its doorway, limned by the interior lights. It too was wearing combat armor. Lescar squinted, trying to recognize the make of armor, the small painted insignia, and the face inside the helmet. The armor was not Templar, of that much he could be certain.

As Harivarman eased their vehicle to a stop at a

distance of ten meters or so from the shelter, Lescar caught sight of the small one-seater combat ship parked, almost wedged in a corridor, at a little distance on the shelter's other side. It was not a craft with interstellar capability, but it could fight powerfully at close range.

"Who can it be, Your Honor?"

"I expect it's Prime Minister Roquelaure."

Lescar couldn't tell if his master was serious or not.

Without saying anything further, the Prince reached up and closed and sealed his helmet, which he had been wearing open. Lescar silently followed suit.

Then Harivarman was the first to break radio silence. He spoke again, in words that were obviously not directed at Lescar beside him: "You are a little earlier than I feared you might be, Prime Minister. Waiting for your arrival was becoming something of a strain."

"Ah." The voice that answered was well known in all the Eight Worlds and beyond, instantly recognizable. "Thank you. I naturally got here as fast as I could when the courier ship reached my little squadron. Fortunately we were on maneuvers in what turned out to be an ideal place to get the news. Everyone must be ready to respond instantly when there's word of a berserker attack. Everyone, of course, but goodlife." The figure in the doorway made a small mocking bow.

"Or even goodlife, sometimes."

"Ah. Can it be then that you have grasped something of the truth?" The figure in the doorway of the temporary shelter shifted its position, standing now in such a way that its face became partially visible through the helmet faceplate. The prime minister's physical trade-

marks—Lescar had seen him before, at a distance—
were a wild shock of hair that for many decades had
been just touched with distinguished gray, a nobly chiseled profile, a tall spare frame. He was naturally elegant,
as the Prince was not.

"I think I have by now grasped something of the
truth," the Prince replied. "Are you ready, then, for me
to know it all?"

The flyer was still drifting lightly in the corridor, with
the two powerful machines that were its escort maintaining themselves at a little distance from it, one on each
side.

If Roquelaure was in the least perturbed by the arrival
of his enemy with an escort of berserkers, he was doing
a marvelous job of concealing the fact. "Yes, I should
say that the time has now arrived for you to know the
whole truth . . . I've just been looking over your dig-
gings here, General. Fascinating. And I rather expected
you'd be along. With metallic companions."

"Ah? And still you came unaccompanied to meet me?"

"Yes." The figure in the doorway still seemed perfectly at ease. "You see, a lot of people—most of the
Imperial Guard included—might have a hard time dealing with certain aspects of the truth that I wanted to
discuss with you."

"I can well believe that."

"So, I left my soldiers back with my two ships.
Where we landed, a couple of kilometers from here.
They have things to do there to keep them busy. And
they admire my almost foolhardy courage in coming
here without their protection. Actually when I really

wanted was this little talk with you alone. Lescar is there with you, of course—how are you, Lescar?—but he doesn't count.''

The Prince said: "Speaking of little talks, I've just been having one with Captain Lergov.''

"My dear man. I thought you said you were concerned with truth.''

"I believe I heard some of it from him, this time. The Templars are going to hear it too.''

The prospect of revelations by Lergov seemed to have no more effect on the prime minister than did the presence of berserkers. Roquelaure only shook his head inside his helmet. "Ah, truth. A chancy business, trying to deal with that.''

In another large airless chamber half a kilometer away, Chen Shizuoka was watching Colonel Phocion patch another communications connection into another utility box. The journey to this point from the interior had seemed a long one to Chen, though in fact it had taken only minutes.

The self-propelled gun, here with them in near-weightlessness, was clinging to a wall nearby.

Phocion had stopped frequently en route, at each stop using his old base commander's key, gaining secret access to the various communications networks of the Fortress. He kept looking as they progressed for traces of berserkers or other people in areas nearby.

This time his caution was rewarded.

Beatrix moved closer, watching with the men as a picture appeared. The colonel had managed to get a remote video pickup working in an area ahead of them, where preliminary readings had indicated there was activity.

"It's Harry," she breathed, as the picture steadied. "Harry, and . . . ahh."

Harivarman ordered the controller to send its companion machine scouting, to check whether Roquelaure had really come here unguarded and alone.

"Affirmative," the controller replied, after the other machine had been gone for a couple of minutes, searching the nearest other rooms and corridors.

The Prince said: "You appear to take your status as my captive quite calmly, Roquelaure. Are you so sure I won't give the word to my machines and have you pulled to pieces?"

"I'm not sure what word you will give them. Are you sure of the result?"

"Yes, I think so. I've had some time to get used to it, watching berserkers operate at close range, having their power at my command. Have you ever tried to imagine, Roquelaure, what it would mean to a man to have the berserkers' control code in his hands?"

"Oh, I have tried to imagine that, yes. I too enjoy power, you know. Though perhaps my imagination is not as fertile as yours, Prince. Anyone would be able to make certain deductions about you, though. Anyone who saw you come here escorted by berserkers. And I suppose that you have been holding the surviving inhabitants of the Fortress hostage until you are somehow provided with a getaway ship."

"It would seem that I can now count a prime minister among my hostages."

"It might seem so to you. But in reality, it is not so at all." The prime minister turned his head calmly to one side, looking directly at the controller. "Your berserkers are not going to harm me. Because, you see, I am not here at all. It is a mere phantom that discourses with you. The real, historical meeting between us is coming a little later, in an hour or so. I am going to catch you without your escort then and kill you, earning the cheers of billions of people by eliminating the despised archgoodlife. Meanwhile my men will be defeating the berserkers and driving them off, saving the precious population."

"I see. I hadn't realized all that . . . but did I understand the first part correctly? At the moment, you are not here?"

"That is correct."

Prince Harivarman shook his head. "My eyes and instruments assure me that the image of a somewhat overly handsome assassin before me is not a creation of holography. So explain that claim to me, if you will."

"Tut. You could be sued for that, calling me an assassin. You seem to be projecting all your own little flaws upon me . . . I mean that my presence here, tolerated by the machines escorting you, is going to be invisible to history—because only I will survive to tell humanity about this talk that we are having. This moment of history is going to be exactly what I say it is. No more and no less."

"Oh indeed?" Harivarman sounded as confident as

ever, but suddenly very curious. "And how do you plan to accomplish that? What bluff is this?"

"No bluff at all, my dear Prince." Roquelaure gestured offhandedly at the controller. "How long would you say our friend here, and its auxiliary machines, have been on the Fortress?"

"I have seen evidence that they have been here for several centuries. They were even filmed with dust—"

"No. Not at all. There you are wrong. Dust can be arranged. Several months is much more like it."

Harivarman smiled slightly. He raised his control device near the window at his side. "You have carried off some amazing bluffs in your career. But not this time. Can you see this? What would you say this is?"

"Tell me. I want to hear you tell me."

"Very well. Suppose I tell you that I have here the control code for the berserkers?"

"I would say that you are making a false claim—as you have often done. You are not only goodlife, and an assassin, but a fraud!"

"I can demonstrate the fact."

"Oh indeed? Can you? I look forward to witnessing the attempt."

Harivarman thumbed his device. At the same time he spoke in a changed, commanding voice. "Controller, seize that man. Do not kill him, but bring him here, closer to my vehicle, away from his own."

It was a direct order, if Lescar had ever heard one.

The controller ignored it. The tall metal shape, still incongruously trailing cable-ends, was clinging to a wall approximately equidistant from Harivarman and the prime minister. And it did not move a centimeter.

The Prince triggered his device again and again. "Seize him! I order you!"

The controller turned another one of its lenses toward the Prince's vehicle. But it did nothing else.

Roquelaure had begun to laugh when the Prince's first order was ignored. He was still laughing. It was a very confident and a very ugly sound.

The Prince slowly lowered his hand, the radio device still in it. He sat there, his helmet shadowing his face from Lescar's gaze. When his voice came into Lescar's headphones again it sounded more numb, more utterly defeated, than Lescar had ever heard it sound before. "But . . . it worked. I found them . . . I opened the controller unit . . ."

Lescar bent over his seat, hands raised to his own faceplate. But that did not shut out their enemy's laughter, or their enemy's voice. Those came through inexorably.

When he could stop laughing, the prime minister said: "Do I need to explain to you what the real controlling code is? Even berserkers can be—well, no, unlike humans they cannot be corrupted. Unlike people, they remain forever true to their basic drive. But they are honestly, openly, ready to be bought."

"You've bought them, then . . . there's only one kind of coin they'll accept."

"Of course. They have an apt term for it themselves: life-units. For a rather large number of human life-units, scheduled for future delivery, I have actually concluded the bargain that the bad side of your own nature was finally able to wrestle your better nature into making. After I'm Emperor, they can have Torbas . . . it can be arranged. It'll never be anything but a poor and unprofit-able world anyway.''

"There are a hundred million people living on Torbas."

"Pah. Closer to two hundred million. But there is no audience here, don't bother posing. History is going to be blind to your words and actions from now on, General. Two hundred million life-units. Useful coins. Oh, it occurs to me. Are you recording my voice perhaps, my image? Will it disappoint you too cruelly if I tell you that it will not matter?"

"I know," the Prince said, slowly, after a long pause. His voice was hardly more than a whisper. "No, I'm not recording. But will you tell me something? One thing more. For my own final—knowledge."

"Well, possibly. What would you like to know?"

"Colonel Phocion. Did he—?"

"Did he know that it was berserkers he was letting aboard his Fortress? Gods of all space, no. There must have been rather a lot of them—I came past their lander back there; it's rather larger than I had expected. Well, guarding against human treachery of some kind, I suppose. The way the wicked world is, one can hardly blame them for that.''

"But Phocion . . ."

"Look, Harivarman. The man knew he was being corrupted, but he thought it was only some simple smuggling operation, accommodating certain simple civilian needs—all he had to do was create a blind spot or two in the outer defenses for a time—no trick at all for some-one with his knowledge of the system."

"Why do you do it, Roquelaure? You already have wealth, power, everything—"

"I do it because it pleases me to do it. And why should I not use the world and what's in it to please myself? If the universe has any higher purpose than that, I've yet to observe it . . . and the Imperial Throne will be mine now, and that will please me, more than most people are capable of imagining. But you can imagine it. That's why I wanted to tell you. The Imperial Throne, my friend. I will have it, I've made up my mind to that. I'll take it with the berserkers' help if that's the only way that I can manage it."

The Prince's lips moved. The words were hard to make out. He said: "Well. I had hopes . . ."

"Of being the next choice for Emperor yourself. Mounting from the berserkers' backs. Announcing the discovery of the control code"—a chuckle—"after of course some judicious use of berserker muscle to punish your local enemies." Roquelaure had to pause, to laugh again. He was really enjoying this. "It must really have been quite a strain, for you, to turn goodlife . . . but no, Prince. No. The berserker throne is mine, not yours."

And a giant's hand seemed to come slamming against the back of Lescar's seat. The Prince, who could still act quickly enough to take him by surprise, had gunned his flyer into maximum acceleration. The corridor ahead came leaping at Lescar; the shelter with Roquelaure in its doorway, that had been to one side, had already been whisked from sight.

But the try was too slow by far to avoid the controller's weapons. Lescar, saved by his heavy armor, felt and saw the hurtling vehicle torn and blasted open around him. His armored body hurtled free. A huge bone of the

Fortress, an exposed major structural element, came flying at him. The impact was a glancing one and Lescar came through it essentially unhurt.

At first the Prince was a suited figure tumbling beside him. Then the Prince was grabbing his arm, helping him get his bearings, pulling him on. Somewhere. And once more there came the flare of heavy weaponry around them . . .

Beatrix, when she saw on the screen her husband's vehicle shoot forward, tried to rush out from her position of relative safety, to do what she could to help him, to be with him at least. She heard the blast of the berserker's shot echoing down the corridor just outside. The scene she was watching remotely could be no more, she thought, than half a kilometer away.

She had almost reached the door when figures in heavy armor, Templar armor, sprang in from the corridor to hold her back. A tall man gripped her with both hands, then savagely made a gesture that would be understood by any veteran of space warfare, fiercely commanding her to radio silence.

Then the astonishment of the Lady Beatrix was compounded. Looking into the faceplate of the man who held her back, she recognized the craggy features of the Superior General of the Order of the Templars.

Chapter 20

When the heavily armored figures of Harivarman and Lescar went scrambling away from the wreckage of their flyer, they were out of the direct line of sight of the controller, and it forbore to fire after them again.

Nor did the controller attempt to pursue the man who had claimed to be able to control it, whose orders it had in fact been following for days. As far as Beatrix could tell, watching the small screen, the berserker was intent now on nothing but observing the prime minister.

Prime Minister Roquelaure, launching himself out of the plastic workshop's doorway with an expert push and drift, moved through the low gravity toward his own small fighter ship. Glancing back over his shoulder, he saw the controller following him slowly, and he said to it: "I see that you understand. It does not matter that he should get away for the moment. If he does not take his own life somehow now, I'll soon take it for him.''

The radio whisper of the berserker's reply, relayed by pickups in the room where it was speaking, came thinly to the ears of the people watching in the chamber half a kilometer away. ''You are right in that it does not matter. I will kill him soon.''

The man who was alone now with the controller paused. It was taking him long unhurried seconds to drift the last few meters to his fighter. ''No. No. I see that after all you do not understand. You can kill any number of life-units you wish to in the Fortress, as long as you save a few to testify to my heroic rescue of them—all as we discussed. But in the case of the badlife Harivarman, it will be better if you are not the one to kill him. I want to claim his death for myself; that will make me something of a hero. If later it appears that he was killed by a berserker, that could cast doubt on my story. It could even tend to make him a martyr in the eyes of many badlife units. Do you know what a martyr is? We don't want that.''

In the gloomy chamber five hundred meters away, Beatrix met the eyes of the SG; slowly, with a last warning gesture, he let her go. More gestures had already been exchanged between him and Beatrix's companions. Working in almost complete silence, though for the most part in darkness, Phocion was tapping into the communications nexus again, this time in a more elaborate way, making multiple connections for some purpose that Beatrix could not immediately comprehend.

People in Templar armor, with more electronic equipment in hand, were helping him.

Other armored Templars were, with an agonizing effort for speed and silence at the same time, unlimbering Colonel Phocion's heavy gun and turning it out into the adjoining corridor.

"We?" the controller asked.

"You and I. I was speaking of our common interest." The tiny figure of the prime minister on the small screen had now finally reached the open hatchway of his fighter. Roquelaure was pausing there, casually, seemingly nerveless, with one hand on the door before he got into the ship.

The controller had come drifting—just as casually— after him, and was now no more than three or four meters away. The other berserker machine still had not returned; it had evidently found other business of some kind to occupy it.

How many more berserkers were there, Beatrix wondered, still prowling in the interior of the Fortress, surrounding the beleaguered base? A few of them had been destroyed. There might be forty left. Even if the controller were fired upon, destroyed, it was very unlikely that they would all simply go dead. No. Berserkers did not work that way. . . .

The tiny berserker on the screen was asking the prime minister: "How far do you consider that our common interest now extends?"

"To a considerable distance . . . don't tell me that you're having second thoughts about our agreement. If you don't go on with it now, all that you've done so far would make no sense from your point of view. So far you have helped me, but I have not helped you. You have derived no substantial benefit.''

"My computations on the subject of our agreement have not changed in the slightest.''

"Good." Roquelaure turned his head, about to enter the ship.

"And you have helped me. With the badlife unit Harivarman now effectively out of the experiment, most of my immediate goals have been achieved.''

Roquelaure's head turned back. "But you have killed very few so far. Your long-range goals, all the life-units—''

"Two items remain.''

"Excuse me for interrupting.'' The prime minister sighed faintly; irony, of course, was lost. "All life on the planet Torbas will be yours, in time, as I have promised.''

"All life everywhere will be mine, in time.'' The words were spoken with mechanical certitude; they seemed to hang endlessly in space, all along the airless, ancient Dardanian corridors.

Roquelaure drew a deep breath. "No doubt. Then what are the two items that you say remain? I warn you, you will jeopardize my ability to help you, if you do anything here that will interfere with my accession to the—''

"You have already given me almost all the help that I have calculated on receiving from you.''

For the first time the attitude of the small armored

figure appeared other than casual. "I have pledged you my future help, which we agreed will be to my advantage to give. But I have as yet actually given you almost no—"

The controller interrupted again: "I repeat, you have given me almost all that I expected to receive. The first item I still want here is the destruction of all life within the Fortress. The second is information. Most of the information I sought here I have obtained, but a few data remain. To gain them I intend to observe your reaction when you learn the truth."

This time Roquelaure paused for a longer time before he spoke. "If you are bargaining for more—"

"The time for bargaining is past. I will now disclose the truth to you, that I may observe your reactions to it. The life-unit Prince Harivarman was calculating in error during its dealings with me. Yet it was closer to the truth than you have realized. A very important experiment has indeed been in progress here, concerning the means by which a dangerous opponent can be controlled, perhaps rendered totally harmless and ineffective, by nothing more than transmitted information. A control code, as you have termed it. I was able to convince the life-unit Harivarman that he was conducting such an experiment upon me."

"I know that. All according to our agreement. I—"

"Even as I convinced you that you were bargaining successfully with me."

There was silence. To that statement Prime Minister Roquelaure appeared to have no answer at all.

"The truth," said the controller, "is that I am the

experimenter. You, like the life-unit Harivarman, are a subject. From the beginning I have been testing you and your fellow life-units. We that you call berserkers have long sought a control code for the life-units that call themselves humanity, particularly the more prominent leaders among them. It has been an exceedingly difficult search, and I must compute that the results so far are still uncertain. It is doubtful that any perfectly reliable code exists or can as yet be devised for the control of units of such complexity.

"Nevertheless, much information of great importance has been gained. What does a human life-unit seek that I can offer it? With a very high degree of probability, it seeks power over other life-units of the human type. Also, the motive called revenge must be classed among the most powerful inducements. Also greed, the affinity for wealth as measured in your systems of finance. Using the proper codes of information, I have been able to control you both.

"You, life-unit Roquelaure, have been a very valuable subject."

The prime minister was only a second, perhaps two seconds, of fast movement away from being inside his fighter with the hatch slammed closed behind him. But he did not move. He whispered something. Beatrix was unable to make it out; perhaps the berserker heard it and recorded it as information for study.

Around her in the room from which she watched, the feverish maneuvering of equipment was going on, still in a strained effort to maintain silence. The clang of tools or weapons, the tread of feet, might come traveling through the fabric of the airless outer Fortress corridors to alert the keen senses of the berserker to their presence. She yearned to grab the Superior General and make him tell her what was going on—but she did not dare distract him now.

The people who were making the effort with the gun and with the communications equipment did not appear to need her help. This is my job just now, she thought, looking at the screen. I am a witness.

The controller went on: "My purpose from the beginning of this experiment, from the first indirect bargaining between your emissaries and mine, has been to measure what temptations of power may best serve as a control code for the badlife. To gain such information, the sacrifice of a number of machines, the tolerance of the continuance of many lives, has been very much worthwhile. Now I wish to observe your reaction to this information. Express your reaction to me."

Roquelaure did not speak or move, and in a moment the berserker spoke again: "It is very probable that you are the final fully aware human victim—that the remaining human life-units here on the Fortress will still be without understanding of the situation when I destroy them. And I have already observed the truth-reaction of the unit designated Prince Harivarman."

At last the prime minister had found words. "A control code. I see. All right, maybe you were playing that sort of a game. If so, you've won. But there's no reason why we can't conclude a bargain now. Now that you've studied our reactions. And I could still go through with—"

The berserker had evidently heard enough from its last subject. The screen flared brightly, almost dazzlingly in Beatrix's face. At the same instant light flared in from the corridor, leaping from a distance to wash around the newly positioned heavy gun. At the same instant the communication channel went silent.

But the small screen cleared again, almost at once, to show the berserker turning quickly. At last, in the flare of its own weapon, it had sensed the watchers' presence down the corridor.

It turned with weapon hatches opened, just in time to take the full charge of Colonel Phocion's cannon on the front surface of its upper body. When the small screen had cleared again, there were nothing but fragments of berserker to be seen.

The men around the communication connection were thrown into frenzied activity, but not yet of jubilation. At least radio silence could now be broken. "Get the gun in here again! They might come this way. We don't want to block the corridor."

They? thought Beatrix. The SG had her by the arm again, a lighter grip this time. His voice came clearly to her over the standard channel. "We've been working with the Prince for a couple of days now, ever since I got here; tell you the details later. We've just duplicated one of the controller's signals to its troops—we hope—and transmitted it from a hundred places within the Fortress. If all goes well, they're going to be heading for their lander, and—get it in here!" This last was directed at his troops, who were once more in a frenzied scramble, this time to get the gun turned again and drawn back into the room with them.

It crowded the dozen people in, backing them against the walls at back and sides.

And then the waiting resumed. Presently, at a gesture from a Templar at the communicator, radio silence was reimposed.

And then Beatrix was distracted, to her vast relief, by the entrance of her husband, Lescar's figure beside him. Even in the darkness she could be sure at first look that it was the Prince. She knew his movements, his size, his . . . for minutes she did not worry particularly about what might be going on outside.

The Prince and the SG exchanged firm handgrips. Then all were quiet again, waiting. Bea could feel her husband's armored hand resting on her suited shoulder.

At last there came a faint sound from outside the room, that of an impact made faintly audible in vacuum by its passage through beams and frame and floor and boots and bones. And only seconds later there began a massive but almost silent passage through the corridor outside. It was a parade of sizable machines, gliding through near-weightlessness in darkness, heard only through their occasional contact with the framework of the Fortress.

At last the parade had passed. Colonel Phocion turned on his remote video gear again, and drew in a signal from the proper pickups. The fourteen people huddled in silence were able to watch the approximately forty berserkers enter their lander and reembark, gliding off silently into space.

"The outer Fortress defenses are all yours, Commander," said Phocion's voice. And Anne Blenheim's face appeared briefly on the small screen, acknowledging.

The Lady Beatrix heard the Superior General giving orders to the gunnery officers of his two ships.

And then the night of the universe outside the Fortress was lit by titans' flares and forges. Seconds later there came sound again, the wavefronts of blasted particles hitting the outer surface of the Fortress hard enough to awaken roaring resonance in stone and metal, sending an uproar rolling and rumbling on toward the far interior.

The Prince was first to put it into words: "Got 'em. Got 'em. Got 'em. I think we got every last bloody one."

Epilogue

There were two statbronze statues now in Monument Plaza. That of Exemplar Helen, of course, was there as it had been for many centuries, portraying a beautiful woman wearing a toga-like Dardanian garment, with a diadem in her hair. But now, facing Helen from an equal dais, stretching out an arm toward her as if to offer comradeship and support, was a metal version of the late Prime Minister Roquelaure, who had been martyred a year ago in the latest heroic saving of the Fortress.

The statbronze prime minister had one striding foot planted on a berserker, half-crushed but still malevolent. There were critics of the statue who said he looked like he was standing on a chair.

The new statue had been unveiled some months past, but a formal rededication of the plaza was to take place today, and the Emperor himself was coming to preside. Some thousands of people, including a few old friends and acquaintances, were waiting for a chance to greet him.

Two enlisted Templars, who happened also to be husband and wife, had been excused from regular duties for the occasion, and were at the moment standing at one side of the plaza, the less prestigious side today, content to be lost and ignored amid a nervous crush of comparatively minor dignitaries.

Olga was wondering aloud how the Emperor's appearance might have changed since they had seen him last. Chen, married almost a year now, wasn't paying all that much attention to his wife. A politician not far away was trying out a line of a written speech, muttering it under his breath. Chen with his good ear for voices could understand:

"How strange, how fitting, how lovely, that these two men, fierce enemies for most of their lives, should have put their differences aside to save the Fortress and the lives on it."

"Yes, fitting enough I should say, the way that it worked out." This last was a remembered voice, closer at hand, and Chen turned to see Colonel Phocion, a little fatter, dressed in the natty civilian garments of retirement. "It's been a long time. How are you two kids getting on?"

On the far side of the plaza, Commander Anne Blenheim had just got out of her staff car, to greet the Superior General, who had already arrived. Then both Templar officers disappeared into a throng of their fellow dignitaries gathered around the temporary speakers' platform.

There was a muted loudspeaker announcement, sounding across the plaza: "The ship bringing the Empress and the Emperor has docked."

The official story was, of course, that Prince Harivarman had known from the beginning, from the moment he discovered the controller, that the berserkers were out to play a clever trick on the inhabitants of the Fortress, to run some kind of a test. He had immediately suspected something was not as it seemed, and had played along with the enemy to find out what—and because he knew that if he did not, all life in the Fortress would be immediately destroyed.

Chen personally doubted very much that the official story was completely true. Still, it was probably not that far off, as official stories went. And someone had to be Emperor, or Empress, after all, and things could have turned out a whole lot worse.

But, as the Emperor himself officially admitted, it had taken Anne Blenheim's mention of an effective control code, during their meeting under the eyes of the berserkers, to trigger his next flash of insight. He had sent a berserker looking for Chen Shizuoka to try to assure himself of proof. But of course, without the heroic self-sacrifice of the late prime minister—

The late prime minister had millions of political followers who were still alive, and it was necessary for them to be appeased.

Someone else was approaching Olga and Chen and Colonel Phocion. A small gray man, plainly dressed, but the heads of the knowledgeable everywhere across the plaza turned in his direction. Though he still tried, Lescar could no longer manage to be inconspicuous.

Looking uncomfortable in the public eye, he said to Chen and Olga and the retired Colonel Phocion: "Emperor Harivarman would like to see a few old comrades in private. For a few minutes."

Commander Anne Blenheim, immediately after the berserkers' defeat, had been able to show evidence confirming the Prince's story: the Council order for General Harivarman's arrest, with her own and Harivarman's written messages to each other on it, as they wrote them in their silent, secret conference in those early precious minutes when no berserkers watched. She had decided in those moments to trust the Prince, and from then on they had worked together as much as possible.

Even as the human survivors were playing along with each other now, honoring the late PM for political reasons, to appease his many followers.

"I must say the controller tried everything to fool me, even to the point of filming itself and its machines with dust."

Actually the Prince did suspect early on that something about this particular batch of berserkers was well out of the ordinary.

And he had also been wondering why the controller had failed to activate all of its forty-seven units at once when it had the chance, in that first supposed moment of perfect freedom, when it first moved to attack him and Lescar.

The offer of power, even if illusory, has proven well-nigh irresistible.

But it was not quite so.

The SG, alerted by warning relayed from the courier that had got away, had come onto the Fortress at once with what ships he had with him; had been able to land unobserved and unchallenged, thanks to Colonel Phocion's disruption of communications; had managed to use the communications system himself—who knew it better than the Superior General, after all?—to talk in scrambled messages with Commander Blenheim at the base, and through her had learned of the gamble she was trying to win with Harivarman.

Representatives of the whole Council, of all the Eight Worlds and of other human worlds besides, were at the Fortress now, taking part in this year-later ceremony. There were going to be a lot of speeches.

But they couldn't start until the Emperor and Empress were ready. And the Empress and the Emperor took time first to have a small talk with a few old friends.

Then Harivarman I, the Empress Beatrix at his side, moved out to give his speech.

Chen followed, watching from a distance, his young wife at his side.

Olga was looking at the newer of the two statues. "I don't think it looks like a chair, really," she said.

FRED SABERHAGEN